PLANET OF THE GRAPES

by Kirsten Weiss

KIRSTEN WEISS

Books by Kirsten Weiss

The Witches of Doyle Series
Bound (Book 1) | Ground (Book 2) | Down (Book 3) | Spirit on Fire |
Shaman's Bane | Lone Wolf | Witch | Tales of the Rose Rabbit

Doyle Cozy Mystery Novels
At Wits' End | *Planet of the Grapes*

Perfectly Proper Paranormal Museum Series
The Perfectly Proper Paranormal Museum | Pressed to Death | Deja
Moo

The Riga Hayworth Paranormal Mystery Novels
The Metaphysical Detective | The Alchemical Detective | The
Shamanic Detective | The Infernal Detective | The Elemental
Detective | The Hoodoo Detective | The Hermetic Detective

The Mannequin Offensive

The Pie Town Cozy Mystery Series
The Quiche and the Dead | Bleeding Tarts

Sensibility Grey Steampunk Suspense
Steam and Sensibility | Of Mice and Mechanicals | A Midsummer
Night's Mechanical

CHAPTER ONE

"If there's probing, I'm out." The blue-faced woman crossed her arms and scowled at her tentacled companion.

His violet appendages quivered. "How many times do I have to tell you? It's just panels and funnel cakes and... fun."

I approached the oval-shaped table and clutched the pitcher of OJ closer to my chest. "Um, is there anything else I can get you?" I smiled and hoped for a negative answer.

Late summer sun streamed across the hardwood floor. It glinted off the metal lids of the chafing dishes on the sideboard, covered in a white cloth. The rooms at my B&B, Wits' End, were cozy comfortable, but it was the breakfasts that got the rave reviews.

The mixed bunch of UFO enthusiasts shook their heads and mumbled *no's*. Two Mulder and Scully wannabes steadily shoveled eggs and waffles into their mouths.

Around the breakfast table, other guests chattered excitedly. Blue curtains fluttered in the open windows. A breeze carrying the scent of pine and roses mingled with the heady scents of bacon and pecan waffles.

I set the juice on the table, backed out of my breakfast room, and stepped on a booted foot.

"Ooof! Hey big shot. Watch it. Sue." Dixie crossed her arms over her Army-green tank top. My young cousin had gone for the Cleopatra look today, thick kohl making her green eyes gleam.

I grinned. "Nice hair."

Dixie tugged on a lock of tousled black hair tipped electric blue. "Violet was so ten minutes ago."

And I suddenly felt unhip, out of touch, when I was barely thirty. Dixie had that effect on me.

A collar jingled. The beagle I'd inherited, Bailey, made his way down the stairs to sit at Dixie's feet. He cast a hopeful gaze my way, and I bent to scratch behind his ears.

His tail thumped the faux-Persian rug. Colorful trapezoids of light from the stained-glass above the door cast dizzying patterns on the carpet.

"I thought you'd be off to your dumb festival by now," Dixie said and followed me through the swinging door into the kitchen. She slouched against the butcherblock counter and jammed her hands into the pockets of her cargo shorts.

"Soon." I smiled modestly. It wasn't really *my* UFO festival, but I *had* spearheaded bringing it to Doyle. My stomach twisted with nervous excitement. The X-tranormal festival started today and would fill my B&B to capacity. It would bring more tourist dollars to our small mountain town.

She shrugged. "Whatever. I'm holding you responsible."

Ha. Dixie was clearly a teensy bit jealous about my new VIP status in the UFO community. My cousin obsessed over all things UFO, but she'd been decidedly cool on the X-tranormal festival.

"Holding me responsible?" I asked. "What's that supposed to mean?" Reaching past an aloe plant, I grabbed a box of treats from a thick, plain wood shelf and tossed one to Bailey. My late grandmother had left most of the old Victorian "as is." But before she'd died, she'd modernized the kitchen. White subway tiles lined the walls. A ceiling fan helped push the warm air coming through the open windows and screen door to the porch.

"You're concentrating all the UFO hacks and nutjobs in one place. Here, in Doyle. It's a bad move."

I tugged at my blue-flowered blouse. "They're not hacks or nut—"

The swinging door edged open. An alien in green face paint and silver lamé stuck his head through the open doorway. "Um, where's the Boötes breakfast?"

I pointed over his antennae. "Octagonal room on the other side of the hall."

"Thanks." He disappeared behind the door.

"Boötes?" Dixie asked archly.

"It's the only constellation that starts with *b*." I tightened my ponytail. It's not easy coming up with astronomical alliterations.

"Nothing good can come from this festival."

The beagle curled into his bed by the kitchen table.

"Only economic development." Drawing a deep, satisfied breath, I mustered the arguments I'd presented to the town council. "X-tranormal will bring a full week of extra tourist dollars on Main Street. Plus, publicity for the cutest mountain town between Lake Tahoe and Yosemite." But I glanced uneasily at the swinging kitchen door. I'd worked with the festival company to make sure things would go smoothly. And they would. Our plans couldn't fail.

She snorted. "Save it for the mayor."

"Anyway," I said, "the VIP brunch goes until eleven. I have plenty of time to get to X-tranormal." But I was dying to go now. There aren't a whole lot of power-networking opportunities when you run a UFO-themed B&B. Plus, I was a sponsor! A VIP!

The screen door banged open. Bailey started, tucking his tail.

A teenage girl in jeans and a faded unicorn tee stopped short in the doorway. "Oh. Hi. Am I early?" She ran her hand over her blond ponytail.

"Not at all, Kayla." As an X-tranormal VIP sponsor (ahem), I'd be busy at the festival grounds for the next nine days. Normally, Dixie and I cleaned the rooms, but with me festival-ing, my cousin could use the extra help.

"You're right on time," I continued, my gaze flicking to the agenda on the table. "I thought it would be useful if Dixie gave you a tour before you started. She'll explain how everything works, and then you can start cleaning."

"So, I'm in charge?" Dixie's green eyes narrowed.

"You're always in charge when I'm not here," I said.

She smiled broadly, and a chill crept up my spine. Dixie only smiled at other people's pratfalls.

My cousin crooked a finger at Kayla. "People are still finishing breakfast, so let's start at the reception desk." My cousin strode through the swinging kitchen door.

Kayla shot me an uncertain look and followed.

Bailey trotted after them, his tail wagging.

My stomach rumbled. Time for my own VIP breakfast.

I hurried into my private sitting room and grabbed my purse and cell phone off the table. Stopping in front of the mirror, I yanked my blond hair from its band and finger combed it free. A bit of mascara had smudged beneath my blue eyes, and I rubbed it away, then smoothed the front of my lightweight blouse. I sighed. Nothing could change my wholesome, girl-next-door look, and it was completely out of style. But at least no scrambled eggs dotted the front of my blue capris. It was my first time as a festival sponsor, and I wanted to look professional.

I strode through the kitchen, grabbed my planner, and walked into the high-ceilinged foyer. Behind the low, front desk, Dixie explained how to use the credit card reader to Kayla.

I paused in front of the scarred desk. "No one's checking out until the end of the festival, so you won't have to worry about taking payments."

Dixie rolled her eyes. She pointed at the shelves built into the stairs and weighted with UFO books, playing cards, alien bobble heads, and other chotchkes. "They'll be paying for the souvenirs. I'll shock anyone who even thinks about shoplifting." She pulled a stun gun from a desk drawer.

"Whoa." I blinked, taken aback. "Where'd you get that?"

"Duh." Dixie glowered. "The drawer."

My mouth pressed into a slash. I had a pretty good idea where the weapon had come from. "Right. Well, normally I'd say *no* to stunning guests, so today, I'm going to say *no*. Don't do that. And I'll be back tonight."

Dixie shrugged one bare shoulder. "Whatever. I don't see what the big deal is about this festival anyway. It's not like they're going to solve any universal mysteries."

I tamped down my rising annoyance. It might not be a big deal for her, but the festival was my first attempt at community involvement. "PB Gates is going to be there," I said casually.

Dixie's eyes widened. "You mean your Gran's PB Gates?"

I plucked one of my grandmother's slim UFO books off the shelf. My grandmother had been a huge fan of PB Gates, a UFO expert who traveled the world reporting on UFO sightings and UFO travel in general. Her dream had been to get her UFO-themed B&B, Wits' End, into one of his articles. She hadn't fulfilled that dream in her lifetime, but I was going to do my damnedest to succeed on her behalf.

The Mulder and Scully couple emerged from the breakfast room.

"I don't trust a word from that guy's mouth," Scully was saying. "Chuck Thorpe is a conman. He gives UFOlogists a bad name."

I sucked in my cheeks. Thorpe? He was one of the X-tranormal speakers. I'd heard he was controversial, but surely X-tranormal wouldn't have invited a conman.

"His dad worked for Project Bluebook," her husband said. "Chuck knows things."

"Then his father wasn't a very good Air Force officer," Scully replied tartly, passing the scarred front desk. "They're not supposed to blab to their families about top secret alien encounters."

They mounted the stairs.

Dixie's lip curled. "Scully's right. Thorpe's a phony and a parasite. If that's the caliber of speakers at your festival, it's going to be a bust."

This festival was going to be absolutely wonderful, even if I had to kill someone. "Thank you for your opinion." Nose in the air, I sailed out the front door and collided with six-foot-two-inches of bronzed muscle.

CHAPTER TWO

"For what opinion?" Arsen Holiday's hazel eyes glinted.

I stumbled back a little on the porch and cleared my throat. "Oh. Just. Nothing." The front door swung shut behind me.

A lock of Arsen's whiskey-colored hair stuck out on the side. I jammed my hands in my pockets to keep from reaching out and fixing it. Arsen and I had been best friends since childhood. It wasn't fair he'd grown up to look so damn good – tanned, sinewy, and with big hazel eyes you could fall into.

Heat rose to my cheeks. I wanted to think it was due to the excitement of the morning, but I knew better. "What are you doing here?"

He smiled winningly, his head dangerously close to brushing a hanging fern. "Breakfast."

And... he was bumming free waffles.

Again.

"Sorry," I said. "We're all out."

"Really? I smell bacon." His muscles bulged beneath his polo shirt, the logo for his new security company embroidered in one corner. "And waffles."

Yes, Arsen could tell the difference between pancakes and waffles by scent alone. "All gone," I lied.

"I can hear silverware clinking through the open window." A blue-patterned curtain fluttered through said window. The fabric batted a broom someone had left angled beside the front door.

I grabbed the broom and hung it on its wall hook. My Gran had always kept a broom by the front door, and I'd kept up the tradition. "An aural hallucination. You should get that checked. Did you give Dixie a stun gun?"

"She said she wanted it for self-defense."

"Arsen, it's Dixie," I hissed.

"So?"

"So, she's threatening to stun my guests."

"Come on," he said. "She wouldn't."

"That's easy for you to say. You won't be named in the lawsuit if she does."

"She said she'd keep it at her trailer, and Dixie should be able to protect herself. She's vulnerable out there all alone."

"The stun gun's in the front desk," I said.

He looked thoughtful. "I'll talk to her about legitimate weapons use."

Dixie opened the door and leaned out. "You getting breakfast or just talking about it?" My cousin scratched her bare leg with the toe of one army boot.

Arsen looked a question at me, and I waved him inside. "Leave your dishes in the sink," I said. Arsen had installed new electronic locks at Wits' End for cost, so I sort of owed him free food. Of course, he'd been cadging breakfasts from me long before he'd done me that favor and would be long after I repaid him for his labor.

I edged sideways on the screened, wraparound porch so he could get past.

He touched my arm. "Maybe I'll catch you at the festival?"

"Since when do you attend UFO festivals?" I asked, intrigued and vaguely alarmed. Where Arsen went, a sort of lackadaisical chaos followed. "I thought you were with Team Dixie on the subject."

"I was until I heard there'll be food trucks."

Dixie made a face. "They'll probably be called photon trucks."

"Then I'm definitely in." He winked at me. "I'll see you."

"Groovy!" I bumped into the screened porch door, fumbled around, and escaped down the front steps. *Groovy? Who says groovy anymore?*

I crunched down the gravel driveway and past the rose garden to my blue Subaru Crosstrek. Unlocking its door, I slipped inside and set my planner in the passenger seat.

I rolled down the window and relaxed in my seat. Wits' End in all its glory rose beneath the alpine hills. Vanilla-colored wood slats. Burnt red and deep brown gingerbread trim. A crashed UFO in the shingled roof. My grandmother might have been a little nutty, but she'd had style.

I smiled at a nearby rosebush, one of many she'd filled her garden with. "Wish me luck, Gran," I whispered.

Starting the car, I backed onto the court. The next two weeks were going to be amazing. Between X-tranormal and the following week's Harvest Festival, Wits' End was booked solid.

I cruised slowly through Doyle, my favorite small town in all the world. It had started as a mining town in the Gold Rush, and the shops on Main Street still sported old-time false fronts.

Today, a banner hung across the street and proclaimed: *Welcome X-tranormal!* I beamed at a trio of paper aliens decorating the window of the ice cream shop. Doyle was getting into the X-tranormal spirit, and I was partly responsible.

I drew a deep, gratified breath and straightened in my seat. Gran had always said that good deeds first benefited the giver and then the receiver. Now I understood why. Helping the town felt great.

An elderly woman in a billowing black dress stopped to stare as I passed, and I waved. "Hi, Mrs. Steinberg!"

"No names!" she shouted.

Chuckling, I drove on. Mrs. Steinberg was the most paranoid person in Doyle. I'd once believed the old lady to be a dark figure, with secret, inside knowledge of the town. It was *half* true. She worked in town records.

I drove down the narrow mountain highway to the festival. At the X-tranormal sign, I turned down a long, curving dirt road. The land, a flattened area of dried grasses and oaks and odd stone formations, belonged to a winery, and lines of grapevines rippled along the surrounding hills. The road opened to a wide parking lot, and my SUV bumped past a PARK AT YOUR OWN RISK sign. I shook my head at the precaution. *Ridiculous.* What criminal was going to find his way to this out-of-the-way place?

I rolled across the uneven ground. Since the festival didn't officially start until noon, I easily found a spot not too far from the front gate. My dash clock read eight-thirty, and I smiled with satisfaction. I was right on schedule.

Digging my badge from my purse, I looped the lanyard around the collar of my blouse, grabbed my things and strode to the gate. Oaks and brush backed up against the fencing, hiding all but the tops of the white tents inside. Multicolored flags drooped from the tent peaks.

A bored-looking woman in a green *X-tranormal* tee looked up from her clipboard. "The festival doesn't open until noon."

I lifted my badge and glanced up at the silvery UFO over the gate. "I'm here for the VIP brunch." I'd never been a VIP before, and I was determined to enjoy my privileges to the max.

She grunted, unimpressed, and made a tick mark on her clipboard and handed me a map. "Second tent on the right. And *Planet of the Grapes* will open at ten-thirty for VIPs," she said in a bored tone.

I smoothed my lanyard. "The wine tent? I couldn't possibly." But I was definitely going there, even if ten-thirty was a little early for the grape. What was the good of being a VIP if I couldn't wine taste secluded from the hoi polloi? "Thanks." Checking the map, I hurried past the guard.

The X-tranormal festival had been laid out in a contorted spiral. Its twists and turns accommodated the oak and elm trees that had been here first. Shuttered stalls squatted between the tents, and it felt a bit like a medieval ghost town.

A breeze whispered down the empty road, and the sides of the tents undulated. In the distance, thunderheads piled above the Sierra peaks. I eyed them warily. Rain wouldn't exactly ruin the festival, but it wouldn't be much fun.

I adjusted the industrial-sized purse over my shoulder. Stopping to admire the VIP tent, I jammed my hands in the pockets of my capris.

Someone had painted portholes on the VIP tent's canvas sides. Colored lights flashed at its seams in a passable version of a flying saucer. This was going to be so much fun! Low chatter flowed through an open tent flap, and I eagerly brushed through.

Inside, a buffet had been set up along one wall, and throw rugs littered the floor. A second flap, on the opposite side, had also been strapped open. A warm breeze smelling of dried earth flowed through the tent.

An elfin woman with shoulder-length, blazing red hair walked up to me and smiled, her hand extended. "Hi, I'm Maisie, the conference organizer." Her serious brown eyes crinkled.

"Oh?" I'd thought a woman named Rachel was the conference organizer. "Hi. I'm Susan Witsend."

Maisie pumped my hand. Her wedding ring pinched my finger, and I flinched.

She turned the diamond, so it faced outward. "Sorry about that." Maisie looked to be in her twenties. She wore an official green, X-tranormal t-shirt and conference lanyard. "I've lost some weight, and it keeps twisting. It's so nice to meet one of our sponsors."

A burly man with white-blond hair stood near the buffet table. In a corner, a silver-haired woman sat on a folding chair and picked at the food on her paper plate.

She sighed. "And the only sponsor actually interested in attending the brunch, it seems. You must be a glutton for punishment."

"I'm always interested in brunch." I motioned toward the long table lined with champagne flutes. "Especially with mimosas on the menu."

She laughed. "Then it's great to have you. Let me introduce you to one of our speakers." She led me toward the buffet. Pastries lined up beside cardboard coffee containers from a local shop, Ground. I smiled. I *knew* the festival would bring the town business, and Doyle was already benefiting.

"Um, is Rachel here?" I asked. Rachel had promised to introduce me to the infamously reclusive PB Gates.

Maisie shook her head. "There was a family emergency, and she asked me to step in. I normally manage steampunk conventions. But since she had already done most of the work for X-tranormal, I agreed to pinch hit. Why? Is there a problem?"

"No, no problem. I'd hoped to meet PB Gates, and she said she could set it up."

Faint lines appeared between her brows. "PB Gates? Who's that?"

"PB Gates?" the bearlike man boomed. He gripped a plate piled with eggs and sausages. "Only one of the most popular writers on UFO sightings." He extended his free hand to me. "Spence Bradford."

I tried not to squeal. I was among UFO royalty! "Of *Out There*? It's great to meet you. I'm Susan Witsend. I own the local UFO B&B, Wits' End." *Out There* was one of the largest amateur UFO hunting organizations in the US.

He rubbed a hand across his bristly jowls. "Hoped to stay at your B&B for the conference. Booked up before we had a chance."

I winced. A word from Spence on the UFO message boards would have sent Wits' End through the stratosphere. "I'm sorry to hear it. I would have loved to host you, but we don't have that many rooms."

"That's all right," he said. "Got into the Historic Doyle Hotel."

Urgh! My arch rival! Black Bart had stayed there once – how was I supposed to compete with that? But it was a nice hotel, and it had a lot more rooms than Wits' End. A better location too, curse it all.

A slender, olive-complexioned man with high cheekbones strode into the tent and brandished a briefcase. "Is it true? Is Chuck Thorpe going to be here?" His voice had a faint Russian accent.

"That's Chuck's wife." Maisie nodded toward the plump, silver-haired woman knitting in the corner. "So, he'd better be. Oh, Yuri, this is Susan Witsend. She runs the UFO B&B, Wits' End."

Yuri scowled, ignoring me, and I edged slightly away from the little group. "Thorpe *is* here?" he asked. Lank, near-black hair brushed his shoulders. "Keep that bastard away from me, if you don't want any trouble."

"Now, now," Spence said. "No one wants any trouble."

"Speak for yourself," Yuri growled.

"I don't suppose you saw *my* wife when you were walking here?" Spence asked the Russian.

"Yes, somewhere." He waved his hand vaguely.

"If you're looking for PB Gates," Maisie told me, "the registration tent might be able to help you out. They can at least tell you if he's registered under his real name or a stage name – that may make it easier to find him. If you go there now, you can talk to them before they get slammed with prep work. It's right next to this tent, on the left."

"Thanks. I will." I said, relieved to escape. People made fun of UFO enthusiasts. Nine times out of ten though, they were wonderful people. But I didn't much like Yuri's scowl.

I strode to the tent next door. Its flaps were lowered, and it took me a minute or two to find the entrance.

Finally, I brushed through the canvas opening and stopped short. Boxes of wine stacked taller than Arsen made a small corridor. Vacant chairs stood behind the long metal tables opposite.

"Hello?" I stepped deeper inside the stifling tent and made a mental note to have a word with Maisie about moving the boxes. Wine doesn't store well in the heat. If this morning was any indication, the tent would be broiling by afternoon.

My foot nudged a near-black wine bottle. It rolled across the earth floor and came to a stop beside a curled hand.

I sucked in a breath.

A hand.

An arm.

A prone body.

Blood puddled beside a man's head, his eyes blank and staring.

CHAPTER THREE

Sheriff McCourt glared. The five-foot-six sheriff only had an inch on me, but she knew how to use it. "You. Again." She removed her round, broad-brimmed hat and finger combed her hair. The blond curls fell neatly back into place. In the mountains behind her, thunderheads were rising.

A chipmunk scampered up the oak we sheltered beneath. It raced across a branch and cocked its head, as if contemplating a jump to the nearby registration tent.

The Sheriff and I had worked together before, when her ex-husband had been murdered in my B&B. For most B&B's, a murder would be a black mark. But my UFO-inclined guests seemed to think it gave Wits' End the added frisson of a possible haunting.

It wasn't something I discussed with the sheriff.

At any rate, this time, I was prepared. I was also a little more humble than I'd been on my first run as a girl detective. But I *had* to help. I wouldn't blame the sheriff if she shut down the festival. But good God, if she did... My guests would leave. I'd have to refund their money. Worse, all the town's hard work would be down the drain. And despite what the publicists say, there is such a thing as bad publicity in the tourist industry. Most people had chalked up the Doyle Disappearances/Reappearances as a fraud or myth. If anything, the incident had increased tourism. But murder was concrete, brutal, and terrifying, and my stomach churned.

I flipped open my planner. After the last, unfortunate incident when I'd found a body in guest room seven, I'd redesigned it for future law enforcement encounters. "I arrived at the festival grounds at exactly eight-thirty. The woman at the gate can confirm that I came through a minute or two later. It took me approximately five minutes to walk to the VIP tent. I was inside for no more than five minutes, before I went to the registration tent and discovered the body. Whoever the dead man is—"

"Charles Thorpe." She returned the uniform hat to her head.

"Thorpe? You mean Chuck Thorpe?" An X-tranormal speaker, and one another speaker, Yuri, had threatened? A chill, gray shadow seemed to touch the back of my neck, and I rubbed my skin there. *Everything is under control.* "Oh. Well, Mr. Thorpe wasn't in the VIP tent when I arrived." I glanced up from my planner. "The people who *were* in the tent seemed relieved by that fact, except for maybe his wife."

"If I want your opinion about witnesses you've admitted you don't know, I'll ask for it. Who was in the VIP tent?"

The branch above us rustled. Dried oak leaves showered us.

I brushed flakes of brown off my shoulders. "Um... Chuck's wife. The conference organizer, Maisie Henchcliffe. She's the one who suggested I come to the registration tent to see if someone I knew had arrived yet. And there was Spence Bradford. He's the head of *Out There*, an internationally recognized UFO organization." We'd attracted some heavy hitters.

"What does it mean to be internationally recognized?"

I couldn't tell if she was being sarcastic. I also didn't exactly know the answer. "It means it's big. Anyway, Spence asked Yuri, who'd entered the tent after me, if he'd seen his wife on the grounds. So, presumably she's somewhere nearby. Yuri's from Eastern Europe, I think, if you couldn't guess from the name. I don't know what his story is—"

"I didn't ask."

"But—"

She raised her brows, and I bit back a retort.

Fine. She'd no doubt hear about Yuri from someone else. "And that was all."

"What are you doing here? The festival doesn't open for another hour."

"I'm one of the sponsors. This is a huge opportunity to promote Doyle as a UFO destination..."

Her eyes narrowed.

"And I'm hoping to meet someone at the festival," I finished quickly. It was time Doyle and Wits' End got some love. I was sick of Wits' End getting skunked by a certain UFO hotel in Rachel, Nevada. That hotel got all the attention because it was in the nearest town to the military's top-secret base, Area 51, by Groom Lake. Not that any of that mattered now. "I wasn't sure if he'd registered yet."

"He?" One corner of her mouth wrinkled. "Does Arsen know?"

My face warmed. What was that supposed to mean? It's not like Arsen would be jealous of PB Gates. Arsen and I had never been an item. My buddy had spent most of his adult life bumming around vacation resorts as a dive instructor and ladies' man. He had an impressive collection of airplane barf bags (unused) from those halcyon days.

I glanced at a deputy, unwinding police tape around the registration tent. Though since Arsen had started his one-man security company, he seemed a lot less flaky. I'd started to see Arsen less as an old friend to be exasperated with and more as... I wasn't sure what I saw him as.

"It's business," I said firmly. Besides, PB Gates had been writing for decades. The UFO reporter was probably the age my Gran would have been, or near to it.

The sheriff's look was pitying. "Did you see anyone else inside the registration tent, where you found the body?"

"No, but—"

"Did you see anyone going into or out of the registration tent at any time?" She ran a finger along the inside of her khaki collar. The morning was warming.

"No, but—"

"How well did you know Mr. Thorpe?"

The chipmunk sprinted past her boots and vanished beneath a lichen-covered boulder.

"Chuck?" I shifted my weight. "I mean, Charles Thorpe? Not at all. I mean, I'd heard about him. A little. Mostly today. He's controversial in the UFO community—"

"So, you're in the UFO *community* now?"

I crossed my arms over my chest. "I run a UFO-themed B&B. My guests expect me to have some knowledge of the subject. Anyway, Chuck— Charles Thorpe's father was an officer in Project Bluebook—"

The sheriff groaned.

"You know, the investigations the Air Force conducted into UFOs?"

A muscle worked in her jaw.

"Chuck claimed his father had talked to him about what he'd experienced," I continued. "But Chuck was secretive about his, er, insider's knowledge. His father was dead, so he couldn't get into any trouble for spilling secrets, but Chuck could."

"Doesn't it bother you at all that you have this ridiculous information in your head? What useful data has gotten crowded from your brain because of this UFO nonsense?"

I blew out a noisy breath. "For me, this *is* useful information. And it's helping you now."

"Is it?" She sighed. "Is it really?" A siren wailed in the distance. We both stilled, listening. "That'll be the coroner," she said. "Okay, what else?"

"Charles ran a high-priced UFO-hunting crew. Some people think he's a conman." Or at least, one of my guests and Dixie did.

"What do you think?"

Ha! Despite the sheriff's bluster, she respected my opinion. After all, I had once been instrumental in bringing a murderer to justice. Unfortunately, I'd also put Arsen in danger in the process. "I don't know," I admitted. "Chuck Thorpe's UFO-hunting team is a minor footnote in UFOlogy. At least, it is compared to the disappearances that happened right here in Doyle."

"Those so-called disappearances were because of a gas leak," she snarled. The Sheriff wasn't happy with Doyle's reputation for supernaturally missing persons.

So-called? I don't think so. "Right."

Last year, Doyle had been the sight of a mass disappearance of an entire pub full of people - *plus* the pub. Months later, the people had reappeared, confused and with no memory of what had happened. The pub never returned, and that missing pub remained one of the weirdest parts of the story. What would aliens do with a pub? I imagined the Fox and Thistle now on an orange and purple planet, aliens perched on bar stools and drinking cider beneath triple moons.

Gas leak, my Aunt Fannie. "And that's all I know," I said brightly.

"That, I can believe. And you saw no one else enter or leave the VIP tent while you were there?"

"Um, no. So, I guess Chuck was killed with that wine bottle?" Contra Hollywood movies, full wine bottles didn't generally break over people's heads. Thanks to Arsen, I'd learned this lesson the hard way. (No actual heads had been harmed, but my pumpkin was DOA.)

"None of your business, because you're not investigating."

"But we worked so well together before."

"Are you kidding me? Go!"

"Trouble?" An elegant, middle-aged woman with straight, gray and white hair strode down the dirt road. "I'm Bridget Konrach, a reporter. Sheriff, what's going on?"

The sheriff aimed her pen at Bridget's VIP lanyard. "That doesn't say PRESS."

The woman's cheeks darkened. "I'm freelance, and I'm participating in the festival as a speaker." Her flowing gray slacks and matching tunic rippled in the balmy, morning breeze.

"A speaker on UFOs," Sheriff McCourt said flatly and turned to me. "Thank you, Ms. Witsend. We'll be in touch."

"Oh, okay." I edged backward. *Ms. Witsend?* We'd solved a crime together! But I guess the sheriff had to try and look impartial.

It was unlikely the sheriff would tell a reporter anything she hadn't told me, but just in case, I lingered within earshot.

A local reporter, Tom Tarrant, bustled up to the two. "Sheriff, what's the word?" Broad shouldered, brown haired, and blue eyed, Tom had that all-American look you see in TV shows and clothing catalogs. It's hard not to notice these things in a small town with a limited population of single males. Not that I was interested or anything.

"I heard a man was killed," Bridget said. "Is that true?"

Tom's eyes narrowed. "Giving interviews to non-local reporters, Sheriff?"

"No interviews!" McCourt glowered at me from beneath her hat. "*Thank* you, Ms. Witsend."

Busted, I wandered toward the festival exit. I wrung my hands, realized I was doing it, and stopped.

A murder on the first day of the festival? This was a disaster. Ashamed, I scrubbed my hands across my face. But lost tourist dollars were nothing compared to the loss of a life. In the town council meetings, I'd sworn the UFO-curious were normal, fun-loving people. They were no threat to Doyle.

Obviously, I'd been wrong.

A woman carrying a medical bag and flanked by two deputies strode past. The coroner?

I turned away, feeling sick. A man had been killed at a festival I'd pushed hard for, one I'd sworn would benefit everyone. But it hadn't done much for Chuck Thorpe. Chuck was dead.

And how could I fix this when the sheriff had ordered me not to? I stopped short. But she hadn't exactly told me not to investigate; she'd said I *wasn't* investigating, past tense.

I snapped my fingers. Of course. The sheriff didn't *really* want me to buzz off. She just had to say that to keep up appearances. After all, I was embedded in the festival, her inside woman, just like the last time we'd solved a crime together. Sheriff McCourt needed me.

So, if I was in charge of the festival recently derailed by murder, what would I be doing right now?

Having a panic attack, most likely. Maisie must be going bananas. Swiveling on my heels, I strode toward the registration tent.

Deputies guarded its entrance. The festival organizer, Maisie, spoke with the security lady who'd let me in that morning.

Maisie consulted a map. "We'll be moving the registration to tent B." She pointed at a tent near the gate. "Please direct people there."

My shoulders relaxed. Maisie seemed to be taking everything in stride. That was good for the festival and Doyle. I wanted to hug her, but I'm a big believer in personal space.

The guard nodded. "It would be better if we could register them outside, before they came through the gates."

"Well, we can't," Maisie snapped. She grimaced. "Sorry. This isn't shaping up to be a good day for anyone. There's some rule against putting tents in the parking lot. Inside the gate is the best we can do. Just be sure to check people's registration receipt – they should all have one – before you let them in."

"Will do," the guard said and walked away.

Maisie turned to me. "Susan, I'm so sorry about all of this."

"Is everything, er, under control?"

"We're improvising. How are you doing after..." She trailed off, her fair skin flushing the crimson only a true redhead can achieve.

"I'm fine. How can I help?"

"Thanks, but you don't need to worry about anything. That's what I'm here for."

I smiled thinly. Not worry? Maisie didn't know me very well.

She touched my arm and lightly guided me into the shade of a tent. Staff in green *X-tranormal* t-shirts lugged boxes into the tent and exited emptyhanded. "Fortunately," she said, "no one put the computers or registration packets inside the registration tent yet. Otherwise, the police would have confiscated them as evidence. We should be able to open the con— I mean the festival, on time."

"Really?" I asked. That seemed unusually big of the sheriff.

Her smile was wintery. "The sheriff understands how important tourism is to small towns like Doyle."

My insides tightened with guilt. In other words, pressure had been applied, but by whom? Had the mayor found out about the murder already?

"But now we've lost Chuck," she continued, "one of our key speakers. Um... I don't suppose you could take his place?"

"Me?" My voice cracked. I gripped my planner more tightly. But I *had* offered to help.

"You must know more about the Doyle disappearances than any of our other speakers. I've read the Wits' End brochure. It said you give presentations about the disappearances at the B&B."

My purse slid from my shoulder to the inside of my elbow, and I hitched it up. "You want me to give my presentation? Here?" My heartrate sped. I wasn't prepared. This wasn't in my planner. I couldn't just rearrange my schedule. But the more involved I was, the easier it would be to gather intel on the suspects.

"Yes, and it would be wonderful if you could take over for Chuck Thorpe on his panels too."

"I don't know." I gulped. "I've never done a panel before." It was one thing to give my UFO spiel to a friendly audience of eight. There would be thousands at the conference. What if they all came to hear me? What if no one came? I wasn't sure which was worse.

She knotted her tomato-red hair into a quick bun. "They're easy. You'll get the questions in advance. All you have to do is answer them succinctly."

A bead of sweat trickled down my neck. "I'm not sure I'm the best person—"

"It'll be extra exposure for your B&B."

"And I'd love that. But my work week is already tightly scheduled. I hadn't planned on taking extra time to present or prepare for presentations. I just don't know how I can fit in anything extra and do a good job."

She grimaced and tugged on her lanyard. "I get it. It's too bad though. I think PB Gates is scheduled to be on one of Chuck's panels."

I couldn't deny the appeal of meeting him as a co-panelist. My chin dipped guiltily to my chest. This wasn't about me. It was about Doyle and Wits' End. And the sheriff needed me. "Okay. I'll do it."

"Great! Let me get a copy of the speaker schedule. I'll be right back." She disappeared into the new registration tent.

I opened my planner and scanned its pages. The faster this murder was solved, the better. And if I worked my schedule right, I might be able to combine speaking with snooping.

But this wasn't a game. What had nearly happened to Arsen the last time I'd played detective was proof of that. My throat thickened. But I'd found the body. I'd brought the festival to Doyle. And that meant what had happened was partly my fault.

And my responsibility.

CHAPTER FOUR

I jogged up the steps and pushed open the B&B's front entrance. It jammed against something solid, and my shoulder bounced off the wooden door.

"Hey," a masculine voice shouted from its other side. A mass of voices rumbled from inside the foyer.

Alarmed, I forced the door wider and wedged my head through.

Backpacks lay pell-mell atop the rug, where anyone could trip over them. Guests, their voices raised and irritable, crowded the unmanned reception desk. They seemed to be arguing with each other, which I guess was better than arguing with Dixie, but my stomach flipped. Wits' End was out of control. Where was Dixie?

My cousin trotted down the stairs, her blue-tipped hair bouncing. "Here are your extra towels." She handed the fluffy white towels to a zaftig blonde in layers of burlap-colored shifts.

"Thank you," the woman said, "but what about the murder?"

"It's not the girl's fault Chuck Thorpe was killed." Mr. Jonas, a gray-haired guest in a track suit and khaki baseball cap thumped his metal cane on the rug. "It didn't happen here."

"But Wits' End is a sponsor," the blonde insisted. "She must know something."

A chorus of voices rose in agreement.

The churning in my gut intensified. I'd never seen such chaos in Wits' End. I sidled along the elegantly papered wall and thought fast.

Expecting sponsors to have insight into a murder seemed a little unreasonable, even if the customer was always right. But they weren't going to calm down until they got some information. I could defuse this. While I didn't know what had happened to Chuck, I could talk about the festival. "Excuse me."

Mr. Jonas raised a brow and leaned more heavily on his cane. "I hardly think it's fair to blame the B&B for something that happened at a UFO festival."

Why not blame Wits' End? I blamed myself. I'd helped plan the festival for the town I loved, and I'd thought I'd planned for all contingencies. Wits' End had even sponsored the first-aid tent. But no amount of first-aid could help Chuck Thorpe. "Excuse me," I repeated more loudly.

"If there's even going to be a festival after this," someone shouted.

"Can we get refunds?" The curvy blonde tucked a strand of hair into her high bun.

"There's the owner, trying to sneak into the kitchen," Dixie said, pointing at me. "She just returned from X-tranormal."

The crowd turned to stare.

I hadn't been sneaking! "Um, hi." I waggled my fingers in a limp wave. "I'm afraid I don't know much about what happened. But Chuck is indeed dead, and the police are investigating. As to your other question, the festival—"

"Will the festival be canceled?"

"Or delayed?"

"Was it murder?"

"Why *wouldn't* it be murder?"

Bailey barked, an incessant, eardrum-piercing beat.

I swooped down and picked up the beagle. Bailey was a little big for my arms, but he stopped barking and switched to licking my face. *Ugh.* Beagle breath.

"The festival will still open at noon today," I said. And noon was right about now. "They've had to find a replacement for Chuck's speaking engagements. Otherwise, the festival is going on as usual."

"Who's the replacement?" the blonde asked.

"Er, me."

Silence fell. The guests shot each other skeptical looks.

"They want me to talk about the Doyle disappearances," I said, defensive.

"But you're not actually published, are you?" The blonde prodded the knotted hair on her head, shoving it into place.

I clutched Bailey closer, and the beagle squirmed in my arms. "I edited my grandmother's book and added the disappearance of the Bell and Thistle pub." So, no, I wasn't *exactly* published. But I was sort of published, and in today's world, self-publishing counted. My Gran had put a lot of research into that little book.

"What about the reappearance of the people from the pub?" Her brown eyes narrowed with suspicion.

"That too," I said.

"Chuck's death – was it murder?" the blonde asked.

"I couldn't say." Of *course*, it had been murder, even if the sheriff hadn't exactly confirmed it. He'd been bludgeoned with the wine bottle I'd kicked across the registration tent. But I wasn't a total noob. If I blabbed that info, the sheriff would have my head.

"It had to be murder." Mr. Jonas leaned more heavily on his cane. "After what Chuck did to that Nevada rancher and God knows how many others, he practically had a target on his back."

"Nevada rancher?" I asked.

"He was one of Chuck's acolytes," the blonde said.

Mr. Jonas snorted. "One of his victims, you mean. Giving him money for research, all to be part of Chuck's secret club."

"Hardly a club. And definitely not a secret. Chuck had an LLC." The blonde wandered to the desk and pointed at my grandmother's booklet on the shelf behind it. "I'll take one please."

Dixie handed her the slim volume.

"What happened to the rancher?" I asked.

"It may be an LLC, but it operates like a secret society," the older man said. "The higher up you get, and the more you pay, the more secret information is revealed."

"And the rancher?" I asked, fidgeting with impatience.

He turned to me. "No one knows exactly what Chuck told him. Somehow, the rancher got it into his head there was a UFO base somewhere in the Nevada mountains. He went to look for it and never returned."

"And Chuck had the audacity to claim the man had been kidnapped by aliens." The blonde flipped open the book and rolled her eyes.

"Was he ever found?" I asked.

Bored by the murder talk, Bailey squirmed in my arms. I set him down. The beagle trotted to the kitchen door, pushed it open with his nose, and slipped through. The door drifted gently shut.

Mr. Jonas braced his cane in two hands and leaned forward. "Years later, hikers found the body, or what was left of it. The authorities were somehow able to identify the rancher. Chuck has — had — a lot to answer for."

"He's burning somewhere toasty," the blonde said, "no doubt about that."

"Did the rancher have any family?" I asked. Sheriff McCourt might not know this story, and revenge made a strong motive for murder.

"No," the woman said. "The rancher – what was his name? – was a loner. That's probably how Chuck was able to get his hooks into him."

"Oh," I said, disappointed. So much for my hot lead.

"Wait," she said. "You said X-tranormal is opening at noon?"

"Right. In fact, it's already—"

My words were lost in the stampede for the door.

When the dust cleared, Dixie was sitting on top of the scarred front desk, her legs folded beneath her. "By the way, the mayor called."

I jolted forward. "What? When?" The mayor *did* know about the murder. Was she holding me responsible? Had she put pressure on Sheriff McCourt?

"Like, never? No one called. I'm kidding."

My shoulders slumped. "Very funny. Where's Kayla?" I asked, surveying the foyer. Someone had left behind their backpack, angled against the wall.

She jerked her thumb at the carpeted stairs. "Getting acquainted with the cleaning supplies. What are you doing here? I thought you'd be at the festival all day."

"I'd always planned to return this afternoon. Didn't you see the calendar I left for you?"

Dixie yawned.

"Anyway," I said, "The press meet-and-greet isn't until the day after tomorrow."

Mulder and Scully jogged downstairs. Scully grabbed the backpack, and they hustled out the door.

Dixie cocked her head. "You're really going to speak? At a UFO festival?"

"I talk about UFOs all the time at Wits' End."

She threw me a Look with a capital *L*.

"What?" I crossed my arms.

"And when they ask about how Doyle compares to other historical UFO sightings?"

"People have been reporting encounters with and kidnappings by strange creatures for hundreds of years. Centuries ago, people thought the abductions and probing were carried out by faeries. Reports of bright lights, missing memories, and strangely tall or short kidnappers, are all over the literature." Dixie knew this. She was obsessed with the topic, right down to the not-quite-legal radio set-up in her trailer. "Wait, are you testing me?"

"And Roswell? What about the recent revelations of a secret five-year Pentagon investigation into UFOs? Was the Doyle incident part of that? Was that the real reason an FBI agent was on the scene and lingered in Doyle long after The Disappeared reappeared? How do the Doyle disappearances compare to the disappearance of the Anjikuni village in 1930?"

This *was* a test! "Oooh! I know that one."

"Don't worry. No one will ask." She shook her head. "This is why I don't go to these waste-oid UFO festivals. Half the participants are going to be dressed as green-skinned slave girls or Darth Vader."

"You're a UFO snob."

"Exactly." She hopped off the desk.

"Wait," I said. Dixie hadn't liked Chuck Thorpe either. That didn't make her a suspect, but it did make her a source.

Unheeding, she stomped up the stairs.

"Dix—"

"That seemed a little harsh," Arsen said from behind me, and I jumped.

"I know," I said. "Dixie was super critical."

"I meant you calling her a UFO snob." Arms crossed, bronzed muscles bulging, he leaned against the door frame and quirked a brow.

"Dixie *is* a UFO snob. She said it herself. What are you doing at Wits' End?"

His brow creased. "I heard about the murder, and I knew you'd be here. Are you okay?"

"At least you saw the calendar I left on the fridge."

"What calendar? It was in your planner."

"You read my planner?" I asked, outraged.

"It's not like it's a diary or anything."

"My life is in that planner." I even wrote down the things I was grateful for each day next to bullet point hearts. *Uh, oh.* Had I ever expressed gratitude for Arsen? Because he might take those scrawled hearts the wrong way. I tugged my purse in front of my body.

He grinned. "Your life and your weekly breakfast menu."

That explained why Arsen always showed up on pancake and waffle days. As long as he'd confined his snooping to breakfast menus, I was in the clear.

"What exactly happened at X-tranormal?" he asked.

I sobered. "One of the guests – Chuck Thorpe – was murdered, and I found him—"

"Whoa. *You* found him?"

"It was awful." I gulped. "And then the sheriff interrogated me like I was—"

"A suspect?"

"An idiot." I was trying not to take that personally. "And now I have to take over Chuck's speaking engagements at the festival. Chuck's presentation is supposed to last ninety minutes. The presentation I give the Wits' End guests only takes thirty." I whipped a sheet of paper from my planner. "Plus, I'm on panels, Arsen. Panels! *And* it looks like rain." Had the X-tranormal team planned for rain?

"No, the thunderheads are moving east." His tanned brow furrowed. "Why you?"

"Someone had to fill— Wait, why not me?"

"No, I mean, of course they want you. But you didn't have to say *yes*."

"I'm a sponsor. I've got a stake in X-tranormal."

He lowered his head. "Is that the only thing you think's at stake?"

"What do you mean?"

"I mean, you've been the face of this festival in Doyle. Are you afraid your reputation will be dented if things go wrong?"

"What? No." I shifted my weight. Was I? "Chuck's presentations just need to get done, so I may as well do them." I brandished my planner. "Sorry, I guess I'm a little freaked out by the scheduling changes. I thought I could just expand my usual presentation, but now I'm not so sure. I mean, I can't wing a ninety-minute lecture. I need to write it and practice it, and each time I practice that removes ninety minutes from my day."

"Actually, only about seventy minutes. You'll want to leave time for Q&A."

Why hadn't I thought of that? What else hadn't I thought of?

He braced his broad hands on my shoulders, and my heart gave a little quiver. "Breathe," he said, gazing into my eyes.

My breath caught. His hazel eyes were deep as a dappled forest path, and— I shook myself. And this was a path I needed to get off of. Fast.

"I am breathing," I said, irritated. "I do it every day." But that was Arsen, the yin to my type-A yang. I exhaled slowly.

He smiled. "Okay then, chill. Everyone will know you're a last-minute substitution and why. I'm sure they'll forgive any mistakes."

"I guess," I grumbled.

He shook his head. "I still don't understand why you agreed to do the presentation if your schedule was booked."

"I didn't think, and I felt bad about Chuck. And..." And I'd thought it would allow me to poke around in the murder. Now I wasn't so sure. Where would I possibly find time to detect?

"And?" he prompted.

"And PB Gates is going to be on one of my panels. I thought it would be a good way to meet him."

His dark brows slashed downward. "PB Gates?"

"He's a big-time UFO travel writer. Well, he travels around writing about local UFO sightings. PB also writes a lot about UFO-themed restaurants and hotels."

"Are there that many?"

"You'd be surprised. But no one knows what he looks like. He's so reclusive, it's amazing he's agreed to speak at all. Anyway, since PB's not staying at Wits' End, I thought maybe I could butter him up at the festival and give him a tour or at least a copy of her book. He does book reviews too."

The bottom half of his jaw levered sideways. "Huh. I hadn't thought of the festival as a networking opportunity. I guess there are all sorts of people who go there?"

"Well," I said, "sure. There are some people who are a little, er, extreme, I won't deny that. But most are people who've had an experience they can't explain. Or they understand this universe is too big for humans to be the only intelligent life. I mean, it's a little arrogant to believe we're that unique, don't you think?"

"Right." Absently, he patted my shoulder. "Well, if you need anything let me know." He wandered from the B&B, his footsteps clunking down the front porch steps.

Arsen was right. I needed to chill. I'd agreed to speak, and panicking wasn't going to get me anywhere.

Unsnapping the cover of my planner, I headed to the kitchen.

What I needed, was a plan...

CHAPTER FIVE

The candle flared beneath the last chafing dish, and I waved out the match. I'd baked a buttermilk blueberry coffee cake to go with the scrambled eggs, bacon and country-style potatoes. The usual suspects – yogurt and jams and bread for toast - neatly lined the sideboard. Watery sunlight streamed across the white tablecloth and winked on the selection of juices in glass carafes.

Outside the screened window, a stellar jay twittered. The curtains billowed in the early morning breeze. Chuck was dead, and the world went on, oblivious and impersonal.

I worried the cuff of my loose, white blouse. It was day two of the festival, and all I could think of was what I planned to do. The sheriff and I might have teamed up once before, but she'd seemed less enthusiastic about my help this time around. But I'd learned my lesson. All I had to do was gather evidence from the inside and leave the apprehension of the killer to McCourt. I'd play to my strengths, and she'd play to hers.

I removed a slice of coffee cake – just so no one was shy about being the first to dig in – and walked to the kitchen. One of the low, blue cupboards around the sink was open, and I shut it. Dropping onto a wooden chair at the table, I slathered butter on top of the steaming coffeecake.

I flipped open my laptop and proceeded to step one in my plan: research Chuck Thorpe. Chuck had an annoyingly coy website, little more than a name and contact number. But lots had been written about his group elsewhere. The articles could be divided into two groups. Chuck was leading a cult, and Chuck was on to a government conspiracy. There wasn't much about Chuck's personal life. So, I wasn't any further into figuring out who would want him dead.

I bit into the coffeecake and closed my eyes. Oh, yeah baby. The buttermilk blueberry cake hadn't needed the butter, but I wasn't complaining.

I returned to my online research.

UFOLOGIST FOUND MURDERED AT X-TRANORMAL
FESTIVAL

By Bridget Konrach

The Doyle Sheriff's Department is conducting a homicide investigation after famed UFO expert, Charles Thorpe, was found dead inside the X-tranormal festival.

Just before nine A.M., emergency services received word about an unresponsive man in one of the tents. When officers arrived, they found Mr. Thorpe dead at the scene.

The cause of death has not been released. But the Sheriff's Department announced that Mr. Thorpe's death was a homicide.

Mr. Thorpe is a controversial figure within the UFO community. He managed a nameless organization dedicated to the investigation of UFOs. Mr. Thorpe and his organization have been the subject of multiple lawsuits.

If you know anything about the incident, you are asked to contact the Doyle Sheriff's Department.

The article had been in a fairly big-name online paper. Though she was a freelancer, Bridget must have kept up her contacts to get the article published.

I reread it. *Lawsuits?* Records of any legal actions might be online. However, I'd learned the hard way not to expect a lot of detail from court websites. And unless I knew where the lawsuits had been filed, I had little chance of tracking them down.

In his dog bed, Bailey lumbered to his feet and wagged his tail.

"No people food for you." I nodded at his full bowl on the floor by the sink.

He yawned and shook himself, collar jingling. In spite of his subtle begging, Bailey was a trim beagle.

Footsteps thumped up the steps of the kitchen porch, and Arsen breezed in through the side door. "Hey, Sue. What's for breakfast?" His voice rumbled through me, and my stomach fluttered.

Stupid stomach.

"Was that a rhetorical question?" Surreptitiously, I licked crumbs from my lips. "Or did you forget the menu when you spied in my planner?"

"I have to keep up appearances." One corner of his mouth lifted, and he stooped to pat the beagle.

Bailey wagged his tail harder and shut his eyes, ecstatic.

"Coffeecake and potatoes," I said, relenting. "And eggs."

"You're the best. Thanks." Arsen beelined through the swinging door toward the breakfast room.

I snapped shut my laptop. Was that all I was to him? Just a free breakfast?

More footsteps on the side porch, and Dixie ambled into the kitchen. She yawned and scratched Bailey's head. "Yo. Breakfast?"

I nodded toward the breakfast room. Dixie slouched out, tugging her tank lower over her cargo shorts. In spite of my grumbling, I wasn't worried about Arsen and Dixie cleaning me out. I always calculated their breakfasts along with my guests'.

Arsen returned to the kitchen carrying a plate piled high with food.

Bailey sat up straighter, alert for dropped morsels or weakness of character.

Arsen forked scrambled eggs into his mouth. "So. What's with the fairies?"

I blinked. *Fairies?* "The what?"

He cocked his head toward the drapes fluttering in the window above the sink. "Outside. The guys with the signs."

"There are fairies outside with signs?" Baffled, I walked through the door to the side porch, leaned over the wooden railing, and craned my neck toward the street. A crowd dressed in fairy wings and funny hats clustered outside the picket fence. They brandished placards.

"The natives seem restless," Arsen said through a mouthful of food.

I started. I hadn't heard him follow me from the kitchen. I squinted at the signs.

TEAM FAIRY!

ALIENS ARE FAIRIES TOO.

There were more, but they were either angled wrong or the print too small for me to read.

"That's not something you see every day. Maybe they're friends with one of the guests?"

"I don't think so," Arsen mumbled. "It looked like they were gearing up for a protest."

"It looks like they're gearing up for a parade," I ducked back into the shade of the porch and returned to the kitchen.

Arsen followed.

Dixie plowed through the swinging kitchen door. "Who are the weirdos in the street?"

I consulted my planner on the kitchen table.

Nope, I definitely did not have the bandwidth today to puzzle out a fairy gang. It's all about prioritizing, and murder came first. "Don't know, don't care. Okay, I'm on a really strict schedule today. I've got a panel at eight. Then I've got to rewrite my Doyle UFO presentation." Somewhere in between, I wanted to talk to suspects about Chuck's death. But Arsen and Dixie didn't need to know that.

I cleared my throat. "Then lunch."

Dixie yawned again. "Skip to the good stuff."

Plates clattered in the sink, and Arsen frowned down at them, as if wondering what to do next.

"After lunch," I said, "I have to practice my presentation."

"That's not good stuff, and we don't need to hear about your boring life," Dixie said. "When do you get back?"

I glared. "I'm working at the festival all day, and then after dinner I have to introduce the band—"

"What band?" Dixie asked.

"Um..." I consulted my planner. "Peter and the Aliens."

Her lips curled. "Has-beens. What's your point?"

"The *point* is," I said, "I won't be able to return to Wits' End until late tonight. Are you and Kayla going to be able to cover everything?"

She sniffed. "We did yesterday, didn't we? Besides, the guests aren't even going to be around. They'll be at the festival all day."

Arsen raised a hand. "Sorry. But I'm on a mission today. I won't be able to help you out, Dix."

Her brow furrowed. "When have you ever helped me out?"

"But before I go," he continued, "I think I'll have a word with that crew out front. Those wooden stakes could be dangerous."

I tried not to roll my eyes. Ever since Arsen had started his security firm, and I use the word *security* loosely, he'd been pointing out the hidden dangers at Wits' End. I'd already installed new room locks, put red tape on the edges of the steps, and improved the bathmats. It was getting expensive. And irritating.

I washed my hands, dried them on a blue dishtowel. "I'll come with you, Arsen. I'm curious about our supernatural friends."

"There's nothing supernatural about idiots in wings and fake antennae," Dixie said.

I straightened. "They have antennae?"

"Maybe you should stay inside," Arsen said, in what I was coming to recognize as his security specialist tone.

"Come on," I said. "This crew has got to be from the festival, so they're harmless. And they're outside my front yard." Besides, we both knew I was going no matter what.

"All right, but stay behind me."

I followed him out the side door and across the damp lawn.

My grandmother's roses were miraculously still in bloom and winking with dew. The scent of mauve, Angel's Face roses, orange Arizonas, pink Queen Elizabeths, and Scarlet Knights twined through the garden. Then a breeze carrying the crisp scent of pine floated down the mountain. It whisked the rose aroma away and puffed a blue-sky gap in the mist pressing against the B&B's gabled roof.

We stopped behind the roses and the picket fence that formed a barrier between us and the street.

Someone started a chant, "NO, NO, UFO! NO, NO, UFO!" Others joined in, signs bobbing. The volume swelled.

"Do you think they're anti X-tranormal festival?" I rubbed the back of my neck. "They can't be anti-tourist, because they're not from around here."

Some of the grumpier residents, with independent income streams, weren't happy with Doyle's growing tourist trade. Vocal at the town council meetings, they'd hated the idea of another festival, and a UFO festival to boot. I hugged myself, feeling a sudden chill.

Arsen's brows angled downward. "Maybe. But this is Doyle. Angry fairies are par for the course."

We neared the group, and a few people booed.

"Hey," Arsen said. "What's going on?"

A balding, bearded man with long gray hair, stepped forward. "Aliens didn't kidnap those people. Fairies did!"

"Sure." Arsen extended his hand. "I'm Arsen Holiday."

Automatically, the man took it. "Jack. Jack Bauer." His t-shirt stretched across his broad belly.

"Cool," Arsen said.

"Seriously?" I asked.

The protestor scowled. "It was my name before that guy on TV's."

"Sorry," I said.

"There's nothing wrong with my name!"

"I know. I meant…" *Never mind.* "The kidnappings you mentioned… Do you mean the Doyle Disappeared?"

"I mean fairies are responsible for all the abductees. Everywhere!" The protestor thrust his fist into the air, and the group cheered.

"Hm." Arsen rubbed his chin, as if considering the theory.

"It's a theory," I said, exasperated. One I'd thought had died out with the Victorian era. "But what are you doing *here*?"

Jack Bauer, who seemed to be their leader, pointed his sign at the fake UFO crashed into the B&B roof.

In the turret room, a curtain dropped, as if someone had been looking out.

"Your guest Jonas knows," Jack said.

"Jonas? What—?" My shoulders sagged. I didn't know what Mr. Jonas had to do with abduction theories, but I wasn't selling out an old man who needed a cane. "I think you have the wrong place," I said, squirming at the deception. It wasn't entirely a lie. I did think it was *possible* they had the wrong Jonas and the wrong B&B. Unlikely, but possible.

"We know he's here," a woman wearing elf ears shouted.

I grimaced. "No... The name doesn't seem quite right." It was *Mr.* Jonas, not Jonas, like a first name. "And if you don't leave, I'll call the police."

"This is a public street," their leader said stoutly. "You can't make us leave."

I checked the time on my phone. *Urgh. Really?* I couldn't let this bunch harass my guests, but I needed to get to the festival.

"Don't worry," Arsen said. "They'll leave as soon as they realize this Jonas guy isn't here."

I turned my back on them. "But he is here," I whispered. "What are we going to do?"

"He's a festival goer?"

I nodded.

"Okay. I can bring my Jeep around back and take him to the festival myself. I'll make sure the protestors see us and draw them away from Wits' End."

"Would you? Thanks." I hugged him, and quickly broke away, my face warming. "I'll give Mr. Jonas the bad news."

We returned inside, and I climbed the stairs and knocked on Mr. Jonas's door. I straightened a black-and-white UFO photo, picked a gum wrapper off the green carpet.

Locks rattled, and the door cracked open. The older man peered out. "Are they gone?" he asked, hoarse.

"No. Arsen, our um, security expert, has offered to take you out the rear entrance and drive you to the festival. Arsen's bringing his Jeep around now."

He brightened. "Really? Now that's service."

"You can go when you're ready, but I'd suggest you leave soon, before the people out front figure it out."

"Excellent advice. I'll be ready in five minutes." He began to shut the door.

"Er, what have they got against you?" I asked quickly.

He cracked the door wider. "Since you're suffering for my crimes, I suppose it's only fair I tell you what's going on. I do some writing for *UFO Monthly*, and I'm afraid I was a little... caustic about Bauer's claims. He took it personally. I'm sorry they landed on your doorstep. I had no idea anything like this would result. Usually people *like* my writing."

I winced. "Actually, there's a second part to the plan, if you agree. We'd like to let the picketers know that you've gone on to the festival."

"So, they'll follow and leave the rest of your guests alone?" He nodded. "That seems only fair."

"Great," I said, gusting a breath. "Well, in that case, I'll wait for you at the back door." I gestured to the end of the hall.

He retreated into his room. I walked to my post at the end of the green-carpeted hall and peeked out the door. Arsen's black Jeep Commander waited, engine idling, at the bottom of the wooden stairs.

Mr. Jonas joined me exactly five minutes later, and I escorted him down the steps to the rear driveway. His wobbly gait gave him an air of frailty, but he stepped easily enough into Arsen's high Jeep.

"Good luck." I shut the door and waved.

Arsen drove off, revving the engine as he reached the front street. The picketers gave a shout and chased after his Jeep.

Rolling my eyes, I returned inside and grabbed purse, planner, and granola bars, and waited nine minutes. Steeling myself, I walked out the front door to my Subaru.

The protestors had mostly disbursed. A van with a seventies-era fairy-scape on the side pulled from the curb and drove down the street. A few remaining picketers booed me, and my muscles tensed. But they didn't launch an assault as I backed from the driveway, and I zoomed away, unscathed.

Now off schedule, I drove as fast as I dared down the mountain highway. The clouds vanished as I descended to the vineyard, and my shoulder muscles relaxed. I parked in the festival's VIP lot and hurried to the gate, where a long line of people snaked around the fence. Above the arched, metal entrance, fake fog drifted from the UFO's tailpipe.

Guiltily, I walked to the front of the line and flashed my lanyard at the security guard. Even though my pass gave me cutting rights, it still made me feel like a jerk.

"VIP. You can go on in," she said.

"Thanks!" I hurried inside, not making eye contact with the people fuming behind me in line.

The festival was in full swing. Vendors had set up shop between the warren of tents. They'd decorated their stalls with blinking lights and flying saucers and dazzling backdrops of outer space.

But the real attraction was the guests themselves. A couple with giant eyeballs for heads and cotton candy hair led a dog in an alien costume. The dog seemed to be eating its own hindquarters.

I walked past a life-size cutout of Patrick Stewart in a starship uniform and entered the VIP tent.

Maisie paced inside. "There you are! Unfashionably on time, my favorite type of person to work with."

"It's a curse. How are you doing?"

"The show goes on." She led me outside and through a maze of tents.

"I met another VIP yesterday," I said casually, "a reporter named Bridget Konrach?"

"Right, Bridget."

"Do you know what time she arrived yesterday?"

"About thirty minutes before you did. She stopped in the VIP tent, grabbed a bagel, and went to explore. Or at least that's what she told me. Why?"

"Just curious." So Bridget had had the opportunity to kill Chuck, but why would she take it? "I think she's going to be on one of my panels."

"I'll have to check my notes." She flipped through the pages on her clipboard. "According to her bio, she used to be a UFO reporter, whatever that is." She stopped short and blushed. "Sorry. I didn't mean to be snarky. The people here are great, really."

"It's okay." I laughed, dodging a woman pushing a baby in a UFO-shaped stroller. "The UFO scene *is* wacky. That's what makes it so much fun." *Unless one member of the scene is a murderer.* I sobered.

"We laid the festival tents out in a spiral, with arms leading to the exit, the concert area, and the food area. Tents with permanent exhibits, like the art tents and *Planet of the Grapes*, are scattered throughout. There's a sign outside each tent with its name, and they're on your map."

She handed me a sheet of paper I already had. "And here's today's agenda. Most of the tents are for panels, lectures, and discussion. The schedule is here." Maisie pointed. "I've highlighted the panels Chuck was involved with. Your first is *Writing UFOs*." She stopped in front of a tent. Beside its opening stood a lamp post with a UFO-shaped light and a placard that read: *Roswell*. "Most tents also have rear exits, directly behind the panelist table. That way panelists can make quick escapes." She winked.

"Is there a reason we'd need to escape?" I asked, my gaze flitting past the groups of aliens and heroes hustling down the dirt road.

Maisie smiled faintly. "You'll see." She hustled me into the tent and settled me behind a long table.

People stared from their folding chairs and waited for me to do something fascinating. I tugged my blouse more firmly into place.

"Okay," Maisie said. "Here's your panel moderator, Pam Marsh. Pam, this is Susan."

A motherly-looking woman in a fuchsia top and stretchy black pants smiled, and we shook hands.

"Since you and your grandmother wrote that booklet," Maisie said, "you should do fine." Distractedly, she patted my shoulder and hurried off.

Pam grimaced. "Thanks for jumping into the panel at such short notice."

"Is PB Gates here yet?" Hopefully, I waved at the two other people seated behind the table. Was the man PB?

"He had to cancel. Said he was having traffic problems."

"No!" I bit my bottom lip. *Priorities!* "I mean, that's a shame."

Pam checked her watch. "Oh. We should start."

The best I can say is the panel wasn't a complete disaster. The male panelist spilled his coffee on Pam's questions. A guest vomited, setting off a chain of sick. But we made it to the end.

I scooted back my folding chair and checked my phone. Nine o'clock. That gave me thirty minutes for snooping. Then I *really* had to get to work on expanding my Doyle UFO presentation. At least the press interviews wouldn't be until tomorrow. I'd need to find some time tonight or tomorrow morning to prep for those.

I let the guests leave first, then I emerged from the tent. An enraged hoard of protestors in pointy ears and fairy wings swarmed me.

"Liar!"

"Collaborator!"

"You're complicit in the cover-up!"

"I run a B&B with a UFO in the roof." Ducking my head, I hunched my shoulders and tried to sidle past. "I barely have time to get breakfast on the table. How am I supposed to manage a coverup?"

The winged rabble blocked my path and chanted slogans. They might have been funny if I hadn't been so eager to escape.

I caught Jack Bauer's eye. "Look," I shouted over the abuse. "I agree the fairy theory is intriguing. The reports of fairy abductions are eerily like those of UFO abductions. I'm not dismissing your theory, but this isn't the way to go about proving your point."

Jack lowered his fleshy arm, his sign scraping the ground. "Hold up. You agree?"

The shouts died. Were they going to be reasonable after all? "I'm open. No one has all the answers. But I'm not the enemy, and I don't think Mr. Jonas is either. Wouldn't you, you know, rather have an open, public debate instead of shutting down people who disagree with you?"

Team Fairy looked at each other.

"No!" They howled.

Yeesh. I darted back into the tent and squeezed through a gap I'd noticed behind the panelist table. Quick escape, indeed. Had Maisie known Team Fairy was here and looking for blood? But she couldn't have. They couldn't have gotten to the festival much before I had.

Darting glances over my shoulder, I wound between the tents. No one seemed to be following me, but I had no idea how they'd found me at the festival.

I stopped beside a stand selling alien-head nightlights. Pulling out the schedule, I reviewed today's agenda. My eyes bulged. I was supposed to be in the press tent *now*? How had I misread that?

Rechecking the festival map, I hurried toward the press tent. I dodged and wove between people, then gave up and crept along one side of the dirt road to better evade the crowds.

Three pastel people drifted past. Their parasol hats dripped with long, blue, pink, and green tendrils, like giant jellyfish.

"I'm doing it this year," a purple jellyfish said. "America's UFO highway. I'm driving it all the way across the States."

"You say that every year," a blue jellyfish retorted.

Something thunked nearby, and I stopped, cocking my head.

Yuri chucked a rock at an oak tree.

The palm-sized stone hit the trunk dead center. He turned to me and smiled the smile of a movie madman.

Hairs lifted on the back of my neck. I lifted my hand and waved limply. "Hi?"

CHAPTER SIX

Ignoring me, Yuri scanned the dry ground, picked up another rock, and hurled it. It thunked off the oak.

I swallowed. This *was* an opportunity to interrogate one of my suspects in his natural element. I wasn't thrilled about Yuri's rock-throwing, lunatic-abductee vibe though.

Discretion being the better part of valor, I jogged around a tent. I glanced over my shoulder and nearly plowed into Spence. I wavered, torn between schmoozing the head of the biggest amateur UFO hunting organization in the US and Doing the Right Thing. But my inner conflict was moot. Intent on a strong-jawed woman with Frida Kahlo hair and eyebrows, Spence hadn't noticed I'd nearly flattened him.

"He's dead." The woman wore a purple tank with an open back, and a miniskirt in a matching fabric over brown leggings. "If that doesn't make it over, then what will?" She stormed off.

I averted my gaze and pretended to be invisible. My foot struck a rock, sending it skittering across the earth and into the ankle of his hiking boot.

"Whoops," I said. "Sorry about that."

Spence rubbed his hand across the rounded front of his black *OUT THERE* t-shirt. He grimaced. "You married?"

I started. "Um, no."

"Huh. Would say you were lucky, but Aleta's really the best." He jerked his head toward the woman, who'd vanished in the crowd. "My wife. Next time, I'll introduce you. Where you headed?"

"Press tent."

"Wrong direction. That way." He pointed.

"Oh. Thanks."

"Headed that way too. Want company?"

"Sure," I said.

We walked in silence, and I tried to think of a decent segue into Chuck's murder. The crowd thinned, festival-goers disappearing into tents for the scheduled presentations and activities.

Ask about Chuck! But I was weirdly tongue-tied. This was Spence, the groundbreaking leader of *Out There*. He was internationally known!

"Wife shares my interest in the unknown," he said abruptly. "Gets anxious in crowds."

"I don't blame her," I stammered, trying to make sense of his truncated sentences. "I ran into a group of protesters. They believe fairies are responsible for the abductions, not UFOs."

He barked a laugh. "Fairies. Luck with that. Who believes in fairies?"

I cleared my throat. "So, *Out There*, have you been running it for long?"

He smiled. "Since 2005. There." He nodded toward a tent with a big *PRESS* sign above the entrance. On its sides, painted aliens scribbled in notebooks, snapped photos with old-fashioned cameras.

X-tranormal had gone all out with the décor, I thought, impressed. "Thanks." I strode into the tent.

Maisie looked up from her clipboard. "There you are. Right on time for your interview."

"I almost wasn't." And I really hated being late. "For some reason, I thought my interview wasn't until tomorrow."

"Oh, we changed the schedule. It was on the new agenda I gave you this morning. Didn't you read it?"

I smothered my annoyance. "Is PB Gates here?"

People sat in folding chairs in groups of two. The reporter, Bridget, interviewed a serious-looking man dressed like a college professor. She brushed her mercury hair over the shoulder of her tunic, a sleeveless number in red.

"Sorry," Maisie said. "I don't think PB is registered as press for the festival this year."

My breath hitched. "But he's a UFO reporter," I bleated.

She shrugged. "If you don't register, you're not press. But he's definitely here. I checked with the registration desk."

"I don't suppose they have a photo of him?" Maybe I'd run into him in the crowds.

Maisie winced. "No."

"At least we're on another panel together. I was told he had to cancel the last one."

"Right," she said brightly. "And I've got someone who wants to interview you."

I might not get Wits' End into one of PB's articles, but at least I'd get the B&B some fresh publicity. Determined, I scanned the reporters. A Sacramento paper, a San Francisco paper...

She motioned toward local reporter, Tom Tarrant.

My mouth pressed tight. *Great.* Tom's article for the *Doyle Times* would not send business to Wits' End. Locals don't stay at their friendly neighborhood UFO-themed B&B.

He brightened and waved. "Hey, Susan! Ready for your interview?"

I walked to the high, empty chair across from him and sat, looping my purse over its back. "Why not?"

The reporter touched his cell phone's screen. "Do you mind if I record our interview?" Tom shot me a boyish smile, but his youthful good looks were deceptive. Like me, he was in his early thirties.

I sighed and plucked at my blouse. Despite the humming fans, it had already begun sticking to my back in the tent's warmth. "I guess not."

"So, I understand you found Chuck Thorpe's body?"

I shifted in the high canvas chair. I hated it when my feet dangled. It made my thighs look fat. "Um. Yes. But I don't think the sheriff wants me to discuss the case."

"I've already spoken to her. Was there anyone around the registration tent when you arrived?"

"Um. No. I mean, the festival hadn't opened yet, so there weren't many people around. Only the security people, and maybe some vendors." *Stop talking about it! Stop talking!*

"And the other VIPs," he said. "They were here too, weren't they?"

"Er, right." Had one of them gone into the tent and killed Chuck, then returned to the VIP tent in time to greet me? It was possible.

"Who do you think might have done it?"

I crossed my dangling legs, and the chair creaked. "I shouldn't speculate. It would only land me in trouble, and with good reason."

He grinned, unrepentant. "You can't blame a guy for trying. How are you enjoying the festival?"

"Finding a body was horrible, but..." I hesitated. What was I supposed to say? Murder aside, this place is awesome? If only I'd had time to prepare some sound bites.

He smiled. "It's okay. I know you're here to build business for your B&B. I'm not trying to trip you up. Let's talk UFOs."

I relaxed. Flying saucers, I could do.

He shifted in the canvas chair, angling his knees closer to mine. "I ran into some folks who think the Doyle disappearances are due to fairies rather than UFOs. Comment?"

"It's a theory," I said, noncommittal. "And I can't deny the similarities between the described UFO and fairy abductions. But I'm on team UFO."

"Okay." He touched his phone screen, and it went black. *Okay*? "Is that it?"

"Yeah, I hoped for intel on the murder, but I don't want to get you into hot water." He grinned. "And it made a good excuse to chat. I've seen you around town, but you always look so busy, I haven't wanted to bother you."

"Bother me?" I unhooked the purse from the back of my chair.

"Can I ask you a serious question? Off the record."

I shrugged. "Sure."

"What do you think is really going on in Doyle?"

"You mean, The Disappeared?"

In the tent, a woman brayed with laughter.

"I mean everything," he said. "The Disappeared, our bizarrely high murder rate, even the roses at Wits' End—"

"The roses?" I stiffened. "What's wrong with the roses?"

"They bloom all year. Roses aren't supposed to do that."

I sucked in my cheeks. *So?* What did my roses have to do with anything? "My grandmother used a special mulch."

He raised a skeptical brow. "That keeps them blooming all year?"

"It's a *very* special mulch." I wish I knew what was in it.

"Uh, huh. But you can't dispute our high crime rate. This is a small town, and the economy's good. The Sheriff's Department is professional and clean – uncorrupt, I mean, or at least as far as I can tell. We've got wineries in striking distance of ski slopes. The downtown is disgustingly adorable. And yet..."

"Doyle's a great little town," I said, blood pressure rising. "It's not... I mean..." Laying it out like that, Doyle did seem weird. But Wits' End had nothing to do with that. Did it? "I guess I never really thought about it."

He nodded slowly. "It's the Doyle disease. No one ever really thinks about it."

"The sheriff does. I mean, she has to." Sheriff McCourt read the crime stats. She was in the thick of everything that happened, whether she liked it or not.

He smiled wryly. "McCourt's not a big talker."

I laughed. "That's an understatement."

He stood and stuck out his hand. "Well. Thanks."

I slithered from the chair, and we shook hands. He clung to mine a second longer than I expected.

"Hey, do you want to grab a bite some time?" His deep-water blue eyes gleamed with purpose.

"A bite?"

"A date."

"A date?" I parroted.

"How about tomorrow night at the Barn and Brew? Eight o'clock?"

Well, why not? Arsen wasn't exactly throwing himself at me, and Tom seemed... nice. "Um. Sure. It sounds fun!"

A date with Tom... Stepping lightly, I walked outside the tent, unsnapped my planner and entered the date. I had a date. I rapped my fingers on the pages. An actual date with an attractive man. Did I have time to buy something new?

My planner said *no*.

Oh well, I needed to save my money.

I checked where I had to be next: *Paranormal California - From the Mountains to the Coast*. The panel with PB! I scanned the blurb.

Join writer PB Gates, Spence Bradford of Out There, and Ufologist Chuck Thorpe. They'll discuss everything from the Doyle Disappeared to the recently revealed UFO sighting off the San Diego coast. Want to know more about Bigfoot, the ghosts of the Queen Mary, and other paranormal entities? This is the Q&A panel for you!

The festival grounds were quiet, most visitors occupied at lectures. I strolled the looping dirt road and passed the occasional alien with antennas in their hair.

Spence Bradford stood outside the tent reading his notes.

The reporter, Bridget, paced nearby. Her flowy black slacks swished, her arms folded over her simple scarlet tunic.

"Hi, again," I said.

Spence looked up and ran a hand through his shaggy blond hair. "Susan, right on time. Maisie told me you'd be taking over for Chuck."

Voices rose and fell inside the tent.

Bridget paused and eyed me. "Susan Witsend, correct?" She tugged on the long pendant dangling from her neck.

"That's me. I run the B&B, Wits' End."

"Fine," she said. "I'll be sure to introduce you. I'm moderating."

From within the tent came a burst of applause.

I scanned the small clearing. "I guess PB's not here yet?"

Bridget tossed her silvery hair. "Oh, he had to cancel."

Again? "The whole festival?" I asked, dismayed.

"Only this panel, I believe," Bridget said.

"He missed an early morning one as well," I said. Maybe he'd decided against revealing himself to the world. Would my grand plan to give Gran's booklet to PB come to naught? If I couldn't manage that simple scheme, how was I going to help solve a murder?

"Don't worry, you'll meet the great man." Spence's bristly face crinkled in a smile, and I started. Was he a mind reader too? "Things have a way of working out," he finished.

"They didn't work out very well for Chuck," I muttered.

Chattering people in t-shirts and alien costumes streamed from the tent.

He shrugged his rounded shoulders. "Was a tough person to like."

Bridget busied herself with her cell phone. "He should never have been invited."

"Would have come regardless," Spence said.

"I read his organization was sued," I said. "Where was that?"

"Lincoln County, Nevada." Bridget's mouth flattened. "We don't have much time to set up for our panel. Let's get in there."

Inside the tent, rows of metal folding chairs faced a long table.

A man in a brown waistcoat and top hat collected his papers and a book. "Do you need the projector?" he asked, nodding to the device on a stand.

"No." Bridget brushed back a length of her sleek, gray hair. "We're panel only."

Two rotating fans rattled and spun in opposite corners of the tent, but the air around the panelists' table was brutally still.

"All right then." He tipped his top hat and, whistling, he strode from the tent.

"He's a Bigfoot specialist," Spence said. "Wish we could afford a festival that was UFO-only. Opening it to other paranormal phenomena increases the guest count."

"You're one of the festival organizers?" I asked, surprised.

He walked behind the table and pulled out a chair. "In a minor way. On one of the many festival committees. Takes a lot of volunteers to pull something like this together."

I sat beside Spence, and Bridget took a chair next to me. My hands trembled slightly, and I pressed them flat on the plastic table. Why was I nervous? I'd already done one panel. This was no big deal.

Festival-goers shuffled into the tent.

Bridget announced us, and we were off. Fortunately, Spence was all too happy to fill in the gaps when I had little to say. I really wasn't an expert on anything paranormal aside from UFOs. But the Doyle incident fascinated the audience.

A middle-aged woman in yoga pants raised her hand. "I heard a local romance writer recently disappeared and returned."

I nodded. "Karin Bonheim. She went missing in the woods a bit east of here for over a week. When they found her, she was in good condition, but claimed to have no memory of what had happened."

"Claimed?" the woman asked sharply.

"I can't prove if she did or didn't lose her memory. But there's no reason to disbelieve her. Even experienced hikers can sometimes get lost."

"But lots of people do go missing around here and then return with no memory of what happened," the woman insisted. "Isn't that a little unusual?"

I folded my hands on the table. "It's very unusual. The disappearance of the Bell and Thistle pub is inexplicable."

A tentative hand rose amidst the rows of people.

"Yes?" Bridget asked.

A weedy, bespectacled man with a wispy beard stood. "Is it true Chuck was killed by the Men in Black?"

"What a fascinating theory," Bridget said coolly. "Would any of our UFO experts like to comment?"

I shrank into my folding chair. My fellow panelists and I looked uneasily at each other.

Jack Bauer leapt up from the back. The leader of Team Fairy punched his meaty fist in the air. "FairIES! FairIES! FairIES!"

I smothered a groan. But at least he'd saved me from having to talk publicly about the murder. My gran had been right. There was always a bright side.

A group of winged men and women stood and joined the chant.

And... that bright side was dimming.

"Thank you," Bridget shouted. But her voice was drowned out by the racket.

My pulse sped. This was getting out of control. I took deep breaths. This wasn't my fault. I wasn't responsible. The protestors weren't violent, and I didn't need to be in control.

Oh yes you do, the gray shadow whispered behind me, and I almost turned. Almost. But the shadow of my puppet-master parents wasn't real. It only *felt* that way.

A competing chant started up: "U-F-Os! U-F-Os!"

"We're here to discuss and share information," Spence hollered, "not shout at each other."

The chanting grew in volume. Spence shook his head.

Gripping her phone, Bridget rose and slipped from the tent.

"Where's she going?" I asked Spence over the din.

"Hopefully to call security. Never seen anything like this."

I sank lower in my folding chair. "They were at my B&B earlier. They found out I'm sheltering an anti-fairy-theorist."

Spence burst into laughter. "Seriously? That's what this is about?"

"I think they're following me," I said shakily. An image flashed into my head – a rueful, older man with silver hair. The detective my parents had hired to follow me when I'd first moved to Doyle. I'd had no idea I was being followed until he'd fessed up and walked off the job to retire in Costa Rica.

Spence shook his head. "Couldn't have known you'd be here. You're not on the main program."

"And yet, they were at my B&B, they cornered me on the grounds after another panel I wasn't supposed to be at, and here they are." I thought I'd gotten smarter, paid more attention to people around me. But if the anti-UFO crew was tracking me, I hadn't done a very good job.

His brow furrowed. "Cornered you? That's a little disturbing. Right. Stick with me until security arrives. Don't like the way this is going."

The audience was on their feet now, but their expressions were more amused than angry. The competing groups synchronized their chants, so as not to shout over each other.

"Oh, the fairies and the aliens should be friends," Spence sang to a tune from *Oklahoma*. He checked his phone. "And... time's up. We're done. Let's beat it." He stood and slipped through a break in the tent behind our table, and I followed.

Behind the tent, he chuckled over the dull roar of the chanting inside. "Eventually they'll notice we're gone, but I think we've given them the slip."

We walked through the narrow tent corridor to the main road.

"I'm so sorry," I said. "What a mess." I hefted the elephantine purse on my shoulder. How had it grown so heavy?

He lifted an unkempt brow. "You kidding? This will be the talk of the festival. We're a huge success. Was only the Q&A that got cut short."

Enough dwelling on things I couldn't control. It was time to investigate. Spence had known Chuck. But what did he *know*? "Chuck's murder didn't get this festival off to a positive start."

"Least the sheriff didn't shut us down." One corner of his mouth tilted upward. "Would have been a riot if she'd tried."

"Sheriff McCourt's no dummy," I said. "But she doesn't really understand the UFO scene. I take it you've spoken with her?"

He nodded. "I don't think I was much help though."

"Who do you think would want to kill Chuck Thorpe?"

"All I can say is the sheriff's lucky he was killed *before* the festival started. Otherwise she would have had a suspect pool of thousands."

"He was that bad?" I asked.

"Abrasive, arrogant, and he sure made a lot of money off people. Some of his marks could afford it - Chuck got smart about targeting people with money. But in the early days, he wasn't choosy. And UFO hunters can be... obsessive. When the truth is out there, what price is too high?"

"Susan!" Arsen strode around the corner of the tent.

In spite of everything, my heart lifted.

The festival organizer, Maisie, trotted beside him, and my muscles stiffened. Sheesh, what was my problem? I had no reason to be jealous. She was wearing a wedding ring, and I had a date with Tom. Arsen and I weren't a thing.

Arsen tucked a computer tablet beneath one arm. "Are you all right?"

"We're fine," Spence said. "Protestors were harmless."

Arsen gripped my shoulders and gazed into my eyes. Misplaced desire surged through me in response. *Get a grip!*

"Bridget told us what happened," he said. "Was anyone hurt?"

"No." I glanced away. "Spence was right. The whole thing was loud, but silly. Team Fairy is no threat."

Maisie choked back a laugh. "Team Fairy? Is that what they're calling themselves?"

"It's what I'm calling them," I said.

"Well, kids, got to get to my next panel." Whistling an *Oklahoma* tune, Spence ambled down the dirt road.

"How did it go with Mr. Jonas?" I asked. "Did you get him to the festival all right?"

"Yes and no," Arsen said. "He decided at the last minute he didn't want to stir up any controversy, and I ended up taking him back to Doyle."

"What?" The fairies had driven a perfectly nice old man away from the festival? That wasn't funny.

He shrugged. "He seemed happy enough."

"Then what are you doing at X-tranormal?" I asked.

"Maisie asked me to beef up security after Chuck's death." He smiled at the festival organizer. "It looks like you had the right idea."

"I hope it's not a case of too little, too late," Maisie said.

"I'm worried less about that silly protest than about Chuck's murder," I said. "Anyone who was here that morning could have committed the crime."

A kid dressed like a space pirate blasted an air horn, and Maisie and I jumped.

Arsen eyed me askance. "It almost sounds like you're investigating. The last time—"

"I found Chuck's body and was questioned by the sheriff," I said hotly. "Of course I'm interested."

"But you—"

"Will tell the sheriff whatever I learn, like last time."

"Last time?" Maisie asked.

"Susan got involved in a murder investigation this summer." Arsen's green-brown eyes darkened. "She used me for bait."

Heat flushed through my veins. "That was an accident," I said shrilly. And I still felt terrible about it. But the sheriff and I'd had everything under control. Mostly.

"So..." Maisie's gaze ping-ponged between us. "You're like the sheriff's spy?"

I was a confidential informant – big difference. "No," I said, offended.

"Yes," Arsen said.

Maisie shook her head, her red curls tossing. "I can't believe any of our volunteers would have committed murder. Everyone working the registration tent, where Chuck was killed, was away at breakfast. They all alibi each other." Her cheeks pinked. "I asked. I guess I was playing amateur detective too."

At least I wasn't the only one. "Have there been any threats against the festival itself?" I asked Maisie.

A troop of aliens in body paint and gold lamé costumes trooped past.

"Threats?" she asked. "No."

Relieved, I blew out a breath. Then this probably wasn't the work of an anti-tourist Doyleite. Not that any locals really had reason to be upset with the festival.

Yet.

"What about Bridget?" I asked. "She wasn't in the VIP tent with us, but she couldn't have been far when Chuck was killed."

Maisie glanced around the curving road. "I probably shouldn't say anything, but it's public knowledge. In fact, you may already know this. Someone fire-bombed a car belonging to Chuck some years ago. There was a rumor Bridget had done it, but no charges were ever filed. I guess the police didn't have any evidence."

Whoa.

"Why would she set his car on fire?" Arsen asked.

Maisie grimaced. "You'll have to ask Bridget." She tucked an arm in his.

I crossed my arms, my stomach hardening. "I will."

"Now that we know Susan is safe and sound," she said, "we really need to tour the fence line. I want to make extra sure no one's getting inside the festival grounds without permission."

Arsen didn't budge. "Are you going to be okay?" he asked me. His handsome face creased with concern. "Maybe you should come with us?"

I fought my instinct to agree. *Could* an outsider have snuck through the fence and killed Chuck? It didn't seem likely. "Thanks," I said, "but I can't. I've got to prep for my presentation. I'll work in the VIP tent. No one will bother me there." Also, the VIP tent had bagels.

"We can walk you to the tent," Arsen said.

Maisie's doe-like eyes widened. "Of course, Susan. If you're feeling threatened, we'll come with you."

My cheeks burned. Feeling threatened? I was an experienced investigator. "I'm fine. You go ahead." I strode in the direction of the VIP tent.

Nothing today had gone according to plan. But at least the press interview was over, and I'd knocked off two panels. PB Gates hadn't been at either, but things could only get better.

Right?

CHAPTER SEVEN

I staggered beneath the afternoon sun. My feet were on fire. I knew I should have worn my good walking shoes.

Flyers and bookmarks and brochures stuck at every angle from the top of my purse. They weighed a ton. But I couldn't stop myself from taking more from the colorful stands I passed. Yes, I *did* want to know *The Truth about Bigfoot in California,* and *The Seven Signs You've Been Abducted by Aliens,* and *How to Tell if Your House is Haunted!* I presumed the latter would apply to B&Bs. Not that I'd actually experienced any haunting, but the sheriff's ex *had* been murdered upstairs not that long ago.

I paused at a fork in the dirt road. One branch led to a shaded depression where someone had built an alien-themed playground. I took that low road and reveled in the temperature drop beneath the oaks.

Collapsing onto a wooden bench, I grabbed a brochure and fanned myself with *Everything You Never Wanted to Know About Alien Implants.* In thirty minutes, I was supposed to introduce the opening band, Peter and the Aliens. But after a day at the festival, I still hadn't found the main stage. Maybe it was at the Interplanetary Meeting Ground?

A giggling, blue-faced couple walked behind a head-in-the-hole board. They stuck their heads through two Martians, and a red alien snapped their photo.

I stopped fanning and dug out my festival map. The Interplanetary Meeting Ground, where I probably was supposed to be, was on the opposite side of the festival.

I had to move.

I couldn't move.

If only teleportation devices were real.

I sighed. Since when did I let achy feet get the better of my schedule? Feet and legs aching, I hauled myself from the bench and trudged toward the Meeting Ground.

Starship personnel and aliens thronged the curving road. Most of the speaking events had ended at this late hour. Festival goers lined up for last minute purchases from kiosks. They sold everything from green snow cones to glow-in-the-dark necklaces.

I paused across from a wooden stand with a sign that said: OUR SPONSORS. I was a sponsor. The stall carried hand-drawn maps of the locations of Doyle "incidents." I checked the clock on my phone. Maybe they could help me find my way.

I limped to the stand. A young woman in a green X-tranormal shirt braced one elbow on the wooden counter and yawned. "Welcome to the X-tranormal sponsor kiosk. What can I do for you?"

"I'm one of the sponsors, from Wits' End. I'm a little lost, and I also wanted to check if you needed any more maps or brochures."

"You are officially no longer lost. You're here. And more brochures wouldn't be a bad idea." She motioned to the plastic brochure stand.

Only three brochures remained. My *Doyle Disappearances* maps were gone.

"But I should warn you," she continued, "most people take stuff because it's free. Later they throw them out when they realize they're carrying too much."

I shifted my purse, packed with alien-themed magnets, brochures and bobble heads. "Well, thanks for managing the booth. I hope you're not bored."

"Are you kidding? I'll take this gig over working the registration tent any time. That's where everyone goes to ask questions and complain."

"Were you working the registration tent earlier? You weren't here the morning Chuck Thorpe died, were you?" I knew being an insider would pay off. I might have found a source here.

She pinked. "Um, yeah. Maisie wasn't too happy."

"Why? What happened to Chuck wasn't your fault."

PLANET OF THE GRAPES

She braced her other elbow on the wooden counter. "We were supposed to be back from breakfast by eight-thirty. But Devon was doing this really funny thing with the muffins, and time sort of got away from us. We didn't get back until around nine, when the police were there."

"When did you leave for breakfast?" I asked, repressing my curiosity about funny things you could do with muffins.

"Just before eight, which Maisie wasn't happy to learn either. We were supposed to leave the registration tent at eight and be back by eight-thirty. But when you add the time to walk to the food area, that's hardly any time at all. So, we left early."

"What time did you leave the registration tent, exactly?"

She looked up at the green awning and frowned. "Exactly? I don't know about exactly, but I figure we left maybe five or ten minutes to eight. Why?"

I shook my head. "I was the one who found the body, and I can't help wondering when Chuck died. It sounds like it must have happened sometime between seven-fifty and eight-thirty."

"Is that when you found him?"

"No, I got there a bit later, but... Who knew the registration tent would be empty?" Because the killer had taken a big chance. Anyone could have walked inside.

She frowned. "Aside from us? I went to the VIP tent around a quarter to eight to ask Maisie if we could duck out early for breakfast. She said *no* and reminded me we had exactly thirty minutes to get to the food area and back. And she wasn't quiet about it either. Anyone nearby would have known the tent would be empty for thirty minutes." She flushed. "Or so."

Even after a telling off by Maisie, they'd abandoned their post a little early, but that was between Maisie and the staff. "Do you remember if anyone else was in the VIP tent when you were talking to Maisie?"

"The dead guy was there. He was alive then, of course. And I guess his wife. They were standing together and had that couple look, you know?"

I nodded. "Anyone else?"

Someone jostled me from behind, and my purse slipped to the ground. A UFO stress ball rolled out. I muttered a curse and stuffed it into my bag.

"Sure, Spence Bradford and his wife, Aleta. That reporter, Bridget. And the abductee, Yuri." She sighed. "He's soooo good looking."

Lank-haired Yuri? Good looking?

She grinned. "I'm kind of a UFO buff. That's the payoff for working the festival, I get to meet everyone and attend some of the events for free."

I needed to talk with Aleta and Bridget – and to Yuri, Spence, and Chuck's wife, too, whatever her name was. "Did any of the staff or food servers leave the breakfast between eight and eight-thirty?"

She shook her head. "The police asked us that too. We were all there, eating."

And doing fun things with muffins. "Who else was on the grounds at that time? There was security. I know, because I met a guard at the gate."

"She was the only guard on duty. The festival didn't open to vendors until nine. I don't think the rest of the security team was expected to arrive until around nine either. It was only the one guard, the VIPs, and us volunteers. Oh, and the lady from the café that brought the food."

"Who was that?" I asked.

"I didn't get her name, but it was a café with one of those clever coffee names."

"Ground?"

"That's the one."

I didn't know Ground catered breakfasts. But I did know the owner, Jayce, so that made things easier. "How many volunteers were there that morning?"

"The fateful eight. That's what we called ourselves."

"And all eight were there, at your breakfast?"

"Yep."

"Well, thanks. You're well informed."

She laughed. "Registration is more than handing out tickets. It's also about answering questions. We have to know everything about the festival."

"I'll bring more brochures and stickers by tomorrow. And the concert stage is...?"

She pointed. "Thataway."

I started to turn.

"Look out!" she said.

A plastic light saber whacked me in the face. The kid wielding it raced on, unaware.

I rubbed my eye. "Ow."

"Are you okay?" she asked.

"Yeah. Don't worry, I won't need directions to the first aid tent."

"It's in Rendlesham Forest," she said promptly, "right in the center of the festival."

"Rendlesham?"

"Britain's Roswell incident. There were multiple sightings there."

"Oh, right." Rendlesham was also near a base being used by the American Air Force at the time. I was pretty certain most UFO sightings around air bases were human aircraft. But you had to wonder if a crashed UFO or two wasn't being held at Area 51 in Nevada.

I trudged onward, and the road widened, branching.

Maisie waved to me from beneath a massive oak. "Susan! Over here!"

I smiled, relieved my journey was almost over. There had to be some chairs to sit in backstage, right? "I guess this is the place?"

"Almost." Maisie ruffled back her red hair, cooling herself. "I'll take you backstage and introduce you to the bands."

I followed her down a narrow drive. The oaks formed a canopy above us providing delicious, delicious shade.

We left the trees and walked into a wide, flat area of dried grass. A stage with high, black curtains had been set up on the far end of the field. Concertgoers had already claimed spots, and picnickers had spread blankets on the cropped, dried grass.

A few people were enjoying bottles of wine, and I silently vowed to pay a visit to the *Planet of the Grapes* tent tomorrow. The owner had created a special label for the festival. If Chuck hadn't been bashed in the head with a bottle of the stuff, I'd probably have bought a case.

Maisie led me behind the stage and up a set of metal stairs that trembled with every step. Who'd put this pile of junk together?

I grasped the railing for balance. "Say, I heard the only people at the festival when Chuck died were the registration staff, a guard or two, and the VIPs. Is that true?"

She gave me a startled look. "Well, yes. I suppose so. Plus the woman from Ground who brought breakfast."

"And there weren't any other guards aside from the woman at the gate?"

"We didn't need more than one guard at the time," she said. "We weren't opening for hours, and we're on a tight budget. Why?"

"Chuck," I said, looking for a chair and finding none. "I can't stop thinking about finding his body."

"No one can, not really. Am I selfish to hope that the murder was an isolated incident? That it was something personal? Because if there's a madman out to wreck the festival..."

"A random madman is loads more disturbing." Though the idea someone would kill a person they *knew* didn't exactly fill me with peace and joy either.

Men in headsets and black *X-tranormal* t-shirts taped cables to the metal floor, shifted equipment across the stage.

Maisie pointed to a group of men in black suits and made a face. "There's the band. I'd really hoped they weren't going to dress as Men in Black tonight. It's so cliché."

She introduced me to the band, and I made notes in my planner about how they wanted to be introduced. The band prepped, discordant notes screeching through the sound system. Gritting my teeth, I stood in the wings and worked on my introduction.

The crowd's volume rose, and I rubbed my sweaty palms on my capris. The audience was bigger than I'd expected. But it was just an introduction. No one cared about me. They were here for the music. I could manage this.

"Nervous?" Maisie asked.

"Is it that obvious?"

"You don't have to say much," Maisie said. "In fact, if you don't keep it short, you'll rile up the crowd."

I scrunched my notes between trembling hands. Why the devil had I agreed to this? I'd never spoken in front of so many people before.

"The band's a lot of fun," she continued, "and the group that comes next is even better. Their chords are based on the music of the spheres, and they use sounds collected from space in their music. I'm not a UFO person, but it's pretty groovy."

Ha! I wasn't the only one who still said *groovy*. "I'm staying for one song, and then I'm out of here. Unless you need me for anything else?"

She laughed. "You've done more than enough."

"Good, my feet are killing me."

"In that case, can I get you a drink? Your choices are beer, beer, beer, and water."

"I'll have a beer."

Maisie left the stage and returned twenty minutes later with two beers. I was halfway through mine when klieg lights flashed above.

The crowd roared. No biggie. Just because I hadn't planned this didn't mean I couldn't do it. My breath quickened. After all, I'd had some time to plan. It was just an introduction.

Maisie clapped my shoulder. "You're up," she shouted over the noise.

Stomach roiling, I walked on stage and squinted into the sun, lowering over the western hills. Just an introduction. "Welcome—" My voice cracked. "Welcome to X-tranormal!"

The crowd shouted their approval. Talking too fast, I raced through my spiel and hustled off stage, making way for the band.

"Great job!" Maisie screamed over the thunderous music.

I gave her an uncertain thumbs up and fled. Making my way down the steps, I moved along the edge of the writhing crowd. Even though all I wanted was to go home and take a bath, I forced myself to stay for the first song. Then I escaped onto the festival roads. Empty tents flapped eerily in the warm breeze.

The back of my neck prickled with unease. I glanced over my shoulder. Lots of people were headed in my general direction, toward the exit. If someone was following me, I couldn't tell. They trudged in groups of twos and threes, heads bent, speaking in low voices or not at all.

I shook myself. *Ridiculous.* I wasn't being followed, and I wasn't in danger, because I wasn't alone. But I lengthened my strides.

The fact that I thought I was being followed probably meant I wasn't. My parents' detective had trailed me for weeks, and I'd been oblivious.

I walked through the main gates and into the dirt and weed-covered lot. Another perk of being a sponsor was the VIP parking. It wasn't next to the gate – those spots were for vendors lugging inventory and equipment – but it was reserved.

The lot was half empty now. Beneath a tangerine sky, I strode across crushed, dried grass, past an oak, past an antique water pump.

My blue Subaru waited alone in the VIP area, and I smiled with relief. Weaving through the parking cones marking off the VIP lot, I dug my keys from my purse. I aimed my fob at the small SUV.

Something whizzed past my head.

A splintering sound.

I gasped.

A spiderweb of cracks blossomed on my windshield. I jumped. *What the...?*

A rock thudded to the soft earth.

I started to turn.

Pain splintered my neck. The parking lot accordioned to blackness.

CHAPTER EIGHT

"Susan? Susan?"

My eyelids fluttered open. Filaments of pink cloud stretched across the sky. The light had taken on a misty, twilight quality. It softened the silhouettes of the oaks and rolling hills, the tops of the tents rising above the fence.

Arsen cradled my head and neck in his broad hands, the setting sun haloing his brandy-colored hair. His hazel eyes crinkled with concern, and he was close, close enough for me to smell the peppermint of his breath.

Arsen was here, and I wasn't surprised. He was meant to be here. Relaxing into drowsy warmth, I understood. I didn't want to fight this. I loved him.

"Susan." His voice was a tender ache.

Hot insanity flowed from my heart. I raised my hand to his rough cheek.

He lowered his head to mine.

I kissed him.

God help me, he responded. Heat seared my veins, and his mouth parted mine. And even with a rock digging into my lower back and my skull splitting, it was better than our long-ago first kiss, wild with summer stars and dried lake water on my skin.

But that had been followed by a more awkward morning after, me knocking on the door of his aunts' house and discovering he was gone. No reason. No explanation. I hadn't known until later that it had been a farewell kiss, an experimental kiss, a pity kiss.

We'd never spoken of that first, teenage kiss.

Arsen's hand shifted.

Pain rocketed through my head. I gasped and jerked away.

"Are you okay?" he asked anxiously. "Have I hurt you?"

"I'm fine, I—" I'd kissed Arsen, my best friend. I'd ruined everything. I clapped my hand to my mouth.

"Can you sit up?" he asked.

"Can't I just stay here for a minute?" I had the strong suspicion I might throw up if I moved. And I'd kissed him. My cheeks flamed.

"Do you know what happened?" he asked, all business.

My lips pressed tight with disappointment. He was pretending nothing had happened. Which meant it hadn't happened or he'd wished it hadn't kissed me either. My breath hitched. But he'd kissed me back, hadn't he?

Gingerly, I touched the side of my neck. "I think I got hit by a rock. My car—" My car! I pushed myself up then, swallowing the bile flooding my throat.

A massive starburst of cracks decorated the Subaru's front windshield. I gaped. "Are you kidding me?" No amount of windshield glue was going to fix that.

Arsen's nostrils flared. "Then you *were* attacked." He looked away and cursed softly.

"By someone with good aim." Someone like Yuri, who'd been practicing his rock throwing. I blinked rapidly. Of course, the blow had lowered my inhibitions. Maybe I'd hit my head when I fell. The kiss hadn't been my fault. I blamed the rock thrower. Maybe it hadn't happened at all.

Gently, he grasped my arm. "Hey, it's going to be all right," he said in a lower tone. "You're just a little, uh, out of sorts. I've called the festival medics. They should be here in a minute."

Out of sorts? "Forget the medics." Throat tight, I rolled onto one hip, cast around for my purse, and saw Arsen's computer tablet by his feet.

My purse was behind me. Brochures and stickers and my planner spilled onto the dirt.

I scrabbled in my bag. My wallet was still there, and so was my phone. "Thank God. Everything's here. It wasn't a mugging." My insides hollowed with relief.

"A mugging would make more sense." His brows drew inward. "Did you see anything? Hear anything?"

"No." My chest clenched. "But I thought someone was following me through the festival."

"Are you sure? You were hit pretty hard. That sort of injury can confuse things."

"But I sensed someone behind me before I was attacked. Unless it was you? How *did* you find me?"

"I saw your car," he said.

"And?"

"And I was going to leave a note on the windshield."

"What was the note going to say?" I asked, suspicious.

"Don't piss off any killers."

"Ha ha. Too late." I dragged my purse closer, clutching it to my stomach. "I saw Yuri Polyak throwing rocks at trees earlier. He seemed to have pretty good aim."

He frowned. "Who's Yuri Polyak, and why would he want to mug you?"

"It wasn't a mugging, and he's a guest speaker, an abductee." Roughly, I stuffed the fallen UFO materials back into my purse. "I've got no idea why he'd want to attack me, and I didn't see who threw the rock, so maybe it was someone else. We should call the sheriff."

Two green-shirted X-tranormal medics trotted across the parking lot. They examined me with their medical gloves, said I might be concussed, and suggested Arsen take me to a hospital.

I shook my head, setting off sparks of agony in my neck. But worse was the feeling of vulnerability, of being out of control, that tightened my muscles and sped my pulse. And then there was that kiss...

"I'll drive you home," Arsen said. "We can leave your car here overnight. I'll bring you back to the festival tomorrow morning." He smiled faintly, and my legs went wobbly. "After breakfast."

Arsen helped me into the high seat of his massive Jeep Commander and waited while I called Sheriff McCourt. For reasons I won't go into, I had her personal cell phone number.

"What now, Witsend?" the sheriff asked.

"Someone attacked me outside the festival." I glanced at Arsen, staring across the grounds, and my lungs constricted.

A beat. "Who?"

"I didn't see them. Whoever it was hit me from behind – well, the side – with a rock." A cooling breeze flowed through the open doors, and I rubbed my arms, suddenly chilled.

"Probably hit the Vagus nerve," Arsen said.

"I think they threw it," I said, "because I didn't hear anyone close behind me. They broke my windshield too."

"Did they get your purse?" she asked.

"No, they didn't take anything." Cold fear rudely intruded on my Arsen confusion. Someone had been following me. Someone had wanted to hurt me. And they'd succeeded. Who had attacked me and why? "This must be connected to the murder."

"Must?" the sheriff asked. "Or could it have just been some drunken idiot throwing stones?"

Thanks to *Planet of the Grapes*, there *had* been some red-faced and tipsy aliens at the festival. "I guess it could have been," I said, doubtful. "But is it likely? Chuck was a VIP. So am I. I discovered the body."

"And?"

"And maybe the killer thinks I saw something, or maybe he's targeting VIPs?" Or maybe the killer was aware of my connection to the sheriff's investigation. All of Doyle knew I'd once helped catch a killer. Of course word had gotten out.

"Or maybe the incidents aren't connected at all," she said.

"That doesn't seem—"

"But it hardly matters," she went on more loudly, "since you didn't see who did it, and we're not likely to get fingerprints off a rock. Though the Israelis were working on a technique a few years back," the sheriff mused. "I don't suppose you saved the rock?"

"Um. No." I didn't know which rock hit me. The ground was covered in rocks. What did I care about rocks?

"Then we'll file this away in the interesting but unhelpful category, shall we?"

"But—"

"Goodbye, Susan." She hung up.

I glared at the phone. Honestly? Two VIPs are assaulted – one killed – and that was her response?

Arsen straightened off the side of the Jeep. "What did she say?"

"She said she'd file the information."

His expression tightened. "Is that all?" He slammed my door. Sliding into the driver's side, Arsen started the car, his jaw clenching and unclenching.

"The sheriff knows I can take care of myself," I said stiffly. If you thought about it, it was really a compliment. And the sheriff was right. I had sort of fallen down on the clue gathering. I needed to do better. "Stupid rocks," I muttered.

"What?"

"Nothing."

We bumped out of the parking lot and onto the highway.

Trying not to think of our kiss, I rolled down the window and sank lower in my seat. Golden hills dotted with oaks sped past on the winding road. We drove higher. The oaks gave way to pines, the scent of the air turning alpine.

"How was your day at the festival?" *Casual. I can do casual.*

"Okay, until now. I've promised to give Maisie my security review tomorrow morning."

"You'll have a review done by the morning?" I asked, surprised.

"I got most of it done today. I just need to shine it up and print it out. If Maisie agrees, we can start making changes to her security procedures."

My brow furrowed. For some reason this also caused me pain, and I grimaced. "Is she paying you?"

"Why wouldn't she? I gave her a discount rate." His jaw hardened. "I told her the discount was because I'd like to help her with other festivals, but I really just wanted to get inside X-tranormal. I don't suppose it will do any good asking you to stay away from the festival for the rest of the week?"

"I'm a sponsor."

He sighed. "So that's a *no*. If you did get knocked out because of a blow to the vegus nerve, you're probably not concussed. But I don't want to take chances. What about me spending the night?"

My breath froze in my chest. Arsen? Spending the night?

"To watch for a possible concussion," he said quickly. "Someone's going to need to wake you up every hour."

"Oh." I laughed, the sound high and false. "Right. Sure. That would be great. Thanks." *Casual, casual, casual.*

"You don't mind if I use your color printer, do you?"

I smiled bitterly. With Arsen, there was always an ulterior motive. "Why not?" I massaged my forehead. "It's the least I can do."

He turned onto Grizzly Court. The lights from Wits' End cascaded across the gravel driveway, and my muscles unwound at the sight of home. Arsen hovered over me as we walked up the porch steps, and he ushered me into the high-ceilinged foyer.

Tail low, Bailey beelined for Arsen and gave a happy yip.

Dixie looked up from behind the worn front desk and set down her phone. "Hey." She did a doubletake. "Uh, what'd you two do?"

"What does that mean?" I asked.

"You look guilty," she said.

I shoved her booted feet off the desk. "How did it go with Kayla?"

She shrugged, one strap of her purple tank slipping down her shoulder. "Everything went fine. I don't know why you're always freaking out about organizing things. This place isn't hard to manage."

I bit back a retort. The work went fine *because* I was organized.

She stood and stretched. "Anyway, I'm outta here."

"Can you stay?" Arsen asked. "Susan got clocked on the head at the festival. She might have a concussion."

"Or not," I said.

Dixie lifted a brow. "Do I get overtime?"

I checked the wall clock behind the desk. "Dixie doesn't need to stay. The guests know they can call my cell after hours if there's a problem." There rarely were any problems, because... organized!

"Are you sure?" Arsen bent to pet the beagle.

"She's sure." Dixie crossed the rag rug. "And I've got things to do, places to be." She slouched out the front door. The screen banged shut behind her. A moment later there was a second bang, the screen door at the top of the porch steps closing.

"I'm going to do a security check of Wits' End," Arsen said.

"Go wild." And because we were playing things normal, I grilled cheese and tomato sandwiches in the kitchen.

Outside, he rattled doors and windows.

"Everything's locked tight," he said from behind me, and I jumped. I hadn't heard him come inside.

"Great!" I plated his sandwich and turned too quickly. Odd little sparks of pain shot up my neck.

Arsen was inches away, the only thing between the two of us the blue dish and a grilled cheese sandwich. I thrust it toward him, and he stepped nimbly back.

"Thanks," he said.

We ate at the kitchen table, our conversation stilted. Bailey gazed, hopeful, at Arsen, and he fed the beagle a bit of grilled cheese.

Desperate to escape, I faked a yawn.

"You okay?" he asked.

I yawned for real this time and nodded. "Just beat."

His eyebrows drew together. "I can clean up if you want to lie down."

"Thanks," I said and fled into my private sitting room – the one other room in the house my Gran had modernized. I set a pillow and blankets on the black velvet couch for Arsen, then took a shower and tumbled into my bed.

But I couldn't sleep. My mind hamster-wheeled on warp speed. Had Yuri thrown that rock? How long would Arsen and I be able to pretend that kiss hadn't happened? The festival seemed to be puttering along in spite of the murder, so why did things feel so out of control?

Finally, I gave up. The only way for me to get any sleep was if I started putting together the pieces of this mystery. I pulled out my laptop, turned it on, and conducted an internet investigation from bed.

Yuri was sort-of famous, as abductees went. He'd been part of a psychology experiment on abductees by a Stanford researcher. The researcher had been determined to prove Yuri's abduction memories were caused by a non-UFO trauma, like a surgery. His team had found odd metal implants in Yuri's nose and the back of his neck. The researchers had also been unable to identify any past trauma that might have accounted for Yuri's memories.

Bailey rolled over in his doggy bed and snuffled. I watched the beagle for a moment, the gentle rise and fall of his side, and then I returned to my research.

Yuri's memories were both terrifying and transcendent — humiliating surgeries combined with visions of cosmic awareness. But there were no reports of Yuri being violent.

Dissatisfied, I shut down the computer and fell asleep, and was immediately shaken awake by Arsen.

And he kept waking me – every hour. And even though I'd known he would, that that was the plan, it was really irritating.

But at least I didn't kiss him again.

When I finally awoke on my own, sunlight streamed into my bedroom. The crystal in the window shot rainbows across Gran's tree-of-life quilt, the blue reading chair, the white-painted dresser. The scent of bacon and pancakes wafted beneath the closed bedroom door.

Arsen was cooking?

Alarmed, I swung my legs out of bed, my toes pressing into the soft throw rug. I pulled on a lightweight robe so purple it was nearly black and stumbled from my bedroom, stopping by the mirror near the parlor door. A purple bruise marked the base of my neck. I turned my head experimentally. The muscles were a little achy, but I'd live.

I hurried into the kitchen.

Arsen stood by the stove in the same clothes he'd worn yesterday and flipped a pancake. "Morning, beautiful."

"Hey." I knotted my belt and hurried to the stove. Neck injury or not, I owed my guests a breakfast. "What are you making?" And why was there so much of it?

"I call them, celestial pancakes."

"Celestial..." I stared at the open container of very expensive sprinkles on the counter. About half — pastel planets, white stars, candy pearls, and confetti quins – were gone. I'd special ordered those sprinkles from Canada for Dixie's birthday cake. The shipping had cost as much as the sprinkles. "You didn't—"

"Put them in the pancakes? I was afraid the colors might bleed, but check 'em out." He displayed a pancake on a spatula. It was embedded with colorful stars and planets. "Your planner said today's breakfast was supposed to be flying saucers. I wasn't sure what that meant, so I figured these would work."

Briefly, I closed my eyes. Arsen had done me a favor, letting me sleep while he'd made breakfast. But these were the most expensive pancakes I'd ever served.

I'd *planned* on making flying saucer breakfast sandwiches, but I could do that tomorrow. I forced a smile. "They look fantastic. Thanks."

His bronzed brow furrowed. "Are you okay? You look a little stressed."

"No. It's just, I'd gotten those sprinkles for Dixie's birthday."

"That's okay then. Her birthday's not for another six months. We've got time to get more."

"Right." I mastered my breathing. He was right. No need to freak out. It wasn't his fault we'd just blown past today's carefully designed breakfast budget. It was the fault of whoever had brained me yesterday and tricked me into kissing Arsen. I winced at the memory. Unless I'd hallucinated the kiss? It seemed like a dream now, and I'd much prefer a hallucination to humiliation.

My chest lightened with hope. "Let me get dressed, and I'll help you put the food in the warming trays."

I hurried into my bedroom, took a 30-second shower, and grabbed the first things I saw in my closet – a lightweight green blouse and tan slacks. I'd learned my lesson yesterday and slipped into a pair of ugly but comfortable walking shoes to complete the ensemble. I flipped up the collar to hide my bruise.

Returning to the kitchen, I chopped fruit and poured juices into pitchers.

Arsen flipped pancakes, and I set a collection of yogurts into a chilling bowl. We worked companionably, like nothing had happened. We seemed to be... okay. Maybe I really *had* imagined that kiss?

We shifted the food into the octagonal breakfast room and set out silverware and cloth napkins. I opened a window, and a draft of pine-scented air mingled with the scents of bacon, pancakes, and potatoes.

Mr. Jonas poked his head through the open doorway. He wore a maroon ballcap today and gray sweats. "Am I too early?"

"Not at all." Smiling, I plugged in the toaster. "I hear you skipped the festival yesterday. I'm sorry those protestors ruined your day."

"They didn't, and the festival goes all week. I had a great time just relaxing in Doyle." He stacked pancakes on his plate, then paused and stared at one quizzically. "I suppose planetary pancakes were inevitable." He sat at the oval table and unfurled a cloth napkin.

Mulder and Scully wandered into the breakfast room.

"Star and planet pancakes?" Scully exclaimed. "They're so cute! And sparkly!"

I smothered a grimace. But those expensive silver moons really did look pretty.

"Forget how they look," Mr. Jonas mumbled from the table. "These are the best pancakes I've ever tasted, even if the planets are a little crunchy. I had my doubts about the sprinkles, but this is a Class A breakfast, Ms. Witsend."

"That's for sure," Scully said. "These are so much better than those stupid breakfast sandwiches at that other UFO hotel. Remember hon?" She snorted and nudged her husband. "They called them *flying saucers*."

"Not really," Mulder said.

She gave me a look that said, *men!*

"Right," I said, dying a little inside. "Flying saucer sandwiches? How lame."

"I'm telling everyone about your B&B," she enthused. "We came back early yesterday, exhausted, and just relaxed and drank wine in your gazebo. It was heaven."

"I'm so glad you're enjoying it." And scratch tomorrow's flying saucer breakfast sandwiches. How was I going to top these stupid pancakes? I couldn't make them twice.

"What are you making for breakfast tomorrow?" Scully asked.

"It's a surprise," I said. For both of us.

CHAPTER NINE

Arsen and I walked down the spiraling dirt road. Flags hung lifeless from the tent peaks. Though the air was still, the festival was a swirling chaos of people. I adjusted my collar. It was only nine in the morning and already steaming hot.

Two aliens wearing worried expressions trotted past, jogging in the opposite direction.

Arsen frowned, watching them. We'd stopped at his house, so he could shower and change. He now wore a fresh golf shirt with his security "company" logo and khaki pants with an abundance of pockets.

"Are you sure you're feeling up for this?" Arsen asked for fifth time. He rested one hand on the pocket knife strapped to his canvas belt. Arsen carried a computer tablet in the other hand.

I gripped my purse with the copy of Gran's tiny book inside. "Thanks, but I feel okay." According to today's program, PB Gates would be at the *Other Worlds, Abroad* panel – a discussion of cryptid and UFO sightings overseas. I wasn't about to miss another chance to meet the man.

He checked his dive watch. "I need to meet Maisie at *Planet of the Grapes*. Do you have time to come along?"

My heart gave a little jump. At least he wasn't acting awkward and avoiding me. My hallucinated kiss theory was seeming more and more probable.

But I needed to catch PB, and Arsen...

We strode past tents and green-faced aliens and stalls hawking socks and UFO keychains. The image of Arsen cradling me in his arms flashed into my mind, of him pressing his mouth—

"I know what you're thinking," he said.

I started and sucked in my cheeks. "What?"

"Hanging out with me in *Planet of the Grapes* isn't part of the morning's plan." He canted his head toward my purse, and the planner bulging from its open zipper. "But this is a festival. It's supposed to be fun, and that means spontaneous. Live a little and come with me."

I laughed hollowly. "Have you seen the festival schedule? You have to strategize if you want to catch the interesting speakers."

"Come on. You know more about UFOs then all these jokers put together."

"That's not true," I said, warming. "They're not jokers, or at least, not all of them. And I know about Doyle UFOs. But I'm weaker when it comes to general UFOs history, aside from what Gran told me."

"Like I said, more than anyone."

Angry voices drifted around the bend of tents. We glanced at each other and crossed beneath the shadow of an oak.

Arsen's tanned brow creased. "That doesn't sound good."

We pushed through the tide of families. Parents, darting anxious looks behind them, prodded their children forward.

"But I want to see," a pink princess with bobbing antennae whined. She tugged futilely at her mother's hand.

"No, no, UFO!" a familiar chant drifted between the tents.

A competing chant roared over the second. "SciENCE! SciENCE! SciENCE!"

My stomach plummeted. "Not these guys again."

"This is getting monotonous," Arsen muttered.

We rounded a wooden kiosk selling UFO pops and reached a dead end. In front of a striped tent, Team Fairy faced off against a second group. Their bearded leader, Jack Bauer, brandished a protest sign. The second group seemed to be led by Yuri Polyak. In his shabby, too-big suit, he looked frail and outgunned.

Bridget stood slightly to the side and snapped pictures with her phone.

Veins bulged in Yuri's neck. "You're diverting attention from abductees! The victims need real help, not fairytales."

Jack Bauer shouted something inaudible beneath the chanting.

Bridget licked her lips and tucked her phone into the pocket of her sleeveless tunic and slacks ensemble. It matched her pale gray hair.

"Uh, oh. Arsen—" I turned, but he'd vanished. I jammed my hands on my hips. Some security specialist. Where had he gone? Panicked, I looked for help, saw none. Just what we needed – a brawl at the festival.

Yuri and Team Fairy ringleader stepped closer to each other.

A spark of anger flared at the point between my eyebrows. This was getting out of control. There were children here. What was wrong with these people?

I wedged myself between the two men and placed my hands on their shoulders. "Guys, there are kids around. Let's cool things down."

Yuri shook me off, knocking my oversized purse with his briefcase. It slipped off my shoulder, and I caught it before it could hit the dirt.

"You have no idea how destructive these idiots are to the cause," Yuri snarled.

"We believe in the abductions," Jack said. "Just not what or who's responsible." The bottom of his t-shirt didn't quite cover his round stomach.

"Hey," I said, "we're all here to get at the truth and hopefully enjoy ourselves."

Yuri's eyes bulged. "Fun? You think I'm here for fun?" He shook his head, his lank, black hair flinging outward. "You think I wanted to be abducted and tortured?"

My face heated. "No, of course not, I didn't mean—"

"Leave her alone," Jack said. "She's right. We want to be heard, but we don't want to get kicked out for rioting."

"Of course you don't." Yuri sneered. "You have no conviction, because even you don't really believe your stupid theories. But I know what happened to me." He shoved Jack.

Jack smacked his hand away.

"Don't touch me!" Yuri flailed, briefcase swinging.

I ducked, narrowly avoiding his arms.

Jack bent and blocked a wild slap with the top of his balding head. Yuri lurched forward, jostling me into Jack.

A woman screamed. "Fire!"

We froze, Yuri and Jack gripping each other's shirts and me sandwiched in between.

Flames raced up the side of a nearby tent. I froze, paralyzed. No. *No.*

Arsen stepped forward and raised a fire extinguisher. A whoosh of white foam and smoke roiled the air. I coughed, waving my hand. The smoke cleared.

"You okay?" Arsen asked.

I looked around, bewildered. The fairy and UFO contingents had vanished.

I gaped at Arsen. "You brought a fire extinguisher to a slap fight? How did you *know*?"

He flushed. "I didn't. I was going to use it to cool off those two idiots. Where'd they go?"

I stepped backward and something snapped beneath my shoe – a placard, discarded on the ground.

"No idea," I said. "They're probably hiding, hoping they won't get kicked out of the festival."

"If I catch them," he said, grim, "they will be. What were you doing in the middle of that brawl? Didn't you hear me ask you to wait?"

"Um, no." My hands curled around my purse strap. "I looked around, and you were gone, and things started heating up. I thought they were going to start a riot."

"So you jumped in the middle?"

"I thought I could talk them down. And Jack Bauer was more rational than I expected." Though Yuri had been disturbingly fervent, Yuri of the rock throwing... He'd implied he was committed enough to start a riot and get tossed out of the festival. Was he committed enough to kill? And if so, why go after Chuck? Had he somehow harmed Yuri's position on abductees?

I sniffed. "Do you smell something chemical?"

He nodded. "Accelerant. Those tents are supposed to be fire retardant." He brushed the smoldering fabric. "The fabric didn't burn, only whatever accelerant someone splashed on top of it. Maybe rubbing alcohol? It's got a low burn temperature."

"So," I said, "this was... deliberate."

"I'd say so."

My eyes narrowed. "Where did you learn about accelerants?" Arsen's business model was based on selling security equipment, not fire equipment.

He shrugged. "It's an old circus trick. No biggie." He raised his head. "Now that's a surprise."

I turned to follow his gaze.

Jack Bauer trudged toward us.

Arsen folded his arms. "We need to talk."

The big man hung his head. "I know, I know. I didn't want or expect things to get out of hand. But we didn't start that fire."

"Can you prove that?" Arsen asked.

"I think I can." He dug a cell phone from the back pocket of his baggy shorts. "One of the people in my group – who wishes to remain anonymous – took a video of the demonstration and texted it to me." He handed Arsen the phone.

I peered over Arsen's muscular arm. The video focused on the protestors and seemed to be shot from in front of the tent that had caught fire. There was a shout, a blur of white, jumpy shots of legs and the ground, and the video ended.

"You can see," Jack said, "that the only person near the tent was the person holding the video camera. She—I mean they were too busy filming to start a fire. Their back was to the tent the whole time."

"May I?" I extended my hand, and Arsen gave me the phone. "Arsen, you and Jack stand where Jack and Yuri were standing."

They got in position. I studied the photo and tried to match the image with the men. I ordered them a few inches to one side, then another. "This looks about where this video was filmed."

"And?" Jack asked.

"And you're right." I returned his phone, but not before texting myself the file. "The demonstrators were away from the tent. At least, all the demonstrators within the frame." Jack and his friends were in the clear. So was Yuri. Anxiety twisted my insides. So, who'd set the fire and why?

"*Someone* set that tent on fire," Arsen said, "they just weren't in the shot."

"I'm telling you," Jack said, "none of my team were responsible."

Arsen's face hardened. "All we know for sure is you and Yuri didn't. I don't know the rest of these people. I'll need their names."

Jack paled. "I can't. It's confidential."

Arsen stepped closer and glowered down at him. "You will."

Jack's shoulders slumped. "You're not going to throw them out, are you?"

"As far as I'm concerned, the only real trouble makers were you and Yuri and whoever set that fire."

Jack stuck out his bottom lip. "Fine. I'll make a list."

Maisie hurried toward us, her lanyard bouncing against her X-tranormal tee. "Thank goodness. Someone told me there was a fight and a fire. I see they were wrong."

"They were right." I stepped backward and stepped on another placard, this one with sparkling pink letters. *Fairies R People 2!* "If Arsen hadn't been here with a fire extinguisher, it could have been a disaster."

Her eyes widened. "What? What happened?"

Keeping his eyes on Jack, Arsen filled her in.

The festival manager shook her head. "This is good news. Our processes worked, and so did our fire-retardant tents. The fire didn't spread, and no one was hurt." She brushed at the tall scorch mark. "Accidents happen at festivals. The question is if the response you have in place was adequate. Clearly, it was."

Annoyed, I flicked my gaze toward the cloudless sky. I understood looking at the bright side, but someone had set that fire deliberately.

"*Was* it an accident?" Bridget strolled up to us. The reporter pocketed her phone.

"I didn't see anyone set it," I said. "Did you get any shots of the fire that might tell us more?" Bridget had been here earlier, but I'd lost track of her in the chaos.

She shook her head and smiled faintly. "Not of the fire."

"Whatever the cause," I said, "we got lucky. If Arsen hadn't been around—"

"It wasn't luck," Maisie said, gazing at Bridget. "These tents are flame resistant."

"But Arsen and I definitely smelled an accelerant," I said.

"Accelerant?" Maisie asked.

"That's what was burning," Arsen explained, "not the tent. Someone set that tent on fire intentionally, I'm guessing with rubbing alcohol."

"We don't know that for sure," Maisie said.

"No," Arsen said, "we don't. Which is why we need to call the sheriff and bring in an experienced arson investigator."

"It wasn't *my* group." Jack folded his fleshy arms over his chest. The bottom of his t-shirt rode higher, exposing a swathe of hair-covered belly.

Bridget moved the phone close to her mouth and murmured into the microphone.

Maisie's lips parted. "The sheriff?"

"First a murder," Bridget said, "then a fire. By all means, bring in the sheriff. Then the rest of the reporters in the press tent can write about the X-tranormal curse too."

Maisie's peaches and cream skin turned a shade milkier. "It's not a curse. I mean, what happened to Chuck was terrible, and our condolences go to his family. But this was nothing – a tent that didn't catch fire and a fight that didn't happen. There weren't even any people in that tent."

"A man's been killed," I said. "The fire could have spread. Don't you think it's possible the same person who killed Chuck set the tent on fire?"

"In my experience," Bridget said, "murderers and arsonists are different animals. But not always."

Maisie shot Bridget a startled look. "And like I said, these tents are specially treated. The company that sold them to us gave us a demonstration. It would take a lot to cause a serious fire."

What was *wrong* with these people? I didn't want to shut the festival down either. But I *really* didn't want to be responsible for more people getting hurt or even killed. Chuck's murder was horrible enough. "What if the person who killed Chuck has a grudge against the festival? What if he or she tries something else?"

"I don't think there's much we can do," Maisie said.

Above us, a green, alien-head balloon sailed lazily above the tent tops, and my muscles tightened. Children were at this festival.

I swallowed, hating what I was about to say. "You can shut down the festival."

Jack jerked forward. "What? But we paid for the whole week!"

Maisie planted her fists on her slim hips. "Are you kidding me? There's no way. Even if we did shut it down, do you think this crew would just leave? They'd go on and hold their festival anyway. Trust me, I've seen this before."

"It's okay, Susan." Arsen laid a comforting hand on my shoulder. "I've got this."

I shook my head. I didn't think Arsen would have better luck convincing Maisie than I had, but maybe he'd be able to put some extra security in place. Because I had a sick feeling that if whoever was responsible wasn't caught fast, things were going to get worse.

CHAPTER TEN

Bridget watched, one eyebrow raised, while Maisie and I collected discarded picket signs. We hefted them over our shoulders and followed Arsen down the festival's curving road. An alien whizzed past on a bicycle, and Arsen gripped one of Jack's shoulders to keep him from bolting through the stands.

Maisie shifted her collection of UFO signage. "Honestly Susan, you can stop worrying." She rounded a bend. "It's all under... control..." She stopped short, staring.

A man in a pink and white striped apron stood over Yuri. The abductee lay wrapped around his briefcase beside an ice cream cart.

I clutched the placards to my chest. *What now?*

"Is there someone I should call?" the grizzled ice cream vendor was saying. "A friend? A relative?"

"What's going on?" Maisie demanded.

I set my signs against the ice cream cart, but Arsen was quicker, dropping to his knees beside Yuri.

"Hey buddy," he said in a low voice. "Are you hurt?"

"Only in his mind." Bridget grasped Arsen's shoulder. "This has happened before."

The ice cream man brandished a cell phone. "I found him like this. I wanted to call nine-one-one, but he started freaking out. Freaking out more than he is now, I mean."

Yuri squeezed his eyes shut and rocked slightly.

Feeling helpless, I went to stand between Yuri and the open road to protect him from gawkers.

Maisie cursed beneath her breath.

Yuri covered his face with his long hands. "Don't touch me. Don't touch me."

"No one's touching you," Arsen said, his voice low and steady. "You're safe here, at the festival. Do you remember where you are?"

"It's his PTSD." Bridget brushed her steel-gray hair behind one bare shoulder. "He must have gone off his meds."

I gnawed my bottom lip. There were people in Doyle – I'd heard – who suffered from PTSD. I didn't know any personally, but I knew anxiety attacks. I'd fought off my own gray shadow successfully for years. But when it won, the attacks were horrible. My fists clenched in sympathy.

"Yuri," Arsen said in a low voice. "You're at a UFO festival. Focus. You're at X-tranormal. Yuri? Name five red things that you see."

To my surprise, Yuri responded. "Ice cream stripes." He panted, sucking in ragged gulps of air. "Flag. Balloon. Red shirt. A sign." He pointed at one of the pickets I'd left against the ice cream stand.

"Hey, Jack—" Arsen looked around and swore.

Jack had vanished. My lips tightened. Of course he'd run. I should have—

Yuri's hand shot up and grasped mine, squeezing. I flinched at the pressure.

"Don't let them touch me," he whispered. But his shaking had stopped. Beneath his loose business jacket, his chest rose and fell steadily.

Arsen gave me a look, and I nodded. Yuri's grip was tight, but I was okay.

A pink-haired customer approached the ice cream cart.

The seller waved her away. "Temporarily closed. Sorry."

"You've seen this before?" I asked Bridget quietly.

The reporter nodded. "Once. The attack ended on its own."

"Yuri ended it," Arsen said. "And you're ending it again, Yuri. You're in control here."

I bit my bottom lip. Whatever Arsen was doing, it seemed to calm Yuri down. But where had Arsen learned this technique? Not in the circus.

Maisie checked her cell phone. "Arsen, can you handle this? I need to be somewhere."

"Sure," he said. "We can talk later."

The conference organizer hesitated. "Should I call the medics?"

"No." Yuri gasped. "No doctors."

"You heard the man," Arsen said. "No doctors. It's okay, Susan and I will stay with him."

Maisie turned to leave. Bridget touched her arm. They moved off beside the ice cream cart, and I caught a few of the reporter's muttered words, "I know... Rachel."

I frowned. Rachel, my contact and the original conference organizer? So what if Bridget knew her?

There was a snap, a shadow falling across us. My shoulders jerked.

The ice cream seller locked the umbrella on his cart in place. He shrugged. "He could get a sunburn just lying there."

"Good thinking," Arsen said.

The man shrugged again. "This isn't my first rodeo." He gave Arsen a shrewd look. "I'm guessing it's not yours either. *Semper fi.*"

My brow puckered. *First rodeo? Semper fi?*

"You were a Marine?" Arsen asked. "You're a better man than I."

Yuri's breathing steadied, and he sat up. "I'm okay," he said.

Carefully, I helped him to his feet.

"I need to go someplace quiet," Yuri said.

"The VIP tent?" I suggested. "It's not far."

He closed his eyes again and nodded. "Please."

Arsen stepped toward us.

Yuri shuddered. "Just you please, Susan. Too many people..." he trailed off.

Arsen looked a question at me.

"It's fine," I said, baffled. Yuri barely knew me, and he might have beaned me with a rock. What was this about? "Arsen, I'll meet you in the VIP tent later," I said, knowing he wouldn't be far behind Yuri and me.

Yuri and I made our way down the improvised dirt road. He kept close to the tents and stalls. I walked on the outside, a barrier against the costumed visitors wandering past. Fortunately for Yuri, traffic was light. Muffled voices flowed from the tents we passed.

"You must think I'm mad." Yuri's voice quavered.

"No." I'd never forget my own curled-on-the-floor-and-shaking moments, though I dearly wanted to. *I am in control.* "I think you've gone through something." What I didn't understand was why he'd glommed on to me. He'd obviously connected to Arsen. I glanced at a stall selling UFO-themed jewelry.

"Your grandmother understood."

I stumbled over a stone. "My grandmother?"

He nodded. "I knew her. I was sorry to learn of her passing. I'd hoped to stay at Wits' End this week, but your B&B booked up before I had a chance to make a reservation. She was a good woman."

My eyes heated. I blinked rapidly. "How did you know my grandmother? Were you a guest?"

"Several times. It must sound strange to you, an abductee seeking out a town known for abductions. But I always felt safe at Wits' End. It felt somehow... protected. Maybe that was your grandmother's touch. I'd spend hours in her garden, just sitting. Your grandmother would join me in the mornings, and we'd talk about what was happening in Doyle, what had happened to me."

I swallowed, my throat thickening. "She was a good listener." How many times had she listened without judging to my laments about my parents' impossible demands? I'd put her in an awkward position, but she'd never betrayed my confidence, or criticized my parents.

"Are you friends with any of them?" he asked. "The Doyle Disappeared, I mean, the ones who returned?"

I stilled, one arm held flat against my stomach. "Not really. I was only a summer resident of Doyle until my grandmother passed. And the people who returned... They aren't easy to get to know." They'd isolated themselves, and I couldn't blame them. The media attention when they'd returned must have been overwhelming. I couldn't imagine returning home, with no memory of what had happened. Some had been gone for years, returning to find everything had changed.

Yuri's smile lit his saturnine face with a winter's light. "Does anyone really want to get to know these people? Does anyone truly want to hear what they went through? It's an experience most people can't possibly fathom and don't *want* to believe."

Guilt twinged through my chest. I made money off Doyle's UFO stories. I'd pushed for this festival. But what had I done for the victims? "I could try harder. I should try harder."

He sighed. "No. They'll find you when you're ready. And Susan, they will find you, just like I did."

I looked at him blankly. Why would they want to? Just because I was the local expert on UFOs didn't mean I was an expert at helping people deal with trauma. My gaze clouded. Arsen had somehow known how to calm Yuri though. How?

We reached the VIP tent. Yuri clinging to my hand, we walked inside the empty tent.

Releasing me, he tottered across an oriental rug and dropped onto the worn sofa. "Thank you, Susan." He set his briefcase on the rug, aligning it with a blue-red border.

"Would you like some water?" I asked.

"That would be lovely."

I grabbed a chilled plastic bottle from the ice chest on a long table and handed it to him.

He sat on the couch, his knees bent outward, the unopened bottle held loosely between his legs. "It's hard to believe we were here while Chuck was being murdered only yards away."

In spite of the tent's warmth, gooseflesh rose on my arms. It was as good a segue as any. "I keep wondering if someone was out to get Chuck, or if they're out to get the entire festival?"

"Are you thinking of the fire?"

"That, and other things."

He angled his head. "What other things?"

I hesitated and touched the side of my neck. "Someone hit me with a rock last night in the parking lot." I watched him carefully.

He sat forward. "Children can be monsters. Were you badly hurt?"

"I was knocked cold, but I'm okay. Unfortunately, I didn't get a look at the rock thrower." And if Yuri was the guilty party, he was a masterful actor, showing just the right amount of surprise and sympathy.

"Chuck." Yuri shook his head.

"I know he didn't do it. He's dead."

"But he brought trouble wherever he went," he said. "The man was a parasite."

"What do you mean?"

"He leeched money from people for his supposed UFO research. Chuck diverted funds from real, honest researchers. His greed made him thoughtless, and he hurt many people. There were plenty of people, some who were right here in this tent, who I imagine are glad he's dead."

"Like who?"

"Like Jane, for starters."

"His wife?" I asked.

"I can recognize people who have been damaged by others." He gave me a long look. "Jane is one of those people."

"Damaged by Chuck?" I asked. "Was he abusive?"

"There are many ways to abuse a person." He gulped from the water bottle. "You should ask Aleta Bradford."

"Spence's wife?"

"She and Chuck were... close."

I didn't like where this was headed, and my nose wrinkled. "That surprises me, since her husband is no fan of Chuck's."

His thin lips curled upward. "Or perhaps it is cause and effect?"

"What are you saying? That Chuck and Aleta were romantically involved?"

"It's all innuendo, which as I'm sure you know, is untrustworthy."

"All right." I pulled up a metal folding chair and sat across from him. "Then let's talk about the morning Chuck was killed. Can you remember what time you arrived, and who was in the VIP tent with you?"

He arched a thin brow. "Why do you care?"

"Because I brought X-tranormal to Doyle, and I found Chuck dead, and there's a murderer in my town. Isn't that enough?"

"And perhaps, the feeling of being out of control is also terrifying?"

"I'm not out of control," I said tightly. My hand went to my purse, and the planner inside.

He smiled. "I arrived at the festival around nine. As to who was in the tent, we were all wandering in and out. It was such a beautiful morning, and no one wanted to stay inside. How could they on these grounds, with their oak trees and grasses humming with insects?"

"Did *you* wander in and out?"

"Of course. But as I told your sheriff, I did not notice anyone going into or coming out of the registration tent."

Well, rats.

"I have disappointed you," he continued. "I'm sorry. You and your boyfriend have been very kind."

"He's not my—"

Yuri cocked his head.

"Never mind," I muttered.

"At any rate," he said, "I would like someday to repay the favor."

I perked up. Maybe he could. "I don't suppose you know PB Gates?"

"The UFO travel writer?"

I nodded eagerly.

"No."

I smiled bitterly. "It's all right. I'm sure I'll find him. The festival runs all week." But had I known what the rest of the week would bring, I would have stayed in bed.

CHAPTER ELEVEN

Arsen strode through the opening of the VIP tent and stopped short. "Hey, Yuri. How're you feeling?"

The standing fan whirred, loud in the long silence. Suddenly uncomfortable, I looked away. At the tea urn. The uneven bottles of water. The metal chairs scattered around the tent.

Finally, Yuri rubbed his hands on his baggy slacks and stood. "I am better. Thank you." His briefcase tipped, hitting the faded oriental carpet with a cloudy smack.

"No problem. Sue, could I talk to you for a second?" He angled his chin toward the opening and walked through.

I followed. *Casual, casual, casual.* "What's up?"

He halted in front of a crude wooden stand selling tequila in bottles shaped like alien heads. A sign at the top of the stand read: PSYCHIATRIC HELP (FOR ABDUCTEES). The sign seemed a lot less funny than it had this morning.

"I didn't think the VIP tent would be empty." Arsen frowned, the sun bronzing his wavy hair.

"Lucky for Yuri, it was." The guy needed some quiet time.

Arsen lowered his voice. "He's a murder suspect, Susan. That's why I was right behind you two the whole time."

"And listening outside?"

He nodded impatiently. "You know he might have been the one who attacked you."

"I know, but..." But I was having a harder time thinking about Yuri as a killer. He'd looked too vulnerable curled on the dirt. And I felt he'd been straight with me, even if he had gotten coy at the end about Aleta's connection to Chuck.

"I get that you've got sympathy for the guy," Arsen said. "I do too. But you need to be more careful."

"Says the man who did a handstand off my porch railing last week."

"I'm serious, Susan." His expression hardened, and he looked deep into my eyes. Usually, his "I'm serious" look made me want to laugh. Today I wanted to lean closer.

I looked away.

"Are you all right?" he asked.

I straightened and cleared my throat. "What? Oh. Just thinking." I glanced toward the canvas opening, tied to the side of the tent. "Your point is taken, and I'm way off schedule. Do you mind if we pick this up later?"

"Sure. But we *do* need to pick it up later. Where are you headed?"

"To Spence Bradford's panel. I want to, um, ask his wife about something Yuri said."

A trio of men in monkish white robes strode past, laughing. A breeze rustled the tent canvas, and dying oak leaves drifted onto the wide path.

"I'll come with you."

We walked past a stall selling faux laser weapons, side-by-side with a purveyor of handmade wands. Were the wands part of the *X* in the X-tranormal, or was the fairy contingent making inroads on the abduction concept?

An alien on an old-fashioned tricycle wheeled past, and I checked my map. "We go left on Milky Way."

Arsen grinned. "They've sure *milked* the astronomy references."

"Yuck it up." I sucked in my cheeks. "At least Doyle is getting more tourist dollars from this festival." Without the tourists, I didn't think there'd be a Doyle left. "Even you got business from X-tranormal."

"Yeah, I didn't expect this gig, but I won't say *no*. Most of my business is in the Sacramento area, and I'm getting tired of the commute."

Surprised, I looked up at him. When he'd first started the security business, I'd assumed it was just another one of his fly-by-night careers. Scuba instructor. Hiking guide. God only knew what else he'd done after he'd run off to join the circus. But he seemed to be taking his new project seriously. "How's business?"

"It's keeping me busier than I'd expected," he admitted. "But if I can keep someone from getting hurt, it's worth it." He paused. "I'm not like you. It took me a while to figure out where I belonged. You're perfect running Wits' End. You never wanted to do anything else."

My hands briefly clenched. Wits' End *was* my something else, my second chance. Arsen didn't think of it this way, because he'd been AWOL during my first, respectable accounting career. "After you ran off to join the circus, I toyed with becoming a fire dancer," I said, sarcastic, "but the schedule didn't suit me."

"Were the hours too late?" he asked, looking intrigued by the idea.

"Too erratic."

He laughed. "Who are Aleta and Spence?"

"Spence runs a UFO society. Aleta's his wife. As I'm sure you heard, Yuri hinted she and Chuck were, um, close."

"And you believed him?" His forehead wrinkled.

"I don't know, which is why I want to ask Aleta. But I heard her sort of arguing with her husband, and it sounded... odd."

"Odd," he said flatly. "If she was *close* with Chuck, do you think she'll admit it to you?"

"I've got to try something," I said, my voice high and fast. "X-tranormal was my baby, and now a man's dead. I can't just let this... happen."

"I was afraid you'd feel this way. But solving crimes is what the sheriff's department is for."

But the sheriff had come to me for assistance before. "Someone hit me with a rock and broke my windshield."

"I haven't forgotten." He gave me a sharp look. "You can't control everything, Susan."

"What's that supposed to mean?"

He sighed. "Nothing."

We slowed outside the metal archway to the outdoor food court. Nearby rose the *Planet of the Grapes* tent, covered in fake grape vines.

I eyed the hot pretzel stand, surrounded by red-faced festival goers.

Arsen angled his head. "I don't suppose we have time for food?"

"We'd better. Spence's talk ends in thirty minutes, and I'm starving."

We walked beneath the metal arch and into an oval-shaped picnic area ringed by food sellers. UFO burgers. Cosmic shakes. Galactic fries. It was all ridiculous and mouthwatering, and the tables were packed to the gills, the lines dispiritingly long.

"Has the festival gotten more crowded?" I asked. "Or is it just the food area?"

"Ticket sales have definitely picked up," Arsen said.

"How did you find that out?"

He shrugged. "It's a security issue. The festival is expected to sell out today."

"Because it's a Sunday?" I scanned the crowd and smiled.

Aleta sat alone at a small wooden table beneath an oak. She sipped something tall and orange and frothy. Her slinky festival wear draped suggestively over her curves.

"It must be fate," I said, pointing. "There's Spence's wife, Aleta."

"You don't believe in fate."

"Who says I don't? I believe in the possibility of UFOs." I moved toward her table. "Hi, Aleta." I waved.

She looked up, and her dark brow furrowed. "Hello."

"Mind if we join you?" I asked. "This place is mobbed."

She scooted over. "Why not?"

I stuck out my hand, and she took it. "I'm Susan Witsend, by the way. I run the UFO B&B, Wits' End. Your husband promised to introduce us, but he never got the chance."

Her face cleared. "Oh, right. I should have recognized you. I saw your name and photo in the program."

"And this is Arsen Holiday."

He shook her hand.

She smiled warmly, and jealousy singed by stomach. I looked away, embarrassed. I had no right to be jealous. Arsen and I were *friends*.

It was a shame he was such a good kisser.

"I'm helping with festival security," he said.

"Too bad you weren't here two days ago," she said, "when Chuck Thorpe was killed. Perhaps you could have prevented his death. Or were you here and failed?"

I sat across from her at the wooden bench, and Arsen sat beside me.

"Festival management brought me in after the fact," he said coolly.

Her head bowed. Her hands curled. She looked up, and her lips trembled. "I still can't believe Chuck's gone. Do you have any idea how someone got past the guards and onto the grounds?"

He shook his head. "There was only one guard on duty at the time of his death. The other gates were locked, but someone could have crawled over a back fence."

"Isn't it more likely someone already inside the festival killed him?" I asked.

Aleta toyed with the straw in her orange drink. "I don't know why they would. We all want this festival to be a success."

"I didn't get a chance to meet him," I said, "but I've heard Chuck wasn't well liked. Maybe the murder wasn't about the festival?"

She looked toward the metal arch and smiled faintly. "Chuck was a difficult man to like."

"But you liked him?" I asked.

"That's a strange question to ask about a dead man."

My shoulders lifted, dropped. "I found his body and... it bothers me."

She nodded. "It bothers me, too."

"Then I'm very sorry for your loss," I said.

"A better sentiment for his wife, I think." She exhaled slowly.

"Someone told me you two were close," I said.

Aleta's head snapped around, and her brown eyes narrowed. "Close? Where did you hear that?"

"I'm not sure," I said. She'd definitely reacted, but was that innocence or guilt? "You know how these festivals are. You talk to so many people."

"Then you misheard," she said.

"Do you have any idea who might have killed him?" Arsen asked.

Her squarish jaw hardened. "Are you a detective as well as a security guard?"

He smiled. "We're just talking here."

"Then talk to that reporter, Bridget. She blames — blamed Chuck for her career tanking. Though if you ask me, there's only one person responsible for *that*, and that's Bridget Konrach." She rose and dusted off the rear of her knit slacks. "Excuse me." Aleta strode beneath the metal arch.

Arsen rubbed his chin. "I think we need to work on our investigative technique."

Pressure lifted from my chest. At least that kiss hadn't wrecked things between us. "Thanks for saying *our* technique."

The scent of baking pretzels wafted across the picnic table, and my stomach grumbled. "About that argument I overheard between Aleta and her husband. She told Spence something was over. I wonder if she was talking about her relationship with Chuck?"

"We still don't know for sure she had one, and if she did, just what that relationship was."

I propped my chin on my hand and ignored my rumbling tummy. "No, but Aleta didn't look happy when I asked if they'd been close."

"Chuck was murdered. Anyone might have had the same reaction."

I hated it when he was right.

"There you are!" Maisie jogged to our picnic table. "Arsen, someone reported a break in one of the fences." She did a doubletake, seeming to notice me for the first time. "Oh, hi, Susan. I've been meaning to tell you, I checked with registration, and PB Gates is registered as himself, PB Gates."

"Oh. Thanks." But if I couldn't catch him on a panel, how was I going to find him in this crowd?

"Sometimes people register under special festival names," she explained to Arsen. "You know, Lord of the Galaxy, that sort of thing. It makes identifying people by their lanyard tough. But he's just PB Gates."

"I'm still hoping to find him at one of the panels," I said.

She frowned. "Yeah, well, that's the thing. PB Gates hasn't come through registration at all. He hasn't picked up his festival badge."

My heart stuttered to a halt. "You mean, he's not coming?"

"I don't know what's going on. We've been emailing him, and he hasn't responded. He's supposed to be here. He's a VIP guest, a speaker. But he's just... not here. No explanation."

"You don't think something's happened to him?" I asked, worried.

"He probably just decided not to come and is too embarrassed to respond to your emails," Arsen said.

"I hope that's all it is," she said. "We don't have a phone number for him, just email. First Chuck and now PB — we've lost two key speakers. I know X-tranormal isn't my usual type of festival. Whether it's a success or not isn't on me. But I'm in charge, and I don't want to see things fall apart."

That, I could understand.

"I'm sure we're worrying over nothing. Not that losing speakers is nothing," Arsen said quickly. "Why don't you show me where that broken fence is. Let's deal with something we can actually manage."

"Right." She blew out her breath. "Right. The fence break is this way."

I watched her lead him into the milling crowd, and dread pooled in my stomach. Chuck dead. A tent set on fire. An attack on me. And now PB Gates was missing?

Easygoing Arsen might be able to take the latest disappearance in stride, but I couldn't.

Something was very wrong at the X-tranormal festival. I just hoped PB Gates wasn't our latest casualty.

CHAPTER TWELVE

Since I'd spoken to Aleta, I decided to give Spence's panel a miss. Worry made me hungry, and there was a hot pretzel with my name on it. I stood in line for my treat, and that took a lot longer than it should have.

I sat beneath an oak for a bit of fine dining, then started listing suspect in my planner. Thanks to the power of the internet, I'd found a company that personalized planner pages. My suspects pages were divided into three columns: means, motive, and opportunity. And each had a timeline tracker per suspect. I'd once suggested Sheriff McCourt use something similar.

She hadn't reacted well.

I tapped my pen on my chin. Should I give the suspects different color codes? Pastels for the girls and primary colors for the boys was a little sexist, but it might make it easier for me to *see* any emerging patterns...

Finishing my salty-sweet pretzel, I tucked my planner beneath my arm and ambled to the VIP tent. The timeout with my planner had given me perspective. There was a limited suspect pool. All I needed to do was keep an eye on the VIPs. And I was probably overreacting about PB. I could do this.

I perked up. Plus, tonight was my date with Tom, which was perfect timing after the disaster with Arsen. I rubbed a hand across my face, my stomach butterflying. *That kiss.*

But I was moving on. I didn't want to moon over someone I couldn't have. It was unhealthy, a waste of time. When we were teens, Arsen had left me behind for a stupid circus – he'd just disappeared from my life for years. My throat tightened with a painful ache. I gave him a hard time about the circus incident. But the truth was, I couldn't stand the heartbreak if he flitted off again. Better I find greener pastures, turn the page, hook another fish in the sea.

Inside the VIP tent, Maisie stood at the food table and frowned into a cardboard box. A fan whirred in one corner, shoving around the late afternoon heat.

"Hi, Maisie," I said.

The festival organizer started and pressed a hand to her heart. "Oh, it's you."

I poured a cup of tea from the metal urn and dunked a shortbread cookie. "Was Arsen able to repair the fence?" I bit into the cookie before it crumbled.

"What? Oh. Yes. He's really wonderful. And then we got a call that a naked guy was wandering around the festival. Our entire security team is female, so Arsen went to take care of that. We're lucky he was available on such short notice."

"Naked guy?" I smothered a laugh. Poor Arsen.

"And the best part," she continued, "is none of Arsen's security improvements have to do with equipment. They're all procedural changes, and those don't cost anything but the time to get the word out."

How was Arsen going to get paid for that? I ran my thumb along the edge of the Styrofoam cup. But my friend was a grown man. He didn't need me worrying about his paycheck. Besides, his family money guaranteed he didn't need one. "What have you got there?" I asked, nodding toward the boxes.

"Pamphlets that I need to alter at my hotel tonight to show the new schedule of panelists and speakers. Plus, Chuck's books and swag that he planned to give away at his panels." She nodded toward a box. "I need to get his things to his wife. Jane's staying at the Historic Doyle Hotel. Do you know where it is? I tried to use my phone's GPS, but the reception in the mountains is terrible."

"You're in luck, the hotel's on Doyle's Main Street." I thought fast. If I took the box, I'd have just enough time to interrogate the widow and meet Tom for our date at Alchemy. "In fact," I said casually, "it's on my way. If you'd like, I'd be happy to take her the box."

Her shoulders relaxed. "Would you? I'm staying in Angels Camp, which is in the exact opposite direction, and I'm exhausted."

I sipped the tea and made a face. It was cold. Someone had unplugged the urn. I set the cup on the table. "If you want, I'll take that box now."

"I'll walk with you." She handed me a box. "My truck's in the VIP lot, and I can dump the brochures inside. Besides, after what happened last night, I think we should travel in pairs."

"Thanks." I wasn't exactly scared of walking to my car alone, but I hadn't been looking forward to it either.

She followed me out the gate to the VIP lot and whistled at my Crosstrek's cracked windshield. "Ouch. I'll check our insurance, but I don't think our coverage applies to this sort of thing."

Even though I'd known getting someone else to pay for the repair would have been too much to hope for, my heart sank. I hadn't paid much attention to the PARK AT YOUR OWN RISK sign earlier. Now it seemed prophetic.

I shook my head. "Thanks. It would be great if the festival's insurance paid, but I'll survive if it doesn't."

Maisie walked to the shade of an oak tree, where a vintage red pickup sat.

I popped my SUV's hatchback and slid the box inside.

Walking to the pickup, I ran my hand along the warm hood. "Nice truck." I joined her at the rear.

"I learned to drive in it when I was twelve. It breaks down at least twice a year, but I can't seem to let it go." She closed the tailgate. It clanged shut, rattling the Nevada license plate.

I waited in my car, watching until Maisie was safely back inside the festival grounds, then I started the SUV. My phone rang in my purse. I dug it out and checked the screen. *Arsen.*

Pulse speeding, I answered. "Hey."

"Hey, where are you?" His voice was faint beneath the rumble of the idling engine and the whoosh of the A/C.

I pressed the phone tighter to my ear. "Inside my car, in the parking lot, about to drive to Doyle. Where are you?"

"I'm just finishing up here."

I grinned. "How'd it go with the naked guy?"

"*Sweaty* naked guy."

I laughed. "Enough said."

"Meet you back at Wits' End?"

"Um, I've got some stuff to do first." *Just tell him about Tom. Tell him.*

"Okay. I'll see you when I see you."

We said our goodbyes and hung up. It wasn't like we were dating. I didn't have to tell him about my social life. Why shouldn't I go out with Tom? Feeling guilty for no good reason, I put the car into drive and bumped across the lot, stones pinging the bottom of my Crosstrek.

Grip tight on the wheel, I leaned forward and peered past the cracks in my windshield. Most of the damage was on the passenger side, but I drove cautiously up the winding highway.

Should I have told Arsen about Tom? I didn't report to him. He'd probably just think I was trying to force the issue of that kiss, which he was still pretending had never happened. A lumber truck rumbled past, rolling down the mountain, and I gave it a wide berth.

I turned off the highway and drove past a stand of pines and onto Main Street. The rear end of a delivery truck rose suddenly before me, and I jammed on my brakes.

I craned my neck. The road was packed with cars, and I winced. A traffic jam in Doyle? Because of the festival? The residents weren't going to be happy about the extra traffic. A car horn blared, and I started.

My SUV crawled past converted stone barns, past the old west false fronts of boutiques and restaurants. The parking spots on the roadside were filled, and I had to drive down a side street before I found a spot, several blocks from the hotel.

I hefted the box and hurried to Main Street, passing a wine tasting room. The rows of vines that filled its front yard and twined around its fence were heavy with purple grapes. Resisting the urge to sneak one, I crossed the street to the shaded walk. Though the sun was lowering on the horizon, the day was still hot.

Hanging baskets of ivy and impatiens dangled from the rafters of a gray-painted boutique. Water bowls sat outside shop doors for visiting dogs. A border collie stood leashed beside one, panting and waiting for its owner, inside.

I wove through the stopped traffic to the Historic Doyle Hotel, a two-story, stone and mortar building. Its green metal shutters opened on narrow, wrought-iron balconies. Though it was well past July fourth, red, white and blue bunting still hung from the front balconies. Wisteria climbed the sides of the honey-colored building, the blooms long gone but the green vines still lush.

A bearded hipster in a wide-brimmed felt hat sat on the bench beside the door and strummed a ukulele. His legs were crossed, the toe of his boot hovering over the ash bucket for smokers.

I walked inside the cool lobby, painted cobalt blue with white wainscoting. Its soft, blue carpet felt like heaven beneath my feet, sore from a day of tramping back and forth across the festival grounds.

Erica, a slim, thirty-something with freckles scattered across her tanned nose and cheeks, looked up from the reception window. She smiled, her brown eyes crinkling. "Howdy, competitor! What can I do for you?"

"I'm playing delivery girl today for one of your guests, Jane Thorpe. I've brought some of her husband's things from the festival." I shifted the box in my arms. "Is she in?"

"Let me call up and find out." She dialed a number. "Hello, Ms. Thorpe?" she asked in a subdued voice. "Susan Witsend is here from the festival. She has a box of your husband's things... Of course... Yes... Have a good evening." She hung up the receiver. "She said you can go on up. She's in room 214."

"Thanks. I hear you've got the Bradfords staying here as well."

She rolled her eyes. "Be thankful they didn't book into Wits' End." She leaned through the reception window and lowered her voice. "Constantly fighting. We've gotten several complaints from their neighbors."

"Huh." I guess there always was a silver lining. "I'm sorry to hear that." I walked up the blue-carpeted stairs and turned at the narrow hallway.

A black-clad figure in a headscarf and flowing skirt thumped toward me. She brandished a cane.

I stopped short. "Mrs. Steinberg?"

The old lady pressed a finger to the side of her nose.

I couldn't see past her Jackie Kennedy-style glasses, but I suspected she'd winked.

"What are...?"

She lurched past and disappeared around the corner.

Nonplussed, I stared down the hall. Had she been visiting Mrs. Thorpe? I mentally shrugged and continued on, my feet padding near silently on the carpet.

I knocked on 214. A discarded room service tray lay on the floor nearby.

After a moment, the door swung open. Jane Thorpe leaned heavily on the handle. Her short, silver hair was matted on one side, and her skin looked doughy from a lack of fresh air. She blinked. "I know you."

"I'm Susan, Susan Witsend. I was at the festival, in the VIP tent, the first morning," I said awkwardly. The morning her husband had been murdered. "I'm so sorry for your loss. It's just— Maisie asked me to bring these by." I raised the box in my arms an inch or two.

"Of course. What am I thinking, leaving you holding that? Come in, come in." She moved away from the door, and I walked inside.

The opposite wall had been given the barn door treatment and covered in old wood in varying shades of brown. Metal cutouts of cowboys and coyotes hung on the wall behind the bed. One of the French windows stood open, and the curtains billowed, languid.

"Just put it on the bed," she said, pointing to the queen-sized bed covered by a smooth, white duvet. Tan pillows lay propped against the rustic wooden headboard.

I set down the box. "Was that Mrs. Steinberg I saw?" I asked over the hum of the ceiling fan.

"Hm? Oh, yes. It was kind of her to stop by."

"How do you two know each other?" Because I *might* believe in UFOs, but I did not believe in coincidences.

"This isn't our – my – first visit to Doyle. Chuck and I were here after the mass reappearance. Would you like some tea?" she asked. "It's only tea bags, I'm afraid, and an electric hot pot. And there's no honey, only sugar and artificial sweetener."

"I'd love some tea, but only if I'm not imposing."

"You'd be doing me a favor. I've been stuck in this room all day, with only room service to talk to. That sheriff told me I can't leave town, and I just don't feel up to wandering the streets like the Lady of Shallot."

"Did the Lady of Shallot wander?"

"No." She shuffled to the bathroom with the plastic pot, and a tap ran. "She sat sighing in her tower while the world went by, so I guess I *am* being the Lady of Shallot, but you know what I mean. And at least I'm out of sight."

"Out of sight?" I repeated. The single trick I knew for prompting people to talk was to repeat back the last thing they said. It usually worked.

"I hate being a widow." Her voice echoed from the bathroom. "I feel like everyone is staring at me, wondering if they should do something and wondering if I killed my husband. I didn't, in case you're worried about me poisoning your tea."

I hadn't been... until now. "With sealed teabags and sugar packets?" I asked, uneasy. "That would be unlikely."

Jane emerged from the bathroom. "But not, I think impossible." The widow set the pot on its stand and turned it on. Dropping onto the bed, she burst into tears.

"Oh." My hands fluttered helplessly, my throat thickening with sympathy. Not knowing what else to do, I sat beside her and grasped her hand.

We sat that way until the electric kettle popped and hissed.

She wiped a hand across her eyes and stood, moving to the desk. "Is Earl Grey all right? It's all I have."

"It's... fine."

Jane poured the water into a white mug, ripped open a tea bag, dropped it in. "Sugar?"

"Please."

She tore open a packet and poured it in. "I'm afraid I don't have any spoons. You'll have to swirl it around with the tea bag."

"I'll make do."

She handed me the mug and prepared her own tea, then sat in a wingback chair near the open window. "Don't worry." She sniffed. "I promise not to throw myself out."

My chest squeezed. Was joking about suicide a cry for help? Or was it a coping mechanism? "How are you managing?"

She gestured with her free hand. "As you can see. Crying one minute, making sarcastic comments the next. I can't believe it. I just can't believe it. Chuck and I were together so long. I told him not to come to this vipers' nest."

My spine straightened. "Vipers' nest?" *Doyle?*

She rolled her eyes. "I'm sure you've heard by now. You *must* have heard. They hate him. All of them."

"You mean, people at the festival? But why?" I grimaced at my playacting, because I had a good idea why, and I stared into my mug. But it had to be done. The sheriff was counting on me. I had to learn what I could from Jane, even if she was a grieving widow.

"My husband delighted in provoking people, myself included. Poor Yuri got the worst of it. He was so deadly serious about his abduction and the importance of proper research. As if there's any such thing as proper research in the field of UFOs."

"And Chuck didn't take the research seriously?"

She sipped her tea. "My husband took his livelihood very seriously. What he didn't take into account was the impact he had on others. Even when Yuri started making those threatening phone calls, Chuck refused to go to the police."

"Threatening calls? What exactly did Yuri say?"

"I never got the details. Chuck was always the first to grab the phone. He could *occasionally* exhibit a protective streak towards me. And in fairness, he always heard Yuri out. But then, of course my husband did whatever he liked, just as he always did, and the calls kept coming." Her brow furrowed. "Until about a month ago. I hope Yuri didn't finally decide to act on his threats."

"I heard someone fire bombed your husband's car," I said cautiously.

"*My* car." She studied her tea. "But whoever did it must have been trying to frighten Chuck."

"Was he frightened?"

"Not enough to report the matter to the police. I loved that MG."

I tested the tea. In spite of my efforts, the sugar had sunk to the bottom. "Who do you think might have done it?"

She shrugged. "I wouldn't want to speculate."

"Have you told all this to the sheriff?"

"Of course I have. All she said was, don't leave town." She shook herself. "I'm sorry. You must think I'm an awful gossip. I don't know what I'm saying."

"Not at all."

"I shouldn't have said anything." She set her tea on the desk and looked out the window. A moth fluttered past the curtains. It beat against the overhead lamp. "Please don't say anything. There's been so much rumor and innuendo already. I'd hate to be the one to add to the flames."

"Of course," I said, disappointed. She knew more. What wasn't she saying?

When we'd finished our tea, and I was fairly certain I wouldn't get anything more out of her, I stood. "Thanks for the tea." Surreptitiously, I checked my watch. I still had plenty of time to meet Tom. "Is there anything I can do for you?"

"Find my husband's murderer?" She barked a harsh laugh. "I don't suppose that sheriff will have any luck."

*****

My romantic instincts were awful.

I slammed my Crosstrek's door and leaned against it, trying to master myself.

It hadn't been a date. All Tom had wanted was to interrogate me about X-tranormal and my grandmother's roses. I'd had to pick my way through thirty minutes of murder talk before I could escape. *And* he'd made me split the check. Couldn't he at least have put it on his newspaper expense account?

"Stupid reporters. And what was with the stupid rose obsession?" I nodded to a deep crimson Louis Phillipe rose bush. "Sorry," I muttered. "Nothing personal."

My head angled back, resting on the car roof. I gazed at the stars, so far away and so brilliant.

An ache squeezed my heart. This was ridiculous. I barely knew the reporter. So why did his deception bother me so much? *Not good enough...* my mother's voice whispered down the mountainside and in my ear.

"Bull." Straightening, I brushed off the back of my clothes and made my way inside Wits' End.

Dixie sat with her feet up on the reception desk, her eyes closed, headphones in, blue-tipped hair bobbing to the music.

Bailey looked up from his doggy bed near the desk. The beagle got up, turned his back on me, and laid down.

I walked to his bed and scratched the dog behind his ears. "I know, you're mad I've been away all day. But I couldn't help it. And Dixie was here."

His tail thumped the floor once.

"Hi, Dixie," I said, straightening.

Her eyes remained closed, head swaying.

"Dixie," I said more loudly.

She blinked, yawned. "Oh, hey. How was your date?"

"I'd rather not talk about it. How did it go today?"

She shrugged. "I didn't burn the house down."

My eyes narrowed. Dixie looked awfully relaxed for someone who'd spent the day cleaning rooms. "And Kayla? How's she working out?"

"She's okay. How was the festival?" she asked quickly.

"No one else was killed, so I'm calling it a win. Were you able to clean all the rooms?"

Footsteps bounded up the front porch, and I glanced toward the door.

"Sheesh," my cousin said. "Chillax. They're clean."

"Hey, Susan, Dixie." Arsen strode into the high-ceilinged foyer. "How's it going?"

Bailey bounded from his bed and frisked about Arsen's boots.

"Oh, come *on*," I muttered.

"Susan's freaking out," Dixie said, "as usual."

"I'm not freaking out." Sweat beaded my forehead, and I stared intently at Dixie, willing her to keep her mouth shut about my so-called date. "I just asked—"

"Ladies, ladies." Arsen spread his arms in a pacifying gesture. "It's been a long day, but at the end of it, we all know we can trust each other. Right?"

"You can trust *me*." Dixie folded her arms.

"Susan?" Arsen asked.

Trust him? That was a sure sign he'd been up to something. "I'm still thinking."

He grinned. "Don't hurt your head. Maybe you could use a break. Why don't you come for a swim at my place?"

"I'm in," Dixie said.

Bailey yipped, turning in an excited circle on the faded rug.

Arsen shuffled his feet. "Um, I meant Susan. She took a bad knock to the head and needs to relax."

"That's for sure," she muttered.

"My head's fine," I said.

"You don't mind staying a little longer here," he asked her, "do you?"

"Oh, puh-leeze." She rolled her eyes. "I already stayed late because of her stupid date."

He stilled. "Date?"

"It was nothing," I said, speaking rapidly. "It wasn't even a date. I just met Tom for dinner, and we both tried to get information out of each other. Neither succeeded."

His expression darkened. "He asked you to dinner?"

"Reporters." I shrugged, tried to look… casual. "They'll do anything for a story. But I can hardly complain when I'm helping the sheriff. It's the only reason I even went."

Dixie snorted.

"What exactly was he asking you about?" Arsen said.

"The murder. Gran's roses."

"Gran's roses?" Dixie scrunched her brow. "What does that have to do with anything?"

"Nothing, right?" I laughed, uneasy. "I mean, they bloom all year long, which is weird—"

"It's because of your Gran's special fertilizer," Dixie said. "What's the big deal?"

"Tom's got some weird ideas," Arsen said slowly. "He's become obsessive about The Disappeared. I think you should stay clear of him."

"That won't be a problem," I said. Tom wasn't interested in me romantically, and he'd probably figured out by now he wasn't going to get any good stories out of me either. I tugged at the hem of my blouse. But why had he thought he could in the first place?

CHAPTER THIRTEEN

"Spiral galaxy" cinnamon-roll pancakes steamed in the warming tray. The recipe had been the only swirly-looking breakfast I could come up with on the fly. Arranging the bowl of pancake icing, I double-checked the tea lights beneath the potatoes and bacon.

Nervously, I looked around the octagonal room and smoothed my khaki capris. My confidence had been shaken after my so-called date with Tom and the flying-saucer-sandwich incident. But the silverware gleamed on the sideboard. The blue tablecloth lay neatly on the table. A balmy alpine breeze fluttered the drapes at the open windows. Everything was perfect.

I should have known better.

Retreating to my sitting room, I emailed Rachel, the original festival organizer. I should have reached out to her days ago. We only knew each other online, but I hoped her family emergency wasn't dire. Besides, she might have some insight into Chuck's murder.

At seven sharp, I drove from to Ground, on Main Street. The coffeeshop had provided breakfast for the X-tranormal staff the morning of the murder. Maybe someone from the café had witnessed something.

I opened Ground's red-painted front door. The hum of conversation and clatter of plates stopped as if swallowed by the rough brick walls. I slowly lowered my foot to the ground. Clearing my throat, I walked to the polished wood counter.

Heads swiveled to follow my progress.

Jayce looked up from the register. The sleek brunette beamed. "Hey, Susan. How's it going?"

"A little... weird, actually." I glanced around the café. Yep, everyone was staring at me, and not in a friendly way. "I'll have a large coffee to go, please. Black."

"Sure thing." She grabbed a napkin and dabbed at the base of a hanging spider plant above the counter. "I over watered," she explained.

"And, um, you catered the breakfast the morning X-tranormal opened, didn't you?"

"Yeah, I handled the setup myself." She crumpled the napkin and threw it away in a bin hidden behind the counter. "I wanted to check out the festival, and it was a super-short breakfast, so I didn't have to leave the other baristas for long. X-tranormal's got their staff on a tight leash."

"Yeah. Do you remember if any of the X-tranormal staff arrived late at the breakfast or left early?"

"Nope. I mean, I remember, and they all trooped in together and left together. And they were hungry. I wish I'd had something more for them than pastries, coffee and orange juice."

"Thanks." So, the staff did have alibis for Chuck's murder. I sidled to the end of the counter and waited for my coffee.

A tall, dignified-looking woman waiting for her drink glared. "You have some nerve showing your face here."

I stepped backward. "Sorry?"

"Clearly, you're not sorry enough. This was a perfectly peaceful town until you brought in that UFO festival," she hissed.

"But..." This wasn't fair. And Doyle wasn't exactly peaceful, but I didn't think I should bring that up. "But Doyle has festivals all the time. Next week is the harvest festival."

"Which is more respectable than UFOs by a long shot. Don't you think we have enough of a reputation without you adding to the insanity?"

"Here's your espresso, Mrs. Longway." Jayce handed the paper cup across the counter.

The woman's long nose twitched. She turned and stalked from the café.

"Oops," I said. I guess I deserved that. I glanced uneasily at the staring patrons.

"I think the UFO festival's great," Jayce said in a ringing voice. "It's brought us all sorts of afternoon business. And the extra traffic is only for the week." She handed me my coffee. "Come again!"

"Thanks." I'd known not everyone would like this festival. You never get one-hundred-percent agreement on anything. But knowing that and getting a verbal smackdown in front of an audience are two different things.

Feeling a little sick, I drove to X-tranormal, arriving in the parking lot well before start time.

I checked my hair in my Subaru's rearview mirror and tightened my ponytail. Then I stalled some more and adjusted the collar of my loose, long-sleeved white blouse. Sinking against my seat, I stared at the wire fence circling the festival. Had I done the right thing, helping bring it to Doyle?

I trudged to the entrance, checked in with the guard at the gate, and made a quick right towards the VIP tent. Strings of flashing lights blinked cheerily along its roofline. Painted aliens waved from faux-portholes.

Nearby stood a forklift, the vineyard's name on its side. I frowned. The forklift must have been delivering more wine to the festival. I needed to check out their *Planet of the Grapes* tent later.

Inside the VIP tent, the reporter, Bridget Konrach, texted from the green sofa. A foam cup steamed on a folding chair beside her. Maybe I'd have better luck getting info from her than Tom had had with me. I winced, smarting at that memory.

"Morning, Bridget." I grabbed a bear claw off the table. It was nice to eat someone else's baked goods for a change.

She glanced up from her phone. "It's Susan, right?"

I set my purse on a vacant folding chair. "Susan Witsend. From the B&B, Wits' End." My lips flattened. Had she forgotten, or was she pretending she didn't know me? But why? To make the point I wasn't important enough to know?

She arched a gray brow, her thumbs flying across the phone's screen. "You run a B&B, and you came here for stale pastries?"

"I wanted to get to the festival before things got going." I took a bite and grimaced. Stale indeed. Disappointed, I set the bear claw on a napkin and sipped my coffee. "What are you doing here so early?"

"I'm speaking today, and my hotel doesn't serve breakfast."

"You're welcome to stop by Wits' End for breakfast."

"If you're trying to bribe me to write a story about your B&B, don't bother. I'm a ghostwriter now, not a reporter."

"Really? I saw an article with your byline about Chuck's murder."

Her nose wrinkled. "You read that? The death of a UFO conspiracy theorist was too good for certain outlets to pass up. But one story in the *Weird News* section doesn't make me a reporter. It's not how I earn my living anymore."

"But you were taking pictures of the fairy protest."

"Old habits. The protestors were ridiculous." She shrugged and glanced down at her phone. "And you never know."

"I don't suppose you got any photos of the fire itself?"

"I told you I didn't."

And suddenly I didn't believe her. My jaw set. "And you're a ghostwriter now?"

"Thanks to Chuck." Her nostrils flared.

"Chuck?" I prompted, setting my coffee on the table.

"You don't know?" She folded her legs beneath her on the couch. "I thought you were part of the UFO crowd."

"I'm more a specialist in the Doyle phenomena, not the UFO scene at large."

She shrugged. "It's in my book. Chuck Thorpe fed me misinformation for years. He was a chronic liar, stringing me along with the *truth* about Roswell. And like a fool, I published his garbage."

"You must have had some suspicions." I run a UFO B&B, and even I don't believe ninety-nine percent of the stories I hear.

"Of course, I suspected. Do you think I didn't check out his stories? He had the facts, and he was a master at presenting them. And so, I ran the stories, and then one fell apart, and then the rest fell like dominoes. I was ruined."

I shook my head. How awful. I'd fled my old career, but I couldn't imagine being driven from it. "Surely one mistake—"

She lurched to her feet. "Don't you understand? I was on thin ice with my story of the century already. The world was *ready* to laugh."

I gripped the strap of my purse. "I'm—"

"How would you like it if someone destroyed your reputation and livelihood? What if a reporter wrote there were bedbugs at Wits' End? Or that you covered up for the murder of the sheriff's husband at your B&B last summer?"

I stilled, coldness spreading through my core. Was that a threat? I hadn't covered up anything. In fact, I'd helped the sheriff catch the real killer. But the only way Bridget could have known about that was if she'd researched me, and why would she do that?

"I guess you wouldn't like it at all." She strode from the room.

Shaken, I grabbed my cup, took a sip, and discovered it was only hot water. I'd taken the wrong cup from the table.

Bridget wouldn't write anything nasty about Wits' End, would she?

Needing friendly contact, I called Dixie, which just goes to show how rattled I was.

"Hello?" a feminine, non-Dixie voice answered.

I dropped onto the lumpy couch. "Kayla? It's Susan. Did I dial the wrong number?" I checked the screen. No, I was definitely talking to Dixie's phone.

"... cleaning the kitchen," she was saying when I returned the phone to my ear.

"Dixie's cleaning the kitchen?" That was... unexpected. "What are you doing there so early?"

There was a gasp, and the clatter of a phone hitting the floor.

"Hey, Susan," Dixie said, breathless. "What's up?"

"I just called to check in and see if you needed anything." A motor started outside the tent, and I stuck a finger in one ear to hear better.

"You just left," Dixie said. "What could I possibly need?"

"That wasn't really what I... I guess I just called to talk. It's been a little strange here."

"What? What's that noise? Are you driving?"

I raised my voice over the sound of the motor. "I said it's been—"

A crash, a groan.

I looked up and gaped, uncomprehending. The tent folded in on itself, one half sucked beneath the table. The food table crashed to its side. It pushed the urn, boxes of coffee, and pastries across the oriental rug.

I swore and leapt to my feet, turning toward the exit. But it was gone, sucked beneath whatever was pulling down the canvas.

I whirled, seeking escape.

The tent poles above me bent inward at an impossible angle. An earsplitting screech, a snap. The ceiling collapsed, driving me to the ground.

CHAPTER FOURTEEN

Something thunked to the ground beside me. Dizzied, I flung up my arms to shield my head. I floundered blindly, gasping beneath the smothering canvas.

The motor fell silent. Outside, a gear ground.

The forklift. "I'm inside!" I screamed. "Stop! I'm inside the tent!"

The motor roared, and the canvas shifted. More scrapes and crashes. I wriggled away from the worst noise. Disoriented, I clawed through the heavy folds.

A solid object bumped my hip and shoved me rudely sideways. Curling into a fetal position, I swiveled onto my back. Bracing my feet against the object – the table? – I shoved. But the table – it had to be the table – ground inexorably forward. It scraped me along the carpet. The canvas wrapped me more tightly in a stifling shroud.

My skull bounced off something, and I shouted, reached above me. I touched something both soft and solid. The couch?

The table shuddered to a halt. Gears ground, and the forklift beeped, backing up.

I thrashed, struggling to free myself. The canvas had been pulled taut, unmovable. It pinned me close to the ground. My hands shook. My legs forgot how to work. I was trapped in a tent cave between table and couch. The entire disaster couldn't have taken more than a minute or two, but fear told me the air was running out, I couldn't breathe.

"Help! I'm trapped!" I screamed. My breath came in ragged gulps. Could anyone hear me over the forklift's motor?

I squeezed my eyes shut. *Idiot!* If this was intentional, if someone was trying to kill me, my shouts had just let them know they should try, try again.

The motor rumbled, stinking of exhaust. Sweat burned my eyes, and I blinked. Around me, nothing moved. The forklift seemed to be waiting. For me to let the driver know where I was?

Heart thundering, I froze, playing possum.

The motor cut.

I held my breath.

Through the thick pile of canvas came the sound of muffled voices.

"Help!" I battled the canvas above me. "I'm inside!"

"Susan?" Arsen shouted.

Tears of relief welled behind my eyelids, and I laughed shakily. "I'm over here!" I kicked up with my feet, thunking the thick fabric.

"Is anyone else in there?" he asked.

"No," I shouted, my voice cracking. "I was alone when the tent fell."

The sound of his footsteps traveled oddly through the canvas. The table tilted away from me.

"Don't move," he said.

A blade stabbed through the canvas above me. I inhaled sharply. A rip, and a long opening appeared.

Arsen yanked the fabric wide and peered through the cut.

Fresh air flowed through the gap. I gasped like a goldfish dropped into a bowl of clean water.

He reached through the canvas and helped me to my feet.

I stumbled against the hard planes of his chest. His arms encircled me, his warmth male and unbearably alive.

My hips pressed too hard against the overturned table, and I winced. "Ow."

Arsen swept me into his arms and lifted me free.

This would have been a lot more heart-poundingly romantic if he hadn't dropped me like a hot breakfast scone once he'd set me on top of the collapsed tent.

I bent, hands on my knees, to catch my breath. "Thank you."

He raked a hand through his wavy, brandy-colored hair. "Dammit, Susan! Are you all right?"

Aches and pains began shouting for attention, but I nodded. "I'm fine. Dammit? Why dammit? This wasn't my fault." The forklift sat parked near the center of what had been the tent. Whoever had driven it *might* not have known I was inside. But the destruction of the VIP tent had been no accident.

Arsen turned and stomped away, stopping a few feet from me. His shoulders heaved. Shaking himself, he returned. "Okay. It's okay."

"No, it—"

Maisie hurried down the dirt road and stopped, her mouth falling open. "What...? What happened to my tent?"

"Death by forklift." Gaze flinty, Arsen made a sweeping gesture toward the wreckage. "And the driver knew what he was doing. He hit the poles just right and took the entire tent down fast, with Susan inside. She's lucky she wasn't killed."

"Susan?" Her clipboard clattered to the ground. "Oh, my God. You were in that? Are you all right? Was anyone else inside?"

"No," I said, "just me. And I'm fine."

"All right." She tugged on her lanyard. "I knew a UFO festival would be a different crowd than I was used to, but this is sabotage. Someone could have been killed. You could have been killed."

"I'm calling the sheriff," Arsen said.

She swallowed and bent to retrieve the clipboard. "Good idea. The first aid tent is already open. Susan, I'll take you."

I brushed myself off. A splotch of coffee stained the thigh of my khakis, and I hadn't even felt the burn. "I'm fine." But if Arsen hadn't come... had he scared off the driver? I said a silent prayer of gratitude.

"I hope you're fine," she said, "but I'd feel better if someone checked you out. Please let me do this. It's the least I can do after..." She motioned toward the wrecked tent.

"You should go." Arsen ran his hands down my arms as if making sure I was really okay. My skin prickled with electricity at the contact. "I'll find you," he said.

"No!" My face heated. "I mean, my phone is in my purse. How will you find me?" My purse... which was buried somewhere in the tent along with my day planner. My planner! Where was I supposed to be next? My entire schedule was in that book.

"Call me," Maisie told Arsen. "I'll stick with Susan."

"Gotcha. Don't worry, I'll dig out your planner, Susan."

Unthinking, I hugged him. "Thanks," I mumbled into his chest. He smelled really good. Like soap and a pine forest. I inhaled more deeply, sighing. What the hell. I'd almost been killed. I'd earned this moment.

His muscular arms wrapped around me, and I felt a light pressure on the top of my head. "No worries. I'll get you back on track."

I sighed and closed my eyes, pressing closer.

My eyes blinked open. What was I doing? I jerked away and smoothed the front of my blouse. "Thanks, um..."

He stepped backward, his face reddening, and stumbled over a broken tent pole. "Yeah, sure. I'll catch up with you."

Her apologies a skipping record, Maisie escorted me to the first aid tent. There, a nurse wearing the ubiquitous X-tranormal tee and latex gloves found bruises in all sorts of interesting places. I wish she'd left them as a surprise.

Eventually, and I think reluctantly, she declared me okay. "Your blood pressure is a bit high," she said, "but I expect that's due to your near miss."

"Right." But I knew better. I needed to get over my crush before I really did ruin my friendship with Arsen.

"First the rock thrower and now this." Maisie steered me from the tent. "It's almost as if someone has it in for you." She eyed me. "You *are* okay, aren't you?"

"I'm fine."

"God knows how long it will take to repair the VIP tent." She checked the clock on her phone. "At least we still have the VIP food tent."

"Wait. There's a VIP food tent?" How had I not known this?

She smiled faintly. "Follow me." We walked toward the food area and to a half-hidden, smaller, and deserted tent behind *Planet of the Grapes*. A frayed, fog-gray couch sat against one tent wall, and high round tables anchored the center of the room. Folded wooden chairs leaned against a long table covered in a cloth.

Maisie strode to a long table lined with boxes and pulled out a near-black bottle of wine. "It's five o'clock somewhere, right?" She uncorked the bottle.

"I really couldn't—"

"But I can." She poured the Zinfandel into a clear plastic cup and set it on a table. "At least have some cheese." She motioned toward another box. "I can't apologize enough, Susan. Are all UFO festivals this intense?" Maisie unfolded an Adirondack chair, grabbed her wine, and flopped onto the chair.

"I wouldn't know." I unfolded a chair beside her and lowered myself onto it. "This is my first."

"And my last, assuming I survive." She sipped her wine. "I thought I was doing Rachel a favor by taking over. Now I wonder if she was playing a sick joke on me. Who would want to shut down a UFO festival? The Illuminati?"

"At one of my panels, someone asked if Chuck had been killed by Men in Black," I said glumly. As much as I enjoyed giggling over a good conspiracy theory, I didn't want to help start one.

She coughed, spitting wine into her cup. "Seriously?"

"But I suspect the killer is more down to earth." I studied her rapidly emptying cup. "I guess you wouldn't know how Chuck wrecked Bridget's career?"

Maisie leaned forward, elbows on the knees of her khakis. "Actually, I do. Rachel warned me to keep those two apart." She frowned. "She told me to keep him away from Yuri, too, but... Anyway, I called Rachel after Chuck... you know. She told me that after Bridget's story on the Roswell UFO incident got debunked, Bridget had a hard time finding work. Bridget blamed Chuck."

"Because of Chuck's bad intel?"

"Because Chuck had high-powered acolytes. Bridget believed they'd put the word out not to hire her."

Acolytes? "But why?"

"Bridget turned on Chuck, wrote some critical pieces on his organization."

"I didn't see those." And I'd looked.

"You wouldn't." She sipped her wine. "Even in the age of the internet, things can get buried."

My face tightened. "That sounds..."

"Like a crackpot conspiracy theory? That's what I thought. I should have taken Rachel's warning more seriously."

"What else did she tell you?"

Her hand clenched on the plastic cup, and it crackled alarmingly. "Apparently, Chuck had some sort of pseudo-cult going."

"A UFO cult?" That explained the acolytes comment, but it hadn't been in my research.

She laughed, but her voice had a hard edge. "Well, not *quite*. It was more a group of people with a UFO obsession. I don't think there was a religious element. But some wealthy people were a part of his group, working to uncover the *truth* about aliens." She wiggled her delicate fingers. "Are they out there? Or are they down here? But why are you asking about Bridget?"

"What about Bridget?" Arsen strode into the tent. Shifting a plastic, X-tranormal bag beneath his arm, he handed me my purse. "I found it next to what was left of the food table."

I stood, my laughter uneven. "Thanks. How did you find us?" I opened the purse. My day planner wasn't inside, and my stomach knotted. I rummaged through my bag anyway, just in case I'd somehow missed the leather-bound binder. I pulled out my phone, and a measure of my tension evaporated. At least that hadn't been crushed.

"Maisie texted me," he said. "What about Bridget?"

"I was talking to her in the VIP tent earlier," I said. "She left just before the collapse." Had she been angry enough at me to drive a forklift into the tent?

His expression darkened. "The tent didn't collapse, it was knocked down. What was Bridget doing there?"

"The same thing I was," I said, "looking for food and conversation. If I'd known about this place, I would have come here instead." My hands crumpled on my purse. "My planner—"

"When did she leave the tent?" he asked.

"A few minutes before the coll— the forklift ran amuck." I shifted, uneasy. The reporter could have done it, but if she hadn't, I was getting an innocent woman into hot water. "Maybe she saw the person who did it." I gnawed my bottom lip.

"I'll ask the sheriff to interview Bridget." He angled his head. "What's wrong?"

"It's just... Bridget got a little angry with me before she left," I admitted.

He crossed his arms over his chest, pecs bulging. "That does it. I'm keeping you away from that reporter."

Since I'd once had to rescue Arsen from a gaggle of co-eds who'd trashed his house, this wasn't confidence building. It wasn't that he *couldn't* protect me from Bridget. But Arsen was constitutionally incapable of getting tough with a woman. "Mm..."

"In fact," he continued, "from now on, I'm not leaving you alone, period. Sorry, Maisie, I'll stay at the festival to respond to any problems if you still want me to, but my priority is Susan."

I warmed, then remembered Arsen wasn't exactly making a sacrifice. He didn't need the work. He never had. "Do I get a say in this?"

"No," he said.

"That's all right," Maisie said quickly. "We don't have the money to pay you much more, and after what Susan went through, she's earned some extra protection."

"I don't suppose you found my planner?" I twisted the purse strap in my hands. My investigation notes were in that planner. My *life* was in that planner. "It's got to be under the tent somewhere."

"Sorry." Wincing, he handed me the green bag. "I did find it."

My muscles went limp. *Thank God!* "Don't be sorry." I peered inside at a mess of torn papers and bent leather. A lump swelled in my throat, and I lifted out the remains of my planner. "No," I whispered. The leather cover was in two pieces, its metal rings bent permanently in the open position.

"It's not a total loss," he said. "I found most of the pages."

Pages that were out of order, coffee-stained and torn. All the time I'd spent organizing, color-coding, investigating... I forced a smile. "Yeah. That is good news."

CHAPTER FIFTEEN

"It figures you'd be attacked in a flying saucer." A characteristically grumpy Sheriff McCourt stared at the wreckage of the VIP tent. Forklift tracks ran across one of the painted aliens. No one had bothered to unplug the tent's colored lights, and they flickered erratically. A redheaded man in a winery t-shirt and ballcap paced nearby, talking into his cell phone.

Morning sun warmed my shoulders. "Can you fingerprint the forklift?" I blotted my coffee-stained khakis with a damp towel.

Her jaw clenched. "What do you think?" She jammed her hat harder on her head and scowled.

Okay, that had been a stupid question. But in fairness, I was still recovering from my near-death experience. And at least she'd come personally. She really did respect me as an investigator. And she probably felt a little guilty about putting me in jeopardy, even though it wasn't her fault. I made my own choices.

"Maybe we'll get lucky," she said, "and the driver won't have worn gloves. Or we'll get even luckier, and their prints will be in a database. Or..."

A pair of tentacled aliens ambled past.

"Or?" I prompted.

"Or it was an accident, a forklift versus UFO hit and run."

"Sure." I brushed harder at the coffee stain. It wasn't coming out in this lifetime. When had my life become so messy? "You must see those all the time."

"This is the second attempt on Susan's life." Arsen rested one hand on his pocket knife holster, and his brows drew downward. "You may not be taking this seriously, but I am."

"The *second* attempt on her life?" She arched a brow. "You sure about that?"

Arsen frowned at me. "Were there others?"

"No," I said. "But throwing a rock at me wasn't super effective. It was probably more of a warning—"

"Or prank." The sheriff shrugged out of her uniform jacket and handed it to a passing deputy.

"If you'd fallen badly," Arsen said, "you could have cracked your head open."

"And the person who drove the forklift might not have known I was in the tent," I said.

"Some kids could have got ahold of the forklift," Sheriff McCourt said, eyeing Arsen. "Another prank. Made simpler when *someone* left the keys inside." She jerked her head toward the redheaded man, and he paled.

"The festival wasn't open to the public yet," Arsen said. "Only VIPs and festival workers were inside. Josh had no reason to think someone would steal it."

The sheriff studied me. "So, which of the VIPs were here at the time?"

"I saw Bridget Konrach in the tent before the forklift, um, incident," I said. This is where my notes would have really come in handy. But the sheriff was counting on me. I opened my mouth to elaborate.

"Aleta Bradford, Jane Thorpe and Yuri Polyak were also here," Arsen said. "I checked with security."

"Yuri," the sheriff said. "Is he that abductee weirdo?"

My neck stiffened. Then it ached. I resisted the urge to rub my bruise. "I wouldn't call him a weirdo just because he has panic attacks."

She shot me a look hard enough to flatten a crop circle.

"Doyle can hardly hold itself up as an abductee-free zone," I said, defensive.

She sighed. "All right. I just like to think that our abductees are better."

"Better than what?" Arsen asked.

"Wait," I said. "Are you telling me the Doyle Disappeared really *were* kidnapped by UFOs?"

"No, I'm not saying that," she snapped. "It was a gas leak."

"But you said—"

"Refresh my memory – why would Bridget Konrach want you dead?" She adjusted her hat, angling it to better block the sun. But no matter how she messed with it, she was doomed to look like an overgrown Shirley Temple.

"I don't know. But she blames Chuck for the loss of her prior career. Yuri didn't like Chuck either—"

"You already told me that."

I attacked a smudge of dirt on my white sleeve with the cloth. "I'm not sure what the relationship was between Aleta and Chuck."

"Who says there was any relationship?" the sheriff asked.

"Yuri suggested they might have been an item," I said.

"Allegedly," Arsen said.

Applause burst from a nearby tent.

"Okay," I said, "it's rank gossip. But if they did have a, er, relationship, that could give either Aleta or her husband motive to kill Chuck."

"Thanks so much for explaining that to me," Sheriff McCourt said dryly. "Would you like to teach me how to fingerprint a forklift now?"

"Um, no thanks," I said.

"But Susan's got a good point," Arsen said grudgingly. "Everyone in that VIP tent had a motive to kill Chuck Thorpe."

"And we're investigating *everyone*," the sheriff said, staring hard at Arsen. My stomach jumped. Why was she looking at him like that? She couldn't suspect he was involved.

"Have you found anything connecting Bridget to car or fire bombs?" I asked.

"Why on earth would I?" the sheriff asked. "Has there been a car bombing at the festival no one's told me about?"

"No," I said, "but I heard Chuck's car got fire bombed years ago."

"And Bridget did it?"

"Um, someone told me Chuck's wife, Jane, thought Bridget was the guilty party."

The sheriff's pert nose twitched. "Thanks for not calling her the perp."

"But when I asked Mrs. Thorpe, she said she didn't want to speculate." I stilled. But *did* she suspect someone?

The sheriff's eyes narrowed. "When you asked—?"

"Was it a car bomb or a fire bomb?" Arsen interrupted. "Because there's a difference."

The sheriff gave me a long look. "Interesting you should make that distinction," she said to Arsen. "Because there was an explosion last night near one of your buddy's homes on Pine Ridge. I don't suppose you know anything about it?"

Arsen's face smoothed, a sure sign he was about to tell a whopper. "No. A bombing?"

"An explosion," she corrected. "It *looked* like someone was trying to clear out a bunch of pines with C-4. Whoever the idiot was blew out all the rear windows of a nearby home."

Arsen whistled. "That doesn't sound right."

"Come on," I said, mouth going dry. "Arsen had nothing to do with whatever happened. And aren't we supposed to be figuring out who tried to smash me flat?"

The sheriff's nostrils whitened. "We?"

"What did Cecil say?" Arsen asked.

"I didn't say it was Cecil."

"He's my only friend on Pine Ridge Road."

Her nostrils pinched. "Cecil and his wife claim ignorance."

"Weird," he said.

The sheriff mashed her hat down on her curly, blond hair. "Oh, for Pete's..." She glared at us and strode to the forklift. A gloved and uniformed deputy dusted it with fingerprint powder.

"C-4?" I hissed when the sheriff was out of earshot. What had he done now?

He drew me away from the milling cops. "Keep it down. And it's not what you think."

"I *think* Sheriff McCourt suspects you and your buddy blew up some innocent trees."

His brows lowered. "They weren't so innocent. They were blocking his view. Do you know what losing a view does to property values? Cecil and his wife are trying to sell. They've got a kid coming."

"Arsen! C-4 has got to be illegal."

"Why do you think I wanted to get rid of it?" he whispered.

"How did you even get C-4?"

"It's a long story but in the service of good."

"What does that even mean?" Was he crazy? Had I missed an insanity streak all this time?

"Cecil was a munitions expert in the Navy. He thought we could kill two birds with one stone – get rid of the C-4 and take care of his view problem." He rubbed his chin. "I guess blowing things up on water is different than on land."

I groaned. Why? *Why?* "So that's what you were up to last night."

"At least I wasn't out on a date with that nutjob reporter."

"It wasn't a date."

"Did you know that when you agreed to meet Tarrant?"

"New topic, since this one isn't getting us anywhere. We need to talk to Jane." Because clearly, Arsen was the one who needed watching.

"Agreed," Arsen said. "I'd like to know where Chuck's widow was when that tent came down."

The tent. A wave of fear threatened to swamp me, and I made my hands into fists, forcing it back. Hysterics weren't going to get me anywhere. I needed to follow the plan and take action. "I got the sense she suspected someone in the bombing of her husband's car." I checked the festival schedule. Jane wasn't on it. "I'm surprised she came today. Do you have any idea where she is?"

"Nope, only that she checked in. Maisie's making the VIP food tent the new VIP tent. Let's try there."

Tugging on the bill of his winery cap, Josh hurried to us. "Susan, I'm so sorry. You weren't hurt, were you? I never should have left the keys, but I was only gone for ten minutes, and I didn't think—"

"No," Arsen said coolly. "You didn't."

"It's okay," I said. "I'm fine."

Josh cleared his throat. "I know the winery has liability insurance, but—"

"It's fine." I smiled. "I won't sue, don't worry."

His shoulders collapsed. "Thanks, Susan." He clapped Arsen on the shoulder. "See ya, Arsen."

Arsen muttered something beneath his breath.

"You defended Josh to the sheriff," I reminded him.

"That's different."

We walked to *Planet of the Grapes* and circled to the smaller VIP tent. It was empty. Open bottles of wine stood on the table, the white cloth marked by wine spatters.

We stepped outside.

Maisie walked toward us with two X-tranormal minions in festival t-shirts and lanyards.

"Maybe she'll know where Jane is," I said, hurrying to the trio.

"What did the sheriff say?" Expression worried, the festival organizer pinned a loose red curl behind one ear.

"The usual," I said.

"She's investigating," Arsen said.

Maisie's smile trembled. "I guess I don't know what's usual when it comes to murder investigations."

"What's usual is she asks a lot of questions and doesn't tell you anything," I grumped.

"I read about the murder this summer at your B&B." She bit her lip. "Didn't you clear the sheriff of killing her husband? I'd think she kind of owes you."

"Well..." I glanced modestly at my sensible walking shoes. I didn't like to brag.

Arsen nudged me, and blood warmed my face. I'd also sort of put Arsen in a teeny bit of danger on that occasion. Maybe he wasn't the one who needed to grow up.

"It was a team effort," I said.

One corner of Arsen's mouth twitched. "We're looking for Jane Thorpe. Have you seen her?"

"She's in the booksellers' tent," Maisie said. "She decided to take over Chuck's table. Signed copies of his books are selling at a premium."

"Really," I said. "Why?"

"His signature's gone up in value now that he's... gone," she said.

The books couldn't be selling for enough to make his murder profitable, but the spouse *was* the most likely suspect. Was this a motive?

We thanked Maisie and hurried through the growing crowds to the book tent. On its side, someone had painted bookshelves and browsing, big-eyed aliens. Multi-colored lights dangled around the entrance, but in the late-morning sunlight, they didn't make much of an impression.

Inside the tent, tables lined the walls. Authors pasted hopeful expressions on their faces and sat barricaded behind stacks of books. Banners hung from the front and stood beside tables. One ambitious author had decorated his table with a Martian landscape, complete with rocket.

A trio of space cadets brushed past us, and I checked the clock on my phone. Eleven-fifty. We'd wasted a lot of time waiting on the sheriff and her deputies. The next round of workshops and lectures would start at noon.

"So what if we haven't figured out lightspeed travel?" said a spaceman with gold epaulets on his shoulders. "That doesn't mean others in the universe haven't."

"Speculation." A red-shirt sneered. "Faster than light travel isn't possible. It's physics."

"Physics as *we* understand it," the spaceman said.

"I still can't figure out if this is a fan con or a UFO conference," Arsen said.

"Both," I said, moving toward Jane's table.

Jane Thorpe sat behind a table with a banner on its front and a stand-up behind. Both featured a book cover with her husband's bearded face.

She smiled uncertainly as we approached. "Oh, hello, Susan. Are you book shopping?"

"Yes. But maybe not a signed copy," I said. "I'm not sure I can afford it."

Behind her glasses, her eyes widened. "What do you mean?"

"I heard the signed copies were, er, selling for more?"

Her gray brows furrowed. "Not here. The price on the signed hardbacks reads nineteen-ninety-nine. That's what I'm selling them for."

"Could a secondary market have sprung up?" I asked.

Arsen's gaze narrowed. "If someone's reselling books they've bought from you, I'll find out, don't worry."

"I guess it's not illegal," she said.

"But it's against the rules," Arsen said. "No one can sell here without a California seller's permit and permission from X-tranormal."

Surprised, I glanced at him. Arsen knew more about the festival rules than I did.

The older woman rubbed her temple. "At any rate, it doesn't seem right to charge more." She handed me an oversized paperback. "Here's an unsigned copy, if you like. Only thirteen-ninety-nine."

"What time did you get to the festival this morning?" Arsen asked her.

"Me? Oh, let's see. Not long after eight. I wanted to set up the table. Fortunately, one of the security guards helped me with the boxes. I should have brought some sort of dolly, but Chuck—" Her lips pressed together and trembled. She drew a deep breath. "Chuck never needed one."

"And you've been here the whole time?" I fumbled in my purse for my wallet. I'd swear it was thinner since getting rolled over by that forklift.

"Yes," she said and blushed. "Well, I did leave to visit the little girls' room."

"What time did you leave your table?" Arsen asked.

"Right before the gates opened. I wanted to be here when the customers arrived. Why?"

"Then you didn't hear what happened to the VIP tent." I pulled out two bills and handed them across the table.

She blinked. "The VIP tent?"

"Someone crushed it with a forklift," I said.

She braced her hands on the table, crumpling the money in her fist. "Oh, my."

"Susan was inside at the time," Arsen said. "She could have been killed."

Her eyes grew round. "Was anyone hurt?"

"No," I said, my voice wobbling at the memory. "I was the only one inside." I paused. "And Bridget left the tent right before it happened."

"Bridget?" She clutched the bills to her chest.

"Given everything that's happened," I said, "I have to ask. Did the police suspect her in the bombing of your car?"

"No." She pulled a metal cashbox from beneath the table and opened it, making change. "*I* suspected her."

"Why?" Arsen asked.

"She kept calling the house. Bridget was growing increasingly hysterical. More and more... unbalanced. Or at least, so I thought. She was certain there was some grand conspiracy to destroy her life." She laughed shortly. "Chuck had friends in high places, but why would he persecute Bridget? Whether her story about Chuck was solid or debunked, it was still publicity for my husband. The truth is, the more confusion around what really happened, the better. Her scurrilous book only helped Chuck's cause." She nodded toward a table opposite piled with books.

"If what he told Bridget was proven fake though," I said, "wouldn't he lose some credibility?"

She shook her head. "Not Chuck. His real friends understood that he couldn't tell the press the whole truth." She lowered her voice. "The government wouldn't permit it. They were always listening." She looked around the booksellers' tent. "They still are. The Men in Black, you know..."

I'd seen at least a dozen people dressed as those mythical government agents since I'd arrived. I cleared my throat. "So, Bridget had motive to set your car on fire. That doesn't necessarily mean she was responsible."

Jane leaned closer. "Oh, she was. I saw her that night. It was definitely a woman."

"Definitely Bridget?"

"It was dark, but what other woman would it be?" She handed me my change.

I walked across the tent and scanned the table Jane had gestured to. It was stacked with UFO-themed books.

"Is there anything you're looking for in particular?" the bookseller asked, leaping to his feet.

"Do you have a book by Bridget Konrach?"

"Yes! It's fourteen-ninety-nine."

"I'll take it." I scrounged in my purse for the cash, and Arsen and I left the tent.

I shoved the books into my purse. "We need to tell the sheriff."

"The sheriff was pretty clear she didn't want you interfering in the investigation."

"What? No," I said. She'd made her usual faces, but that was all part of her act. "After that tent blaze, I'm sure she'll want to know that arson is Bridget's MO."

"Jane didn't see Bridget set the car on fire. She said it was dark."

"What are you suggesting?" I asked, annoyed. "That I don't tell the sheriff what Jane said?" Arsen'd always had a soft spot for damsels in distress. If he thought Bridget was falsely accused, he'd defend her to the end.

"I didn't say that," he said. "But you're in someone's crosshairs. You need to be more..."

I glared at him.

"...discreet," he finished.

I exhaled slowly. Maybe he was right. And it wasn't fair to accuse Bridget on such a thin story. "Thanks. I guess it wouldn't hurt to hear Bridget's side of the story first."

Little did I know what a deadly mistake that would be.

CHAPTER SIXTEEN

Moving stiffly, I stepped outside the booksellers' tent. I checked my crumpled festival schedule. "Bridget's giving a talk about writing for UFO magazines," I said over the noise of a robot whirring past. "What do you think?"

Arsen thumbed his ear. "It depends. What exactly are we planning?"

"Asking her about the car bombing was *your* idea."

"I'm not sure that's exactly what I said..."

"She might have tried to crush me with a forklift." My nails bit into my palms, and I blew out my breath, forcing my hands to unclench. Because yes, I was taking this personally.

"A forklift is specialized equipment," he said. "Whoever drove it knew exactly what they were doing. They were also able to maneuver the forklift quickly enough to knock down the tent poles and trap you inside."

"Assuming they knew I *was* inside. And how do you know so much about forklifts?"

He gazed at a tent opposite. "Same place I learned everything else."

Right. At the stupid circus. Honestly, was there anything he hadn't learned there? "If we're going to catch her, we need to hurry. Bridget's workshop is almost over, and it's on the opposite side of the festival grounds."

"No worries. I know a short cut." He strode toward a narrow passageway between two tents, and I followed him into a tight, canvas maze. Something tickled my left ankle, and I yelped. A discarded flyer scuttled past. I scurried after Arsen.

He hesitated at a juncture and headed left. Murmured voices and spatterings of applause drifted through the tents' thick fabric.

"We're almost there," he said. "It's just around this corner."

"Hsst!"

I stiffened. I knew that *hsst.*

Arsen stopped short. "Did you hear something?"

The sides of the tents breathed in and out.

"No," I lied. "Let's keep going."

Someone tapped my shoulder.

Resigned, I turned. "Hello, Mrs. Steinberg."

She planted her cane in the dirt and braced her legs. A warm breeze rippled her head scarf, and the canvas tents billowed, pressing in on us and brushing the hem of her long, black dress. "We should talk." She lowered her glasses and gazed over them at Arsen. "Alone."

He frowned. "Mrs. Steinberg, you know me—"

"No names!"

"It's okay," I told Arsen. "We'll be right here."

"We'll be right *there*." Mrs. Steinberg pointed toward a wider gap between two tents that backed onto a wooden stand selling fake laser weapons.

"UFO NO! UFO NO!" Familiar voices chanted nearby. Picket signs flowed past the top of the stand.

My shoulders tightened. I really didn't want to deal with Team Fairy. But here, behind the seller's stall, at least we were hidden from the road and the protestors.

Arsen angled his head toward the stand. "I'll be on the other side."

We walked into the small space between tents. Arsen slipped past us and the faux-weapon stand, and to the road.

The protestors' chants faded, and I relaxed. "How did you even find us in here?"

"I saw you go in, and I followed." The old woman brandished her cane at me and leered. "You two looked like you were up to no good."

A wash of heat raced up my neck. "We were taking a short cut."

"Well, if you don't cut to the chase with that boy soon, some other young gal's going to snatch him up."

I changed the subject. "Why were you meeting with Mrs. Thorpe last night? What do you know about Chuck's murder?"

"More than you think."

I closed my eyes and prayed for patience. Mrs. Steinberg lived to speak in cryptograms. When we'd first met, I'd thought she was a little bonkers. But her obscure clues always seemed to lead somewhere. "For example?"

"For example, you're on the wrong track."

"How do you know what track I'm on?"

"Bridget Konrach."

A masculine voice rose from a nearby tent and there was a smattering of applause.

"Okay," I admitted. "We are looking for her. What about it?"

"That reporter didn't kill Chuck. Like you, she's a seeker of truth."

"And what's the truth about Chuck?"

She sighed. "He was a conflicted man, trapped between two worlds."

"The worlds of reality and fantasy?"

"You of all people know better than that, Susan."

Another wave of heat flamed my face. "I don't know what you mean." Had my grandmother told her about my panic attacks? She wouldn't have, would she?

"I know about the demons that haunt you. It's nothing to be ashamed of. We all have demons. But when you let them guide your actions, that way lies disaster."

Time to change the subject. "Bridget blamed Chuck for ruining her career. She might have set his car on fire, just like someone set a tent on fire at the festival."

"Bridget didn't set that car on fire. Or the tent, for that matter."

"Then who did?" I asked.

She nodded, smiling. "Now, you're asking the right questions."

I ground my teeth. *Patience.* "And would you like to share any answers?"

"Do you know how secret societies work?"

"Yes, there's a hierarchy, with different levels of knowledge. People at the bottom don't know what goes on at the top." There'd been a workshop on Victorian secret societies at the festival yesterday. How could I resist that?

"And Chuck was at the top. Oh, Chuck's UFO group wasn't a traditional secret society as we think of it. No secret names or handshakes, but there were rituals, of a sort."

"What sort? Cult rituals? Occult rituals?" I shivered. Had Chuck been a cult leader, or the leader of an incredibly successful fan club?

"Keep seeking, Susan." She barked a laugh and edged sideways, vanishing between an open fold in a nearby tent. I'd swear that opening hadn't been there a minute ago.

I squeezed between the laser weapon stand and a tent and popped out, onto the narrow festival road.

Experimentally, Arsen swung a glowing plastic sword. He shook his head and handed it back to the vendor. "It's the wrong weight for me."

"Where are we?" I asked Arsen.

He pointed to a tent at a curve in the road. "Bridget's writing workshop is over there. What happened with Mrs. Steinberg?"

I scowled. "Lost time." Those were five minutes I wasn't getting back.

"You know," he said, "I'd swear that happened to me last month—"

"Not supernaturally lost time. Wasted lost. And since when do you believe in UFO phenomena?"

"I don't necessarily believe," he said, "but I don't *not* believe. The world's a big, strange place."

That was what I thought too. I smiled. "No wonder my gran liked you so much. Anyway, Mrs. Steinberg didn't have any real information." I hesitated. "Have you seen the sheriff around?"

"No. Why?"

"Nothing." I thought she'd want to keep more of an eye on things, but that's why I was here. I walked toward Bridget's tent.

He kept pace, taking one step for every two of mine. "What's the hurry?"

"Bridget doesn't have any other speaking engagements today." I checked my map. "If we miss her here, who knows when or if we'll find her." I stopped in front of a plain tent with a sign out front that said, WRITING SALON.

We squeezed past people streaming from the tent. Anxiously, I scanned the crowd. A few dismal sheets of paper lay scattered on the folding chairs. A tall, stooped man with the air of a funeral director fiddled with a projector, then unplugged a laptop.

I wound through the folding chairs and toward the man at the projector. "Have you seen Bridget Konrach?"

He nodded mournfully toward the long table, in front of one of the tent walls. "She escaped out the back as soon as she finished, about fifteen minutes ago. I guess she's not one for questions."

"She's gone?" I darted outside and looked up and down the dirt road. No Bridget.

Arsen clapped me on the shoulder. "No worries. You've got the rest of the week to find her."

"Right," I said dully.

Spence trotted past, caught my eye, and hurried to us, his stomach jiggling against his *Out There* tee. "Haven't seen Aleta by any chance?" His pained gaze flitted up and down the dirt road.

My stomach tightened. What now? I dragged my damp palms down my pant legs. "Sorry, no. Is everything all right?"

"Not sure. Supposed to meet her at her exhibition tent thirty minutes ago, but she didn't show. Worried. Artistic temperament. A little high strung, especially in crowds."

"Have you checked the new VIP tent," Arsen asked, "the one behind *Planet of the Grapes*?"

He blanched. "The wine tent. Maybe. She had a little tiff with Bridget—"

"Aleta and Bridget argued?" I asked, my alarm growing. "When?"

"An hour or so ago. Didn't help when I told Aleta to calm down."

Arsen whistled. "Ouch. Women really hate that."

"Yeah," I said, "because it's annoying."

The men shared a look, and that was even more annoying.

Spence eyed the radio clipped to Arsen's belt. "Don't suppose you could call security and ask to keep a lookout?"

"I don't think that would be appropriate," Arsen said.

I blinked. Arsen? Worried about appropriateness? Had I slipped into an alternate dimension? Maybe he was taking his security business more seriously than the scuba diving or mountain guiding or any of his other fun-and-easy jobs. Shame slivered into my heart. Or maybe I wasn't being fair to my old friend. But the memory of his abandonment all those years ago roared into me, and I toughened my heart.

Spence's shoulders slumped. "Right. Not appropriate. Just got a bad feeling about all this."

"It's only that I'm not officially working for X-tranormal," Arsen said.

"So, we'll help you look for her, unofficially," I said and glared at Arsen for slipping out of character. Kissing me back. Being appropriate. What the heck was going on here?

Spence brightened. "Will you? Great. Should split up. Will check the old VIP tent."

"I don't think it's there anymore," I said. "It was wrecked."

"Beauty of tents? Easy to fix." Spence trotted away.

"Which leaves the new VIP tent and *Planet of the Grapes* to us," Arsen said.

I clawed a hand through my hair. At this juncture, any excuse to stop in a wine tent was a good one. I whirled, and a plastic laser sword smacked me in the face. "Ow!"

Oblivious, sword boy, dressed in what looked like zombie rags, marched off.

"Whoa, you okay?" Arsen asked.

I rubbed my nose. "Fine." *Twice?* That happened twice? At one festival?

We slowly made our way through the undulating crowd, the current sweeping us further down one arc of the spiraling road. A flood of people jammed us up at the entrance to the food area, but eventually, we squeezed past to *Planet of the Grapes.*

A CLOSED sign hung from the front of the tent, dripping with plastic grapes and painted with leering aliens. Beside the sign was a cardboard clock, the hands pointing to eleven. Ha. And I'd once believed eleven AM was early for drinking. That attitude now seemed foolish and faraway. After my near-death-by-forklift, I wasn't sure I could wait that long.

I checked the clock on my phone. It was almost ten.

"At least we know Aleta's not here," Arsen said.

"But..." The wine was so close!

He touched my arm, and electricity tingled my skin – not the sort of electric shock you get in high altitudes, the sexy kind of energy. I had no business feeling sexy energy from Arsen.

"I've got a bad feeling about this," he said. "You wait here. I'll check the new VIP tent for Aleta."

Another chill shivered my skin. Normally, I'd get annoyed at him telling me what to do. But Arsen's bad feeling was contagious.

He strode around the corner and vanished into the smaller tent.

I eyed *Planet of the Grapes*. Painted on its canvas side, Dionysian aliens dressed in Greek togas toasted each other.

It wouldn't hurt to sneak a peek inside. I edged closer to the tent flap. After all, I was a VIP. I lifted the flap and backed inside. A vine-covered trellis arched above the entrance. It dripped with plastic UFOs and twinkle lights.

I turned.

Makeshift tables made from wine barrels stood in groupings on the dirt floor. Plastic grapes lay scattered around a poster board sign, angled against a tent wall.

I rounded a wine barrel and gasped. Two feet stuck out from behind the bar.

Breath bottling in my chest, I hurried forward.

Bridget Konrach lay supine and staring on the floor, a pool of blood beneath one leg, a wicked curved knife on the ground beside her.

CHAPTER SEVENTEEN

"I'm surprised she didn't arrest you." Dixie sat on my kitchen counter, the heels of her hiking boots dangling. Morning sun slanted through the windows, knifing across her army green tank top.

A muscle twinged in my back, and I winced. *Stupid forklift.*

My hand tightened on the spatula. I almost wished Sheriff McCourt had put me under arrest.

Two deaths, two murders. And the festival wouldn't be here if it hadn't been for me.

Bacon sizzled on the griddle, its scent filling the kitchen. Swiss Cheese and Prosciutto Galaxies baked in the oven. I straightened my apron over my blue blouse.

Biting the inside of my cheek, I cracked eggs into a bowl. "She knows I had no reason to kill Bridget." I'd tried to save the reporter. She hadn't been in the tent long, and I thought that meant she'd had a chance.

But I'd been too late.

Afterward, the sheriff had dragged me to the station for an extremely long bout of questions. I'd handed over all my notes, every scrap of information I'd gathered. But she hadn't seemed impressed.

"Bridget wasn't your fault," Dixie said.

Bailey gazed at me from his doggy bed, his brown eyes sorrowful.

I shook my head. There had been so much blood. I poked at a strip of bacon and tried to force away the memory.

"I should have called the sheriff right away," I said, gruff, "after Jane told me what she'd suspected."

"From what you told me, if you had, the sheriff still wouldn't have gotten to Bridget in time."

Maybe. Maybe not. I still felt awful. But this wasn't about me. It was about Bridget's life, cut short.

"What's your schedule today?" my cousin asked.

"I probably won't be back until after six." I rubbed the back of my neck. My muscle aches *had* to ease once I started walking and had a chance to limber up. "I need to spend the day at the festival promoting Wits' End." And making sure no one else died.

Bailey turned his back on me and lowered his head to his paws.

Dixie gave me a shrewd look. "Just promoting the B&B, huh?"

"You know what Gran always said, the Lord helps those who help themselves."

"Hm..." Dixie cocked her head.

I glanced at my ruined planner on the kitchen table beside my laptop, and smothered a sigh. I'd have to rebuild my planner too. "Because if you fail to plan," I muttered, flipping a piece of bacon, "you plan to fail."

"That's not one of Gran's sayings. So, what exactly happened? To the reporter, I mean."

I cleared my throat. The blood had soaked into the rugs, the ground... My mouth twisted. "Bridget was stabbed with a pruning knife from the vineyard's exhibit in the *Planet of the Grapes* tent. Arsen said the femoral artery in her left leg had been cut." That had to mean a right-handed person who knew something about anatomy was the killer. Unfortunately, I'd no idea who was right or left handed – yet. And any or none of my suspects could have had such knowledge.

"What does Arsen know about femoral arteries?"

"He knows a lot about first aid," I said, voice rising. He'd known at a glance that we were too late. And that business when I'd gotten knocked out about the vagus nerve – I'd had to look it up.

Bailey lifted his head.

"He has to know with all the hiking he does," I continued. "The mountains can be treacherous."

"Yeah, yeah. Where was Arsen when you found her?"

"In the new VIP food tent calming down Aleta Bradford." My mouth pinched. The artist had become my new top murder suspect. She'd been close to the scene of Bridget's murder, and according to her husband, the two women had argued earlier that day.

Bailey heaved a doggy sigh.

"Aleta Bradford," she asked, "the artist?"

I paused, whisk in hand over the half-beaten eggs. "You know her?"

"I've got one of her night sky posters. But I haven't seen any new night sky paintings from her in years. I thought she'd quit."

"I guess she hasn't, because she's at the festival with her husband."

"The *Out There* guy?" She rolled her eyes. "Yeah."

"What's with the eye roll?"

"I wasn't rolling my eyes."

"You were totally rolling your eyes," I said. "What have you got against Spence?"

"Spence? You're on a first name basis?"

"And I repeat – what's wrong with Spence?"

My cousin sneered. "*Out There* is for amateurs."

And when it came to UFOs, Dixie took a professional interest. "What about Chuck's organization? Do you know what it's called? I haven't been able to find a name for it in any of my research."

"That's because it doesn't have a name." Dixie's heels thudded lightly on the blue cupboard door.

"Scuffs!" I pointed at her heels with my spatula. "How did Chuck promote his organization if it doesn't have a name?"

She stilled her feet. "Someone told me the members just call it, *We*, which is, like, totally creepy. Chuck makes a lot of money off what he does — did — and I have yet to see any results."

"I still don't understand what he does – did," I corrected.

"You know those nerds in the *X-Files*?" she asked. "The ones who gathered information about aliens and government conspiracies for their super-secret newsletter?"

"Yeah." I started beating the eggs again. The whisk pinged off the sides of the ceramic bowl.

"Imagine them without the newsletter, and with a lot more money."

"Okay," I said. "But where'd Chuck's money come from?"

"Duh, from the members."

"And what did the members get out of it?"

"The belief that they were in on it."

"In on what?" I asked, exasperated.

She hopped from the counter to the linoleum floor. "Exactly."

Urgh. My cousin was worse than Mrs. Steinberg. But to admit confusion would be to show weakness, and as much as I loved Dixie, I wasn't dumb enough to do that.

She strode to the porch door.

Bailey hopped from his dog bed and followed her outside.

I watched the screen door slowly swing shut behind them. Bailey was leaving the kitchen before I'd finished breakfast? I tugged at my apron. Was he really that mad I'd been away so much?

I poured the eggs into a skillet, and they hissed at the contact with the hot iron.

Taking a moment to multi-task, I checked my laptop computer, open on the kitchen table. There was an email from Rachel, the original X-tranormal organizer, and I opened it.

Susan:

Thanks for the good wishes. Not sure where you heard I had a family emergency, but everything's fine here.

Maisie told me about the problems at X-tranormal. Give her a hug for me, will you? She needs it.

Rachel

I frowned. Maisie had definitely told me she'd taken over because Rachel had a family emergency. What was going on?

"Shouldn't you stir that?" Dixie asked, returning through the screen door.

Bailey stood, indecisive, on the porch as the screen drifted shut. The beagle woofed, turned, and trotted down the porch steps to the yard.

"I can't believe the way that dog holds grudges." I hurried to the stove, prodded the eggs, flipped the bacon. "He might as well be a cat."

"He's mad you've abandoned the B&B."

"I know, but it's temporary." Though Bailey couldn't understand the distinction. I sighed. "I'll make it up to him. Would you mind putting out the yogurt?"

"I don't do breakfasts, remember?"

I gave her a look.

She scowled. "Fine. But don't think I'll make a habit of this."

I got breakfast on the table and did a final appearance check in the bedroom mirror. Stain-free khakis and blouse? *Check*. Hair in ponytail? *Check*. Makeup complete? *Check*. Sunscreen for hands... I rubbed some into my hands and dropped the tube into a beach tote. *Check*. I stuffed my wrecked planner, laptop, and speaking notes into the roomy bag.

Dixie stuck her head inside my bedroom. "Your date's here."

"Who? Arsen?" Heat flushed my cheeks. He'd insisted on escorting me around the festival again today, so it made sense to carpool. "Don't call him that. It's weird and wrong."

"Whatever." She vanished from the doorway.

Arsen met me on the front steps and handed me a pink rose. "Good morning."

Even though the rose was from my own garden, my heart skipped a beat. "You're bringing me a flower instead of scamming another breakfast? What did you do this time?"

"Can't a guy give a friend a rose?"

My stomach dropped to my walking shoes. *Friend.* Why was I so disappointed? I knew that was how he felt.

We trotted down the steps to the driveway, and I squinted at him. "You didn't blow anything else up last night, did you?" I was not going to let Arsen out of my sight today.

"The rose is for your big day – the Doyle presentation." He opened the rear door of his Jeep Commander.

"You know about that?" I asked, pleased in spite of myself.

"Sure, it's in the program. Hey, that looks heavy." He took my tote bag. "Let me carry that." Setting it carefully on the back seat, Arsen helped me into the high SUV, and we drove to the festival.

The original VIP tent had been resurrected, but the outside looked a lot less VIP without the flashing lights or flag on top. Inside, the green sofa seemed to have survived the forklift attack. Three of Maisie's minions sat lined up on it and listened meekly to her pep talk.

When she finished, they applauded and filtered out, leaving us alone with the festival organizer.

Maisie clutched her clipboard to her chest. "Hi, Arsen, Susan. Are you okay?" she asked me. "Finding Bridget like that must have been awful."

"It was." The memory raised bile in my throat. I swallowed it down. "I wanted to ask you something. I got an email from Rachel today."

Her elfin face paled. "Oh?"

"She told me there was no family emergency."

Blood rushed to the hollows of her cheeks. "I know. I'm sorry. I was just so embarrassed."

Arsen frowned. "Embarrassed about what? What's this about?"

"Maisie told me she'd taken over the festival from Rachel due to a family emergency," I said.

"There was no emergency," Maisie said, her words tumbling over each other. "I needed the money. Rachel was doing me a favor. I'm good at event organizing. Sometimes I think it's the only thing I'm good at. But it's a cyclical business, and right now the cycle is down."

She wasn't lying. I'd become acutely aware of recessions and gas prices and all the other uncontrollable events that affected tourism.

Arsen's brow pinched with sympathy.

"I'm sorry," she said. "You must have wondered... with everything that's been going on..."

"Yeah," I said, embarrassed myself now. "I get it though."

She looked at her shoes, looked up. "I expect your presentation is going to be full. Maybe we should head over there?"

I let her and Arsen escort me into the lecture tent. Maisie introduced me to a reedy IT guy with a wispy beard. He connected my laptop to the projector, while people trickled into the large tent.

Nervously, I reviewed my notes. I'd given this presentation before, but never in front of more than a dozen people, and never quite like this. I scanned the bits I'd added to make my lecture a full forty-five minutes.

Arsen sat in a folding chair near the projector and fiddled with his phone. He glanced up whenever someone entered the tent.

The seats filled, and the butterflies in my stomach morphed into bats. But I was prepared and in control. Totally in control. I checked my phone. Time to start.

Arsen grinned and gave me a thumbs-up.

I took a deep breath and smiled. "Hi, I'm Susan Witsend of Wits' End, a UFO-themed B&B in Doyle started by my grandmother." My voice quavered on the last word, and I coughed to hide it.

Yuri stalked into the tent and looked around. He spotted the last empty seat, in the middle of a row of chairs, and maneuvered around people to reach it.

"My grandmother's interest in UFOs began in the 1950s," I continued. "That was about the time of Roswell. But my grandmother's interest had to do with the startling number of disappearances in the woods around Doyle..."

"*Slow down,*" Arsen mouthed.

I took another breath and slowed my pace.

The audience was attentive, and more people wandered in carrying bags of swag. A half-dozen fairies sat against the rear wall of the tent.

I plowed onward and finally reached the end of my presentation. I'd done it! I was through and hadn't forgotten anything. Had I finished too soon? "Er, what questions do you have?" *No questions, please let there be no questions.*

A blue alien raised his hand. "The reappearance of all those people is compelling. But many believe the entire event was a tourist stunt to revive a dying small town. Your B&B has certainly benefited from the controversy. What do you have to say to that?"

I forced a smile. "The only reason X-tranormal is here is because of the reappearances. I can't deny there have been economic benefits to the town. But the social cost has been real. Can you imagine walking out of the woods and discovering years, sometimes decades have passed?" To be thrown helplessly from one world and into the next – whether it was real or not, The Disappeared *believed*, and that was bad enough.

The blue alien stood. "But that begs the question. It assumes that these people really were abducted."

Yuri bolted to his feet. "Are you saying abductions aren't real?" A fan whirred, ruffling his longish hair.

"I'm saying there's no evidence the Doyle abductions are real."

"Then, where were they?" Yuri brandished his briefcase, and the woman beside him ducked. "What happened to all those people? Where did they disappear to?"

"I don't know," the alien said. "But who's to say they went anywhere? This is a small town. They could have just told everyone—"

Yuri's nostrils flared. "You think they lied to the FBI? Do you think the local sheriff was in on the joke?"

The alien crossed his arms. "She's elected, isn't she? She's got just as much incentive as the rest of this town to bring in tourists."

I shifted. Should I jump in here, or let the Q&A continue on its own? The latter would be easier, but I didn't like the direction the discussion was headed.

"Do you really think an entire town could keep a secret like that?" Yuri's voice rose. "That *no one* would give away the secret? Isn't it much more likely they're telling the truth?"

"I don't see it." The alien's mouth compressed.

"If there's a conspiracy," I interrupted, "I'm not in on it. I don't claim to know what happened. But *something* happened. Anyone else?"

Yuri and the alien sat, arms crossed and glaring.

Jack Bauer, in a green TEAM FAIRY t-shirt, rose.

Whoa. They really *were* calling themselves Team Fairy?

"Isn't it true," he drawled, stroking his beard, "that stories of fairy abductions are nearly identical to tales of UFO abductions?"

"Um, yes," I said guiltily. "For centuries, people have been reporting being abducted by beings who emerged from bright lights. The abductees believed they were taken to fairyland."

Yuri surged to his feet. "Are you kidding me? Fairies?"

"And isn't it true," Jack continued more loudly, "that no one has actually seen an alien spaceship in Doyle?"

"Well, no, they haven't," I said, "but the lenticular clouds—"

"And isn't it true," he said, "that the first settlers to Doyle developed their own folktales about fairies in the local mountains?"

Arsen smiled sympathetically at me, and I felt at least an inch taller.

"Yes," I said. "But it's believed that these stories were references to the indigenous population, which at that—"

"FaiRY! FaiRY! FaiRY!" Jack punched his fist in the air in time to his chant. His cohorts joined in.

"Thank you!" I shouted, but no one could hear. I was losing control, and my pulse skittered. "If you could just—"

A woman in an *X-tranormal* t-shirt and purple hair stuck her head in the tent. "TIME!" she bellowed.

The crowd rose, chattering, and streamed from the tent.

My shoulders sagged. I'd survived. It was over.

Arsen stood and unplugged my laptop from the projector. "You nailed it, Susan."

"Do you think?" I smoothed the front of my blouse. "Things got a little out of hand at the end."

"Are you kidding? Everyone will be talking about your presentation. What's next?"

"The next lecture I want to attend isn't for another hour." It was on British UFO sightings, and I hoped PB Gates might be there. "I thought I'd just hang out in the VIP tent and try to reorganize my planner."

"I'm in."

"You don't have to come." I found my planner fascinating, but I knew he didn't share my passion. Was he that worried about me? And was I a bad person for perking up at the thought? "I'm sure you've got better things to do."

"Come on, we're friends. Friends don't abandon friends."

I wilted. *Right. Friends.* And yes, I was a bad person.

Whistling, he followed me to the restored VIP tent. It was empty. The only thing left of the pastries was a scattering of crumbs on the white tablecloth. The green couch had survived the forklift attack, even if its back did look a little dented.

My back against the couch, I groaned and lowered myself to the dusty rug.

"You okay?" Arsen asked.

"Yeah." My bumps and bruises ached, but they weren't serious. "I'm just feeling a little festival fatigue. X-tranormal is only half-way done." And I had the hollow feeling that I'd let the sheriff down. I was her inside man. Well, woman. The suspects were limited, and I wasn't getting anywhere.

I spread out the remains of my planner. The fan rustled the papers, and Arsen set his phone on top of them.

Grimacing, he got to work bending the planner's metal rings into shape while I organized the loose pages. A few were missing, but I could reconstruct them. I began to relax. It looked like I hadn't lost my calendar and notes after all.

"I dunno." Arsen handed me the small binder. "I don't think I can make these into rings again."

I examined his handiwork. "But at least they'll snap open and shut now. Thanks!"

He grinned. "Why do you look so surprised?"

"I'm not surprised you could fix it. I guess I'm just surprised you're helping me with my planner." I laughed awkwardly. "Don't you sort of see it as a symbol of everything that's wrong with me?"

His forehead wrinkled. "There's nothing wrong with you. I just think you'd enjoy life a bit more if you spent more time in the moment, instead of worrying about plans and schedules."

My heart turned over. He didn't think there was *anything* wrong with me?

Hold on. What was he up to?

"All right, Mr. Live-in-the-Moment. What would you *really* like to be doing right now?"

"I dunno." He looked up at the tent ceiling. "But it's a beautiful day, too nice to be inside. Why don't we check out the picnic grounds?"

"You mean the food area? Are you hungry?"

"No, not there – too many people. But there's a little field—" He sprang to his feet. "Come on, I'll show you."

Carrying my tote, he led me through the grounds. We ducked between two tents and emerged in an open field of high, green grasses surrounded by oaks. He dug through my tote. "And because you're the organized one, you've got to have..." He pulled out a beach towel. "Ha! I knew it."

"Towels are useful," I said, defensive. "You can fold them and put them on dirty seats, you can—"

He unfurled it and laid it on the grass, then flopped onto the ground, his upper half on the towel. Lacing his hands beneath his head, he crossed his ankles.

Uncertain, I gingerly lowered myself beside him and tried not to wince when pain shot through my hip. And then I tried not to wince at the memory of kissing him the last time we were horizontal. Was he thinking of that too?

We were quiet for a time. Slowly, I began to relax. It had always been easy to relax with Arsen, even when he was making me crazy. Because when he was making me crazy, he was usually making me laugh too. Even as a kid, that combination had been irresistible.

"What are we doing?" I whispered. Bringing me here, lying together like this—?

"Looking for UFOs."

I covered my face with my hands. *Head, meet desk.* I was delusional. Why had I thought he was being romantic?

"Look, there's one." He pointed at a saucer-shaped lenticular cloud, drifting over a mountain peak.

PLANET OF THE GRAPES

I blew out my breath and studied the cloud. It was perfect, the edges as smooth as if someone had whipped them into shape with a frosting knife.

A measure of my disappointment evaporated. "You're right," I admitted. "You're right about everything. Sometimes I get so caught up in what needs to be done, I forget how amazing this place is. It's all so beautiful." The mountains. The scent of grass. The cheerful laughter from the festival, and my best friend beside me. It was all... perfect.

He rolled onto his side and gazed into my eyes. "It is. Beautiful."

My breath caught in my throat. I studied the rugged face I'd known so well for so long, and yet hadn't seemed to have known at all. My lips parted.

He leaned down.

"Susan!"

I jerked upright. My nose collided with Arsen's. Pain shot through my face. We yelped, and he reared backward.

Maisie strode toward us.

I rubbed the tears streaming from my eyes. *Seriously?*

Arsen massaged the bridge of his nose and blinked rapidly. "Hey, Maisie. Is something wrong?"

"It's Yuri. He's missing."

CHAPTER EIGHTEEN

"Missing?" Arsen leapt to his feet and brushed bits of grass and earth from his multi-pocketed slacks.

Maisie pressed her clipboard to her chest. Circles bruised the skin beneath her eyes. "He was supposed to be a panelist, but he didn't show." A crow cawed from a nearby live oak, and she glanced up at the bird. "Yuri *always* shows. Maybe I'm being paranoid, but—"

"No," he said. "You're not."

I rolled up the towel and stuffed it into my tote. "Do you know what he drives? Is his car in the VIP parking lot?" I stood. Yuri was probably fine.

The crow sprang from the branch. It soared across the field and over the tent tops. I tracked its path, dread weighting my chest.

"I don't know." Maisie shook her head. "I can look it up though. We collected the make, model and license plates of all the VIP cars." She unhooked the radio at her belt and spoke into it.

A minute or two later, a crackly voice responded. "The car's here."

"Okay," she said to us. "I'll check the parking lot. Arsen, I know you're off our payroll now, but...?"

"I'll help you look," he told Maisie.

"We both will," I said, a horrible sense of déjà vu creeping up my spine. The last time someone had gone missing... I shook myself. The last time, Aleta had seemingly gone missing, but Bridget had died. That had nothing to do with Yuri. I hoped. "Any ideas where he might be?"

"I checked the VIP tent and the VIP food tent behind *Planet of the Grapes*," she said. "He wasn't there. Aside from that, I have no idea. I don't want to call the sheriff yet, maybe it's nothing—"

"It won't hurt to look around," I said.

"Thanks." She bit her bottom lip. "*Should* we call the sheriff? You know her better than I."

"He hasn't been gone that long," Arsen said. "Let's look around first."

I touched her arm. "Hey, are you okay?" Her freckles were stark against her pale skin.

Her smile was wan. "I didn't get much sleep last night." Maisie trotted off, vanishing between two tents.

I frowned. Poor Maisie. I knew the stress of dealing with murder, but she was managing murder plus a festival.

"Let's find Yuri," Arsen said.

"We'll go faster if we split up."

"I know, but too much has happened. I don't want to leave you alone."

"I don't want you to either," I blurted. Another unwanted flush of heat raced up my cheeks. "But splitting up just makes sense. It's broad daylight. The festival is packed. I doubt anyone will try anything."

"I'm not worried about anyone. I'm worried about Yuri."

"Hurting me? Here? Abductees are rarely psychotic or mentally unbalanced. It's okay. We can't stay joined at the hip for the rest of the festival."

He shot me a doubtful look. "Okay, but we text each other our location every five minutes." He fiddled with his watch.

We hurried from the field. When we reached the festival's looping dirt road, we strode in opposite directions.

Gripping the handles of my tote, I walked slowly between the curving rows of tents and stalls and scanned the passing faces. We were "between times" again. Most attendees were inside the tents listening to lectures on Bigfoot or learning to evade capture by aliens. Given how weird Doyle was getting, I was a little sorry I was missing the latter. But duty called. I pulled my cell phone from my pocket. Should I report in to the sheriff?

The ground rose, the oaks behind the tents thickening. A side road peeled off to a playground. Children's shrieks and laughter filled the air.

I hesitated at the fork and gnawed my bottom lip. What were the odds Yuri would be in the playground? But I turned and walked up the small rise and then down into a shady depression stuffed with playground equipment. The festival had turned it into an outer space extravaganza. Plywood painted with planets and aliens with holes for heads had been affixed between the upright bars. A redhead playing alien stuck his head through one and grinned, displaying two missing front teeth.

My cell phone pinged, and I glanced at the screen.

Arsen: I'M AT FIRST AID. NO YURI.

Hastily, I texted back: I'M AT PLAY AREA.

Canvas painted to look like a UFO had been affixed to the play set's round roof. Other strips of canvas fashioned like bits of UFO had been wrapped around crawl tubes. An X-tranormal employee assisted a girl on a climbing wall with a Martian landscape.

Four kids stood staring at a giant, plastic UFO with slides emerging from its sides.

I approached the kids and stared at the UFO too. As plastic UFOs went, this one looked kind of cool. But I had a metal UFO in my roof, so I turned to go.

Someone tugged at the hem of my blouse.

"Can you tell the man he needs to share?" a pigtailed alien asked me.

"The man?" I asked, looking around.

"The man in the spaceship." She pointed at the UFO. "It's *our* turn."

Had a parent got stuck inside? "Mm. I'll talk to him."

"We need to take turns," she shouted after me.

I walked to the ladder, which led to a circular opening in the bottom of the ship, and I stuck my head through.

Yuri sat cross-legged inside. He clutched his briefcase to his chest. His narrow shoulders curled inward.

My heart tightened. Was he having another anxiety attack? "Hey, Yuri," I said gently. "How's it going?"

He rested his chin on the edge of his briefcase. "You look like a head on a platter."

I climbed up a few rungs and rested my arms on the UFO's hard plastic floor. "Better?"

He sighed. "I suppose the children want their UFO back?"

"Something like that."

"You must think I'm ridiculous."

"Nah," I said in a low voice. "It's a pretty sweet ride."

He smiled. "But not as authentic as the one crashed into the roof of Wits' End, I think."

"Maybe not, but you can't get inside the Wits' End UFO."

He shifted the briefcase in his arms.

"Maisie is worried," I said. "You're late for a panel. She thought something might have happened to you."

"Because I'm crazy?" he asked, voice bitter.

I leaned back, and rested my arms on the UFO's floor. *Was he crazy?* Yuri had issues, but he seemed to know what he was doing. "Because two people have been murdered." Why hadn't the sheriff shut the festival down yet? And an even better question, why were people still bringing their kids here? "Do you mind if I text Maisie and let her know you're okay?"

"Fine. Go ahead."

I texted Arsen and Maisie.

"I came here to be alone," he said.

Startled, I looked up from my phone. "And I just ruined it for you?"

"No. It's not fair to the children that I steal their play area." He looked around the UFO's curving plastic sides. "It's actually a lot like I remember."

"Remember? Was this setup at another conference?"

"No, from my abduction."

"Then why did you want to come here?" I asked. "I read about your experiences. They sounded terrifying."

"They were. But... they were something else too. It's strange, but knowing we're not alone, knowing there's more in the universe, is oddly comforting. There is more in this universe than we can imagine, you know."

I knew. Arsen had said something similar.

"I didn't kill them," he said. "Bridget and Chuck. I wanted to kill Chuck, but I didn't. And I liked Bridget. She was on my side."

"What do you mean?"

"Bridget believed me. She wrote a book about me, did you know?"

"She did?" I asked, surprised.

"She had to self-publish. I imagine the signed copies are selling fast in the booksellers' tent now," he said bitterly. "Maybe a deranged bookseller is responsible for the murders, eh?" His laugh was hard and flat and short.

Something scrabbled on the UFO's plastic roof, and we glanced up. Tiny claws scratched the roof and fell silent.

"Where were you yesterday morning, between nine-thirty and ten?" I asked.

"I got to the festival at nine, when it opened. I went to the lecture on evading capture by UFOs."

"They held that yesterday too?" I asked, annoyed I'd missed two chances to catch it.

"They repeat several of the lectures."

"Did anyone see you in the tent?"

"Everyone did. I asked questions during the Q&A." He raised his brows. "Is that a sufficient alibi?"

"I guess so, but I'm not—"

He swiveled and shot down the yellow slide.

"—the sheriff," I said to the empty UFO.

But was it an alibi for Bridget's murder? I rubbed my chin. The Q&A usually came at the end of the lecture. Yuri could have killed Bridget, slipped into the tent during the Q&A, and then asked a question later.

Someone tugged the leg of my capris, and I looked down.

"Can we come up now?" the pigtailed alien asked.

"Oh. Right. Sorry." I climbed down the metal ladder.

A hoard of kids roared past me and into the UFO. I scanned the playground. Yuri had vanished.

Arsen strode over the top of the rise and waved. "Everything okay?" he shouted.

I nodded and walked to him. "Yuri was taking a break in the kiddie UFO. He says he has an alibi for Bridget's death. Yuri was in yesterday's lecture on evading alien abduction and participated in the Q&A."

"That assumes he was in the lecture the entire time."

"Right. I'll tell the sheriff. Maybe she can ask the speakers if they noticed when he arrived."

He snorted. "She'll love that." He checked his dive watch. "*Planet of the Grapes* should be open now. Want to check it out?"

"They reopened it so soon? After the murder?" My enthusiasm for the wine tent had waned since I'd found Bridget's body. But maybe one of the workers knew something about the murder.

"No, the winery opened a new tent by the concert grounds."

"I am curious," I admitted. "But you're not a wine drinker."

"I don't hate the stuff." He took my tote in one hand then laid his other arm, solid and comforting, over my shoulder. We walked through the festival and talked about nothing, and when our gazes met, my heart turned over.

The phone rang in his pocket, and he answered. "Hey... Yeah... I'm with Susan..." He glanced at me. "We're going to the new *Planet of the Grapes*... Okay... Okay..." He hung up. "That was the sheriff. She's here, at the festival."

"And she wants to talk to you?" Why hadn't she asked for me?

"Looks that way."

We found the sheriff scowling outside the new *Planet of the Grapes* tent. It stood in a shaded area beside the gate to the concert grounds. The tent was plain canvas, but someone had hung plastic grapevines around its entrance.

"About time." She removed her broad-brimmed hat, raked her hand through her curly hair, and jammed the hat back on her head.

"What's going on?" I asked.

She pointed at Arsen. "I need you to show me where the fence was damaged."

"Sure," he said.

"Why can't Maisie or one of the other X-tranormal staff show you?" I asked.

Her scowl deepened. "None of them has permission to talk to me, and the organizer, Ms. Hinchcliffe, isn't answering her phone."

My insides tightened. "But I just texted Maisie." I checked my phone. Arsen had replied to my text when I'd found Yuri, but Maisie had not. "You don't think something's happened?"

"No," the sheriff said, "I don't. I think she's avoiding me."

"Why?" I asked.

"Because I saw her dodge behind an oak when I drove into the lot."

"That's strange," Arsen said, his brow furrowing.

It didn't seem that odd to me. The sheriff didn't exactly have a sunny personality. Not everyone knew how to manage her like I did. But being there when she'd found her ex-husband's corpse was the sort of bonding experience you just can't replicate. Not that I'd want to. "You should know," I said, "Yuri said he has an alibi for Bridget's death. He was in the abduction avoidance lecture."

"No kidding," she said. "Do you really think I haven't been collecting alibis?"

"Oh," I said, in a small voice. "He said he participated in the Q&A—"

"Which is at the end of the lecture," she interrupted. "Yeah. Got it. No one can put him in the tent before that, but no one can say he wasn't there either. If he ran, he could get from *Planet of the Grapes* to that tent in five minutes."

My spirits lifted. The sheriff might *say* she didn't want my help, but there was only one reason for her to share information. Sheriff McCourt needed me.

She glared at Arsen. "Now, are you coming, or do I have to arrest you?"

He glanced at me. "After everything that's happened, I'd rather stick close to Susan—"

"No Susan." The sheriff's jaw tightened.

"It's okay," I said quickly. "I'll just wait for you inside *Planet of the Grapes*. I won't be alone." There would be people inside serving wine. And I was fairly certain the vineyard employees had had no reason to kill Chuck and Bridget.

"Are you sure?" he asked. "It may take a while."

"I've got a book I've been meaning to read." I took the heavy tote from his grasp. "I'll be fine."

"Okay, then," he said, but didn't budge. His brows drew together.

"Oh, please." The sheriff snorted. "What's the hold up? Are you trying to figure out if she'll let you kiss her goodbye?"

Arsen colored. "I'll see you soon, Susan."

Cheeks burning, I stalked into the tent.

The rear tent flap, behind the makeshift bar, was open, and a gentle breeze tossed loose strands of my hair. A chic, leather sofa sat in one corner with a low table in front of it. I bought a glass of zinfandel from the bar.

"I like the new tent," I said to the bartender. It beat the VIP area.

She grimaced and tucked her blond hair behind an ear. "The other one was better decorated, but we, uh, had to shut it down."

"I know." I glanced around the tent. A couple stood at one of the wine barrel tables chatting. And this was where I'd prove my worth. The sheriff couldn't engage in idle chitchat with witness. I could. "I discovered the body."

Her cornflower eyes widened. "You did? I was there yesterday too. I must have just missed the killer." She shuddered.

"Really?" I leaned closer and set my tote on the floor. "What happened?"

"I'd gotten everything set up by nine, because I hate doing things at the last minute."

"Me too!"

"I know, right? And then I returned to the tasting room to put my feet up before things got crazy." She nodded to the east, where the vineyard's permanent tasting room sprawled on a hilltop.

"Did you see the reporter who died or anyone else hanging around?"

"No. But I had that CLOSED sign up when I left. I know I did. She had no reason to be inside."

Had Bridget been looking for somewhere private to talk? Or even scheduled a meeting? That would explain why she'd rushed away before her Q&A. But if so, with whom? "You can't help it if people ignore your signs. I saw them, they were plain as day." And I'd gone inside the tent too. My chin dipped self-consciously. "Well, thanks." I hurried to claim one side of the sofa.

Digging out Chuck's book, I took a sip of wine and began reading. I had to admit, the book was compelling. It began with Roswell. In 1947, residents found strange, unexplainable debris, as if something had fallen from the sky. The Air Force immediately began covering up whatever had crashed. This sparked the widespread belief that something dark was in play - a UFO? None of this was new to me, but I'd forgotten a lot of the details.

I sipped my Zinfandel and sank deeper into the leather couch.

Chuck's father had been an Air Force officer working with Project Bluebook in the 1970s. As part of Bluebook, he'd been tasked with investigating the truth about UFOs.

According to Chuck, his father had been tormented by the things he'd seen and done. He'd retired under a cloud in the eighties. In moments of heavy drinking, he'd confided to the young Chuck that alien visitations were real.

Two women with bouffant hairdos and silver lamé miniskirts ambled, laughing, into the tent. I watched them order glasses of wine then returned to my book.

After his father's death, Chuck began his own research into the mystery. His story - if you could believe it - laid out a compelling chain of evidence that UFOs were visiting our planet. But every tale left one wondering, and Chuck had had a habit of teasing other hidden "truths" to the stories that he dared not reveal.

I flipped to the photo section in the center of the book. Portraits of various Air Force generals. A picture of the rancher who'd found the Roswell wreckage. And in the center, in color, the photo of another rancher, who'd disappeared in the Nevada desert on a hunt for UFOs. I studied the man's freckled face and tousled red hair. Was this the rancher my guest, Mr. Jonas, had mentioned?

"Miss me?" Arsen asked.

"Like a stomachache," I joked and looked up from the book.

Arsen dropped onto the couch, jouncing me.

"How did it go with the sheriff?" I asked.

He shrugged. "I showed her where the fence had been broken. She wouldn't tell me why she wanted to see it, but if you ask me, she's clutching at straws. The killer didn't come from outside the festival."

"No." I dropped the book into my tote bag. "There were too many people inside X-tranormal who wanted Chuck dead."

"Well, I'm all yours for the rest of the day. What's next?"

All mine? This was the sort of innocent double entendre I really didn't need to hear. Not if I wanted to keep my emotions in check. "Arsen, you really don't have to play bodyguard."

His brow wrinkled. "Who's playing?"

My lips pressed tight. *Friends.*

"Look, this place is a personal protection disaster. It's impossible to keep any space between you and the people in the crowd. What if someone has a knife?"

After what had happened to Bridget, it seemed all too possible.

"Do you have any idea how hard it is to defend against a knife attack?" He shook his head. "I'd rather face a gun than a knife any day."

I tried not to roll my eyes and checked the schedule. "There's a lecture on the psychology of abductees I'm interested in." My stomach gurgled.

"Or we could get a hot pretzel. I've seen you eyeing them."

Dammit, would he stop being so thoughtful? But I *was* hungry. "The Doyle abductions are important," I said stiffly. "If there's a common psychology—"

"So you want to learn about Yuri. To help him? Or help the sheriff?"

"I don't— Okay, my interests aren't purely academic. But you should have seen him at the playground. He seemed lost."

He played with a strand of my hair. "It's not your job to fix everyone's problems."

I tugged my hair free. Was I that easy to read? "I know, but... when I first took over Wits' End, all I could think about was Gran. And I love the B&B. But now..." I looked around the crowded wine tent. "I told myself this festival was good for the community."

"It is," he said. "Main Street is hopping. Lots of people have gotten temp work here."

"Two people are dead. And even if the murders hadn't happened, not everyone's happy about all these people. Maybe I pushed for this too hard? Maybe I wasn't—"

"The town council approved the festival. It's done. Let it go."

"Live in the present?"

"You really ought to try it some time. Skip the lecture," he said. "There's a pretzel out there with your name on it."

Reluctantly, I smiled.

We ended up getting the pretzel. It was salty and delicious, and we returned to the field he'd found to eat and talk. But if we'd had a moment there before, it was gone now. Nothing happened, and I tried to be okay with that.

Casually, I checked the clock on my phone. "The hour's almost up, and there's another lecture I'd like to hear."

"Where is it?" he asked.

"Same tent as the psychology of abductions."

We walked there and arrived in time to see the last few people wandering from the tent.

"I thought PB Gates's writing was funny." A purple, fur-covered alien gestured to a woman in white, her hair twisted into donut shapes over her ears. "I had no idea he was so hysterical in person."

I restrained myself from grabbing the alien's arm. "PB Gates? PB Gates was there?"

"Yeah." The alien scratched his furry nose. "He hopped in on the Q&A and ended up at the panel table. You should have seen them go."

I looked about wildly. People wandered into tents, examined movie figurines at a nearby stall. "Is he here?"

The woman in white looked around. "I don't see him."

"What does he look like?" I asked, mentally kicking myself.

"Just some guy," she said.

The purple alien nodded. "Definitely a guy." The two wandered off.

My shoulders slumped. PB Gates. I'd missed PB Gates for a stupid pretzel!

"Bummer," Arsen said. "I know how much you wanted to meet him."

"If only I hadn't stopped for that pretzel..." I trailed off. Because I wasn't as disappointed at missing PB Gates as I should have been.

"Arsen?" a woman's voice called from behind us.

Aleta Bradford ambled toward us. Her thin, green t-shirt and ripped and faded jeans hugged her curves. She smiled. "I thought it was you."

"Hey, Aleta," Arsen said. "How's it going?"

She laid a hand on his arm, which seemed like an invasion of personal space. But hey, it was Arsen's arm, and he wasn't complaining. My lips pressed flat.

"I just wanted to thank you again for talking me down yesterday," she said.

"Talking you down?" I asked.

"In the tent," she said. "My art exhibit is opening today. I can sometimes get a little wound up before an opening. And then poor Bridget..." She shook her head.

"You were near the tent when it happened," I said. "Did you hear anything?"

"I thought I heard something," she said, "like a gasp, but it was so quiet afterward, I assumed I'd imagined it."

"What time was this?" Arsen asked.

"Oh, maybe five or ten minutes before you arrived."

So Aleta had been in the tent right next door when Bridget was killed. She'd had opportunity and maybe motive. "You're opening your exhibit mid-festival?" I asked.

One corner of her mouth lifted. "It was Spence's idea. He thought it would generate more interest if I limited the number of days my art was on display. You both should come." She handed us elegant paper cards: *Lights in the Sky - Tent 321.*

Aleta turned to me and opened her mouth, as if to say something, then smiled and shook her head. "I hope to see you there. Cocktails at five." She walked away, hips swaying.

"What do you think?" Arsen asked. "Should we go?"

I thought Aleta had been nearby when both Bridget and Chuck had been killed. I thought Aleta had relationships with both those people that I didn't understand.

We were going.

CHAPTER NINETEEN

The sun dipped toward the western mountains, and I unstuck my blouse from my back. Face paint dripping, weary festival goers trudged past Arsen and I and toward the exit. Oaks and boulders forced a greater degree of separation between the tents, spaced unevenly along the road.

We walked in the opposite direction, toward Aleta's art opening. I wasn't sure what I might learn at so public an event. But I wasn't about to miss a chance to sleuth, even if my muscles still ached from getting jounced by the forklift yesterday. Today's walking hadn't loosened them up.

Two white-robed monks slouched past. "I'm telling you," the bearded one said, "Roswell was a government cover up."

The other waved to Arsen, who nodded back.

"Do you know them?" I asked.

"I've seen them around," he said vaguely, plucking at the collar of his security-company shirt. "I'm surprised there are so many families at the festival."

"Locals, mostly," I said. "It gives the kids a chance to dress up before Halloween. It doesn't look like they're staying for tonight's concert though."

Arsen rubbed his hands together. "And you said we could go backstage?"

"Hey." I pointed to my chest. "You're hanging with a sponsor."

"I knew you'd make good someday." He winked. "I can't believe Pope Whale is playing a UFO festival."

I grimaced. Pope *wail* was more like it. But I could suffer through the metal band for my friend, even if it slightly sickened me that we were only friends.

"Hssst!"

I flinched.

Arsen stopped short, frowning. "Did you hear something?"

"No." My gaze darted around the crowd. "Keep moving."

"Susan!"

Resigned, I blew out my breath. "You know who it is."

Mrs. Steinberg, clad in a black dress, lurked between two massive, lichen-covered boulders, thrusting up from the earth. The boulders were part of a natural stone ring, one of the oddities of Doyle's volcanic past. I'd seen picnickers and members of Team Fairy hanging out in the stone ring's center. But aside from Mrs. Steinberg, it was deserted now.

I waved. "Hello, Mrs.—"

Scowling, she dodged around a boulder and vanished from view.

"I think Madame X wants to talk to me alone." I strode toward the stone circle.

"What am I?" Arsen called after me. "Chopped liver? Maybe she wants to talk to me too." But he didn't follow when I circled the boulder.

Mrs. Steinberg waited on the opposite side, in the shade of the oak. Even from beneath her Jackie-O sunglasses, I could tell she was glaring. "Haven't you learned anything about discretion?"

"We're at a UFO festival with two murders and people wearing antennas. I just passed a man in a top hat on a unicycle."

"Precisely my point." She dug an e-cigarette from her voluminous purse and puffed out a smoke ring.

I hesitated. "How are you?" I asked, watching her closely.

"Worried. Your grandmother would never forgive me if I let something happen to you, even if she did know how damnably stubborn you were."

"I wouldn't say stubborn."

"Persistent then." She blew a stream of menthol-scented vapor in my face. "Persistence is an admirable trait, until it gets you killed."

"Killed?" I paced between the tall stones. "I suppose you heard about the forklift incident. But why am I a target? What do you know about these murders?"

"More than I'd like. More than is good for you."

"Right now, not knowing seems more dangerous."

She nodded. "How much do you know about Area 51?"

"It's a not-so-secret military base in the middle-of-nowhere Nevada desert."

"Not so middle of nowhere. There's a town nearby."

I leaned my back against the warm boulder. "Yeah, Rachel, Nevada." Home of a rival UFO motel. "But it's less a town than a mobile home park."

Mrs. Steinberg rewarded me with a smirk.

"Anyway," I continued, uneasy, "everyone knows about the base. The military only recently admitted it existed, even though it was never exactly hidden."

She blew another smoke ring. "And?"

"And it's been a hot spot for UFO sightings. Most people believe the mysterious lights in the sky are secret military test flights, not flying saucers. But there have been persistent rumors that the remains of a UFO are stored at Area 51. The *X-Files* expanded the theory that the wreckage made its way into military tech."

The older woman's brow furrowed beneath the fold of her black headscarf. "*X-Files*?"

"You know, the TV show?"

"Never heard of it. Must be on cable."

"So, what does Area 51 have to do with this?"

She smiled. "You have your answer."

"What answer?" I asked, bewildered. "Are you saying secret alien technology is responsible for Chuck and Bridget's murders?"

"Are you two okay back there?" Arsen rounded the boulder.

"We're fine," I moved to intercept him. "Mrs. Steinberg was..." I pivoted.

Mrs. Steinberg was gone, vanished as if swallowed by the stone ring, and I shivered.

"Where'd she go?" Arsen asked.

"You mean, you didn't see her?"

"No. Are you okay? You look funny."

"I'm fine." How did she *do* that?

"What did she have to say?"

"The usual vague hints of aliens and Area 51."

He braced a hand on a tall stone. "She does know more than we do about the UFO scene, doesn't she?"

"She acts like she does, but it's hard to tell. And I'm never sure if she's using me for information or if I'm using her."

"She might be worth talking to again – not about UFOs, about the people who are obsessed with them, like Chuck and Bridget and Spence."

"Good luck getting a straight answer," I grumbled.

"Come on. The reception's already started."

We ambled around the stone circle.

Maisie, her movements quick and hurried, strode toward us. She clutched her clipboard to her chest, her smile brittle, her face pale. "Hey, you two. Are you having any fun? Or is this festival all work and no play?"

"We might, if my buddy here would stop investigating." He laughed and mussed my hair.

I jerked away, and I thought he winced. What was *wrong* with him? Did he think I was five? And *buddy?* That was just insulting. "I am too having fun. And we're on our way to Aleta's gallery opening."

"Would I be off-base if I guessed you've got an ulterior motive?" Maisie asked.

"Well, of course we do." I shifted the beach tote on my shoulder. "That's just multi-tasking."

"I got a phone call from the X-tranormal organizers," Maisie said. "They're thinking of closing the festival early."

My breath caught. "What? Why now?"

"Panic. But you know how it is with committees," she said, "they never make a decision quickly. It may not happen at all."

I'd suggested closing the festival. And in spite of all the money I'd lose, I still thought it was a good idea. But there would be a lot of angry people – B&B guests and vendors and tourists. "I guess it makes sense." My hands fluttered jerkily. "But without the weekend sales, the festival won't see much profit, will it?"

"I know," she said, mournful. "I don't suppose you have any good news from the sheriff? Does she have any idea who's behind the murders?"

"Sorry, no," I said. "There are almost too many suspects. It seems like all of the VIPs are somehow connected to Chuck."

She shuddered. "I keep turning his death over in my head — is it a random madman or someone who planned these attacks?"

"Neither option's a good one," Arsen said.

Maisie sighed. "I guess a quick solution was too much to expect. Enjoy the gallery opening. I've got receipts to count." She strode into the river of aliens and earthlings heading toward the exit.

I blew out a slow breath. "It's probably for the best if X-tranormal closes."

"It won't," Arsen said. "Whoever's in charge won't want to lose out on the weekend ticket sales. Besides, it's Friday night. If they make their decision tomorrow, that means they really won't close until Sunday, and that's only one day early. That doesn't make sense."

"I don't know what to want. These murders aren't random, but that tent fire..." Briefly, I shut my eyes. "The murderer doesn't seem to care if innocents get hurt. But if the festival shuts down, the killer will have the perfect excuse to leave town. The sheriff won't be able to keep all the suspects here."

"I know you want to make this right, but sometimes you need to let go."

"And sometimes, you let things go too easily."

His jaw hardened.

"Forget it," I said, and he shrugged, his brows pulling down.

We made our way down the dirt road to the artist's gallery, a warren of small tents. Outside the largest tent, misters kept the crowd cool. People mingled, glasses in hand, and glanced at the tent's closed flaps.

Arsen and I joined the small crowd.

Aleta strode toward us, two goblets in hand. "Wine?" She'd changed into flowing gray knit slacks and a low-necked matching tank. Slim gold necklaces of varying sizes hung around her neck. A massive quartz crystal dangled from one.

"Thanks." I took a glass.

Arsen shook his head. "I'm more of a beer guy."

"There are beers in the cooler." Aleta nodded toward a long table covered in a white tablecloth.

Arsen saluted with one finger and meandered off in that direction.

"There's more to that man than meets the eye," Aleta murmured, "isn't there?"

"To Arsen?" I laughed at her bemused expression. "Sorry, it's just that we've known each other since we were kids." I glanced his way. He chatted with the bartender over the food and drink table. Was I taking him for granted?

She smiled. "That explains it then."

"Explains what?" I tore my gaze from Arsen.

"The chemistry between you two."

Heat surged up my cheeks. "We're friends."

She sipped her wine. "I don't know you well, but I feel compelled to say something to you. May I?"

I steeled myself. "Sure."

"In my brief interactions with Arsen, it's clear he's not the kind of man you can control, or that you'd even want to."

"Of course I wouldn't—"

She raised a finger. "There is no certainty in this world, no matter how hard we try to create it. So, there's little sense in trying to control life, especially when it will keep us from getting what we really want."

I said nothing for a moment, studying her intent expression. What was she really trying to tell me? "No," I said slowly. "Considering what's happened here this week, it would be useless to believe I'm in control. But if we don't try to bring back some order, I'm not sure what we're left with. I've talked to a lot of people about Chuck—"

She stiffened.

"And," I continued, "I imagine that whoever killed him felt justified in doing so. But we can't let it stand."

She blinked, looking away. "Not everyone hated him," she said quietly.

"You mean, you didn't."

"How could I hate Coyote?"

"A coyote?"

Her wine goblet dangled from her elegant fingers. "Not *a* coyote – Coyote, a trickster god of the indigenous peoples. Chuck was trouble, but he was fun."

"And he tricked Bridget?"

"She knew you could dance with Coyote, but you'd be a fool to try and tame him."

What did that mean? That it was Bridget's fault? "But Coyote wasn't only a trickster," I said slowly. "He brought chaos, destruction, death."

"Where did you hear that?"

"Um, a Tony Hillerman novel."

Her full lips twitched. "Well. Hillerman did know his stuff."

"Aleta!" Spence drew her into a hug. "Your guests are getting antsy. When's your big reveal?"

She checked the slim, gold watch around her wrist. "Why not now?"

Spence clinked his beer bottle with his wedding ring. "May I have everyone's attention?"

The murmurs of the crowd subsided.

He motioned to Aleta, and she stepped forward.

She spread her arms wide and bowed, tossing her long hair. "Thank you, everyone, for coming. I'm an artist, and not one for making speeches. But I do want to acknowledge the loss of two members of our small community, Chuck Thorpe and Bridget Konrach."

Her husband's face contorted and quickly smoothed.

"They will both be missed." Aleta's chin dipped, and she swallowed. "And so, I dedicate this collection to them both." She walked to the tent and pulled back the flaps, clipping them in place and stepping aside.

Arsen joined me. "Did you see the look on Spence's face?" he asked in a low voice as people filtered past.

I nodded. "More and more, I'm thinking the rumors about Aleta and Chuck having an affair were true." Had she tried to tame Coyote as well and failed?

The chatter inside the tent rose to a dull rumble.

"Huh." He shook his head. "People are more complicated than they seem."

"Yeah." Was Arsen complicated? I hadn't thought so, but I was starting to wonder.

We walked inside the tent. I picked up a brochure from a stack on a table by the entrance. The tent's front and back flaps were open, and my hair danced in the cross breeze, tickling my aching neck. Paintings blazing with color hung from the interior bars at the tops of the tent walls. Between high fans, freestanding displays dotted the tent.

Arsen steered me toward a painting, and I halted, choking back a surprised laugh.

Fairies. She'd painted fairies. The paintings were like Georgia O'Keefe crossed with J.R.R. Tolkien. And the faces... I stepped closer. Each fairy's face was uniquely real — some haughty, some cruel, some shifty, some beatific. And there was something familiar about them, as if I'd met these creatures.

"I thought she did paintings of outer space," Arsen said.

"I guess her inspiration has changed." I stopped in front of a painting of a silver-haired fairy with a snail for a chariot, a fountain pen for a sword. "Is that... Bridget?" The fairy's chin was raised, defiant, but there was desperation in her expression.

He squinted. "It kind of looks like her, I guess."

"It *is* her." My pulse quickened. But what did a painting of the reporter mean? "Let's see if we can find any others."

And we did. Chuck was a fairy king. In one hand, he held thin filaments like spiderwebs. They connected to the collars of a trio of bowing fairies. His other hand pointed a scepter at a hapless, bearded fairy in chains.

Aleta's husband, Spence, perched on a toadstool and gazed at the clouds.

Yuri was a human, being dragged to fairyland by laughing elves.

"We're not imagining it, are we?" I whispered, unnerved.

"I didn't see Chuck in the fairy king, but that guy's definitely got a Yuri vibe."

"He's not going to like this."

"Like what?" Yuri asked.

I started.

"Uh..." Swallowing, I motioned with my wine glass toward the art. "You seemed kind of anti-fairy."

He shrugged, his shoulders shifting beneath his loose sports jacket. He'd switched his usual button-up shirt for a black tee. "They are a part of our folklore. I have no opinion on them." He studied the painting and grunted. "Old stories. She is a talented artist, but I guess anyone would tire of painting the same thing over and over, no?"

I glanced at Aleta. Spence looped an arm about her shoulders and beamed proudly. Had she painted him as a cuckold, too busy gazing at the sky to notice what was happening on the ground?

"I suppose those ridiculous fairy protestors will think she believes in their cause." Yuri touched his finger to the painting. "But of course, she painted these months ago. See? The paint is dry." He cocked his head. "There is something about this painting... I like it very much."

Yuri studied his brochure. "*Away to Fairyland*," he read. "Maybe I will buy it."

"Mm, hm," I said. "Nice seeing you, Yuri."

Arsen and I ambled outside. The sky had turned a deeper shade of blue. Beneath a string of twinkle lights, I opened the brochure and read the blurbs on the paintings.

"Is there one you'd like for Wits' End?" Arsen asked.

"Don't even think about it. They wouldn't go with my decor," I said absently. He might not care about money, but I wouldn't take advantage of his, even if it meant paying him back with an eternity of free breakfasts.

Aleta had chosen her subjects carefully - her paintings had meaning. But did they connect to the murders? I glanced quickly at the tent. Or had Aleta's subconscious played out on the canvas?

CHAPTER TWENTY

The noise from the stage was deafening, even though I wore earplugs. So Arsen wouldn't notice, I edged slightly behind him and pressed my fingers to my ears.

Colored spotlights shifted across the crowd. The audience moved in disconcerting ripples and waves, as if they were one living organism. The metal superstructure vibrated with the roar of sound, and I glanced up nervously.

Arsen touched my arm. "It's not going to fall."

"I know," I shouted back. How had he even *seen* me when I was behind him?

He shook his head and pointed to his ear, then turned to the stage and resumed bouncing to the music. I couldn't help noticing how fluidly he moved, or the play of his muscles beneath his shirt. My heart tightened – not from regret about that stupid kiss, from wanting more.

My eyes heated, and I blinked away the moisture. Arsen didn't want more. He'd made that much clear by hammering home what great friends we were. And I needed to stop thinking about that damned kiss. I gritted my teeth. These feelings would pass, and the sooner the better.

He turned, grinning. "This is awesome!"

I nodded and forced a smile. Backstage, we were closer to the band, but we only had a side view. Awesome was relative.

My gaze drifted across the crowd and stopped on a familiar face - Yuri. He raised his briefcase in the air and bobbed it in time with the beat.

My breath quickened. What was *in* that briefcase? Even I'd left my massive tote bag and wrecked planner in Arsen's Jeep.

Pope Whale wailed on. Surreptitiously, I checked the clock on my phone. When was this thing over? I needed to find a bathroom. Fast.

"Hey," Arsen said, "great idea." He took the phone from my hand. Turning me so our backs were to the stage, he looped his arm over my shoulders. He leaned in close, his cheek rough against mine, his uneven breath on my cheek, his body warm and strong.

He snapped a selfie and checked the phone. "Nice!"

He looked amazing – the perfect memory of my misery. I took the phone. "I have to find a ladies' room."

"What?"

"Bathroom!"

He moved toward the stairs.

"I think I can take care of this on my own," I shouted.

He nodded and watched me walk behind the curtained superstructure.

I trotted down the rear steps. They jiggled beneath my weight, and I grabbed the cool, metal bannister. I shook myself. Arsen was right. The people who'd set up the stage had known what they were doing.

Pausing at the base of the steps, I scanned the dark clearing to get my bearings. Even behind the stage, the gyrating lights were disorienting, casting jagged, swiftly-moving shadows across the dried grass.

I frowned. There were two bathrooms behind me, on the concert grounds. Unfortunately, I couldn't remember the quickest way to get to them. I dug the festival map from the back pocket of my capris and switched on my phone's flashlight, scanning the page.

A shadow darted at the corner of my vision.

I looked over my shoulder and into the cage of metal pipes beneath the stage.

Nothing was there.

But hairs prickled on the back of my neck. I turned off my flashlight to let my eyes adjust and stared harder into the shifting gloom.

A shadow flitted beneath the stage and vanished.

I sucked in my breath. Had I imagined it?

Stuffing the map in my back pocket, I stepped over two crisscrossed bars and beneath the stage. Wary of braining myself on one of the low metal bars, I raised one hand, letting my fingers trail along the vibrating stage above.

Something flashed ahead and to my right.

I whipped in that direction and squinted.

There *was* someone beneath the stage. In the kaleidoscopic shadows, I could make out a human silhouette.

Get Arsen. But there was something about that flash I really didn't like. Something that said *wrong, danger, fix this fast.*

A strange sense of urgency drove me forward. I clutched the phone in my hand more tightly.

Honestly, I wasn't being one of those dumb females in horror movies who absolutely-should-not-go-into-the-basement-but-did-it-anyway. I had a plan.

Heart pounding, I moved closer. I wasn't worried about whoever it was hearing me – there was too much noise from above. Whatever he or she was up to, the person was too intent to notice me.

I stopped ten feet away, aimed my phone, and turned on its light.

A gray-faced, black-eyed alien jerked upright and flung his hand over his eyes. He gripped a wrench of some sort in one hand. Something small glinted in the dirt – a bolt. He was unbolting the stage.

He looked at the bolt, looked up.

And I realized the first flaw in my plan. My phone's flashlight wouldn't dazzle the alien for long.

Swinging the wrench, the alien charged.

I ducked. The wrench clanged off one of the metal stage bars.

I screamed and realized the second flaw in my plan. Beneath a concert stage, no one can hear you scream.

The alien swung a backhand.

I jolted away. The wrench whizzed past, air whooshing overhead. I tripped over a low bar. My butt hit the ground hard. "Oof!" And *ow.* This is why I should leave these spur-of-the-moment inspirations to free spirits like Arsen.

The alien gripped the wrench two-handed. He swung it over his head. It thunked against the bottom of the stage. The alien staggered.

I rolled and scrambled to my feet.

A light blinded me. Not knowing the direction of the greater threat – fore or aft – I ducked, banged my head on something hard. "Ow!"

The light bobbed toward me.

I half-tripped over a bar and tried to crawl out of the flashlight's beam.

Someone grabbed my shoulder.

I shrieked and rolled onto my back like an upended turtle, arms and legs raised defensively.

Arsen flashed the beam at his own face. "Susan?" he shouted.

Thank God. Using the cross-bars, I hauled myself to standing and looked around. "An alien! It was unscrewing the stage!"

"What?"

"Unscrewing the stage!" I shrieked.

His brow furrowed. "I didn't think you were into that, but—"

"No! An alien! With a…" I grabbed his hand and aimed the flashlight, scanning it across the ground. A bolt gleamed in a tuft of dried grass. "There." Picking my way toward the bolt, I found three more. I dropped them in Arsen's open hand.

He studied the metal bars. Finding the holes they belonged in, he replaced the bolts, screwing them partway in with his complicated pocketknife. He shook his head. "I need a real wrench."

We made our way from beneath the stage.

"I have to call the sheriff," I shouted. "We might not have found them all."

"What?"

"The sheriff!"

He shook his head. "We need to call the sheriff," he bellowed.

I started to argue, realized there was no point, and followed him outside the festival grounds, where the music fell to a dull roar. People could have been hurt. Really hurt. The festival needed to close, even if everyone in town hated me and we all lost income. This wasn't worth it.

Arsen called the sheriff, and I called Maisie. It went to her voicemail. I checked the clock on my phone. Eight-thirty-two.

"I saw someone unscrewing bolts beneath the stage," I said. "I think we got them all back in, but I can't be sure, and we couldn't get them in all the way. We've called the sheriff and are waiting for her outside the south exit." Then I sent her a text saying the same thing, just in case.

She texted back two minutes later - CONSTRUCTION ON WAY. BAND TOLD TO BREAK. SECURITY MOVING PEOPLE BACK.

I showed Arsen the text.

He nodded. "Good. Maisie's on it."

We waited. Well, Arsen waited. I got in line for the ladies room.

When I finally emerged thirty minutes later, the sheriff stood glowering at Arsen in the parking lot.

"Tell me you got a description." She scowled at me and adjusted her hat.

"It was a tall gray alien." I straightened off Arsen's Jeep Commander. "You know, the kind with the really big, black eyes?"

A muscle pulsed in her jaw. "An alien. Is this a joke? Do you know what I do to jokers?"

"Obviously, the saboteur was wearing an alien mask," I said. "And a black long-sleeved shirt and pants. I couldn't tell if it was a man or woman. Sorry. But it was dark beneath the stage and happened too fast." All things considered, I thought I'd done pretty well. Sheriff McCourt could be so demanding. I was glad I didn't work for her officially.

Arsen shook his head. "Susan saw more than I did."

"But you *did* see someone?" The sheriff narrowed her eyes.

He braced his hand on the hood of the black Jeep. "Only from the back. They were running away, and Susan was down," he said. "She found several bolts on the ground."

"Tell me you left them there, so we can get prints."

He grimaced. "Uh, no."

She turned in an angry circle. "Are you kidding me?"

"There were people on that stage," I said, my abdomen tightening. "Arsen had to replace the bolts. Who knows, there might be more lying around for you to print?" I said without much hope.

She swore and stormed past security and into the concert grounds.

"You did the right thing," I told Arsen.

Arsen rubbed my shoulder. "I know. If I hadn't put those bolts back, Maisie's team would have. The sheriff will get over it."

But had Sheriff McCourt been right? My heart plummeted to my tennis shoes. I didn't regret what we'd done. But by trying to save the stage, had we lost our chance to catch the killer?

CHAPTER TWENTY-ONE

"The good news is no one was hurt." Arsen gripped the Jeep's steering wheel. The mountain road raced beneath our headlights in a grainy stream of gray and white.

"I know that's the most important thing." I sighed. "And I'm glad, even if it was way too close a call. But it would be nice, just once, if the sheriff thanked us." Maisie's team had told us the alien was loosening exactly the right bolts to bring down the stage. He'd have needed to loosen a couple dozen more, but he'd been on his way when we'd caught him.

He snorted. "Like that's gonna happen."

Of course it wouldn't. McCourt turned gruff and grumpy when she was upset, and she'd obviously been upset when she'd learned I'd been in danger. So, what was a *thank you* between friends? I knew what she meant.

Engines revved behind us, and two motorcyclists in green alien suits zipped past.

"I don't think McCourt wants our help," he said.

That's because Arsen didn't look beyond appearances. But I laughed, playing along with the sheriff's game. "That just makes me want to give it to her more, good and hard."

He slowed for an RV, huffing up the winding road. "For example?"

"Well, we *are* going to be driving right past the Doyle Hotel, where Chuck's widow, Jane is staying."

"You want to talk to her? Isn't it a little late for a surprise visit? It's after nine."

"It is, but if she was in the hotel during the concert, we can eliminate her as a suspect."

"Is she a suspect?" Arsen asked, passing the RV.

"The spouse is always a suspect, especially when they're married to cheating conmen like Chuck."

"We don't know for sure if either of those things are true."

He might not know, but I trusted my instincts. "Whatever." I dug my phone from my beach tote and called the hotel. They put me through to Jane's room.

"Have you learned anything new?" she asked, breathless.

"There've been some developments," I said. "Do you mind if we drop by? We can be there in ten minutes."

"Of course, of course. I don't sleep much these days. I'm just sitting here in my room."

We said our goodbyes, and I hung up. Jane was at her hotel now, but where had she been when the stage was being sabotaged? I called the hotel again.

"Historic Doyle Hotel," the receptionist answered.

"Erica? Is that you? It's Susan Witsend."

"Oh, hi! I thought you sounded familiar. Was there a problem with your call to Mrs. Thorpe? The line didn't drop, did it?"

"No, I was just wondering, do you happen to know when Mrs. Thorpe got back from dinner tonight?"

"Oh, she didn't. I mean, she had room service."

"You don't happen to have a record of when she called for it?" I crossed my fingers.

"Um... Let me check... Okay, here it is. She called from her room at seven and then called again at eight-fifteen to ask us to remove the tray."

"And you're sure she called from her room and not a cell phone?"

"Yeah," she said, "the computer keeps records of all calls from room phones. Why?"

"There was an accident at the festival. I thought she might have been a witness, but it doesn't look like it's possible." At last, here was one suspect I could cross off my list.

But damn. My list of suspects was on one of the planner pages I'd lost. I needed a new list. "Can you put me through to the Bradfords' room?"

"Sure thing." There was a click, and the phone rang. And rang.

Finally, I hung up. Aleta and Spence weren't in their room. The reception had officially ended when the concert started, but they might have stayed at the tent to mingle. Or one of them could have snuck off to the concert.

"So?" Arsen asked.

"Jane Thorpe was calling from her room phone at eight-fifteen. She couldn't have been the person beneath the stage."

"It was never very likely, was it? She doesn't seem that athletic."

"No, and the alien was definitely slender. But you never know. Jane may have had secret ninja skills." I adjusted the seatbelt across my chest. "Yuri was in the audience. He was wearing a black t-shirt under his jacket. It may have been long sleeved, like the alien's. But I don't know how he could have made his way through the crowd and beneath the stage that fast."

"And where would he have stashed his briefcase?"

My lips quirked. "What do you think's inside it." *Like a wrench?*

"Probably his allergy medication."

"Does he have allergies?"

"Nearly everyone has allergies."

We turned down the short road to Doyle. The road darkened, canopied by trees. And then we were on Main Street and parking in the lot behind my greatest rival, the Historic Doyle Hotel.

The rear door was locked at night to all but hotel guests, so we strolled to the front of the two-story, stone building.

Erica looked up from her desk behind the reception window and grinned. "Our competitor returns. I'm not sure I should let you in. Hi, Arsen!"

"Hey, Erica." He braced one hand on the open window and smiled winningly. "How are things?"

"The festival's keeping us on our toes, even if the crowd is weirder than normal." She nodded to a tentacled alien, walking up the blue-carpeted stairs.

"For Doyle?" Arsen raised a brow. "This is nothing."

The receptionist sighed. "At least no one's disappeared. And the Bradfords have stopped fighting," she said in a lower voice. "I guess yesterday's wine incident cooled things off."

"Wine incident?" I asked.

"Mrs. Bradford threw her glass at Mr. Bradford at the festival yesterday," she whispered. "He had to come back here to change."

"What time yesterday?" I asked.

"Before noon. They must have started drinking early."

Huh. That wasn't long after we'd discovered Bridget's body. "Jane Thorpe knows we're coming," I said slowly. "Can we go on up?"

"Sure. Go ahead." She waved us toward the stairs.

We climbed the steps and walked down the long hallway, its walls decorated with photos of old-time Doyle. I knocked on Jane Thorpe's door.

"Oh, yes," Jane's muffled voice came from inside the room. "Absolutely... I agree completely." The older woman opened the door. "Sorry," she mouthed, pointing at her cell phone. She motioned us inside and walked to the wooden desk. "Yes... yes... Wonderful. We'll talk more next week. Goodbye." She hung up and ran her fingers through her cropped, gray hair. "So much to do! I had no idea."

"You mean, for Chuck's funeral?" I asked.

"No, for the organization."

"The organization," I repeated. Was she taking on Chuck's role? It made sense in an awful sort of way. It also made for a motive.

"Chuck made it seem so effortless." She dimpled at Arsen. "And who is this?"

"Oh, sorry." I shook my head. "This is my friend, Arsen. He's been helping with security at the festival."

"Security consultant," he said, shaking her hand.

"He's been escorting me to the festival," I explained. "Because of... everything."

Her eyes widened. "Goodness! You need a bodyguard? Has something happened? Are you in danger?"

"There's been another attack on the festival," I said.

"Someone tried to sabotage the stage," Arsen explained.

"Sabotage the stage?" Her thin brows lifted. "What does that even mean?"

"He or she tried to make it collapse," I said.

"Tried?" She pulled out the wooden desk chair and sat, motioning to the bed. "I take it they didn't succeed?"

"No." Arsen laid his hand on my shoulder. "Susan interrupted the saboteur."

"You really have been in the thick of it, haven't you?" she said coolly.

I stiffened, perching on the edge of the mattress. "In this case, I'm glad I was. People could have been hurt. What's this about the organization? You're not continuing your husband's, um, thing?"

"It's quite lucrative. Why wouldn't I?" She crossed her legs, her voice hardening.

"I just thought... It seems to have caused you so many problems." My knees nearly touched Jane's in the narrow space between bed and desk, and I shifted backward, wrinkling the white duvet. "Sorry if I misread things, but I didn't get the impression you were a fan."

"One must be practical," she said. "Was that all?"

"Well, no," I said. "You thought Bridget might have set your car on fire, right?"

She nodded. "Not that it matters anymore. I was so angry at her when she came by my hotel room – poking and prodding. As if I'd help her make money off a story after what she'd done. But once I learned she'd died, my anger evaporated. It seems so pointless now."

"Wait. Bridget came by your room?" Arsen asked.

"Yes, asking about Chuck and that poor, dead rancher—"

"The rancher?" I asked. "You mean the man who got lost in the Nevada desert looking for aliens?" Were the deaths at the festival somehow related to the rancher?

She plucked a pen from the desk and rolled it between her plump fingers. "The desert mountains, but yes."

"Did she say why she was interested in that?" Arsen asked.

"No." Her nostrils pinched. "She was never one to give information, only to take."

"What exactly happened?" I asked. "I noticed Chuck had a photo of the rancher in his book."

"A tribute to a fellow seeker." Her chair bumped the desk, and the brass lamp wobbled. "Unfortunately, I can't tell you any more than what was published in my late husband's book. That information is proprietary."

Arsen's brow furrowed. "Proprietary?"

"To the organization."

"How can a man's death be proprietary?" I asked.

Her gaze flicked toward the white ceiling. "Not his death — the reason for his exploration of that part of Nevada."

"You mean, he was there chasing UFOs for Chuck?"

"Of course not, not officially."

"But unofficially?" I asked.

She smiled. "I can't say any more. You understand."

"Not really," Arsen said.

I rose, annoyed. "That's all right. I have a source." And to think I'd felt sorry for Jane. Two people had died at the festival. The rancher was dead. These were real people with real lives, cut short. How could she be so... smug? My gran's voice echoed in my head. *Don't judge. You never know what people are going through.*

"A source?" She started. "What do you—?" Her cell phone rang, and she answered. "Hello, Phil... Yes, it's true, the organization is going on as usual... No, nothing will change, though of course, I'll be the point person now."

"Come on," Arsen said quietly, and we left the hotel.

He started the Jeep. "What was that about?"

"I can't believe she's continuing Chuck's stupid secret organization. It almost sounds like it *is* a cult. Those things are dangerous! Plus, I didn't think she was that interested in chasing UFOs."

"It sounds more like she's interested in the money. Were you bluffing about your source?"

"Are you kidding me? This is Doyle, alien central." I pulled out my phone. "I'm calling Mrs. Steinberg."

"You've got her number? I was sure she'd be unlisted."

"Gran had it in her address book." I'm not certain what had inspired me to program it into my phone, but now I was glad I had. I made the call.

The phone rang once, and she picked up. "Susan? To what do I owe the pleasure?"

I blinked. She'd recognized my number? I'd never called her before. How had she...? *Never mind.*

"What can you tell me about the rancher affiliated with Chuck's organization," I said. "The one who got lost in the mountains and died?"

She laughed softly. "Ah, I was wondering if you'd get there. But you are your grandmother's, er, granddaughter. The poor man was searching for a hidden UFO base."

"A hidden... In Nevada?" Alien bases on Earth? I sank deeper into the Jeep's soft leather seat.

"Of course, you're aware of the theory that aliens have not only visited our planet, but they've built bases here."

If I had heard the theory, it was little wonder I'd forgotten. Why put a base on Earth? As a vacation destination? "Um, right."

"Chuck's organization had narrowed the location of the base to a few hundred square miles of Nevada mountains."

"Wait," I said, "you mean the *alleged* base, right?"

Arsen flicked his high beams at an oncoming pickup. The driver waved as he passed.

"As I was saying," the old lady said, "Mr. Manchin became obsessed with finding the secret base. But obsessiveness is a hallmark of those who join organizations like Chuck's."

"Organizations, plural? You mean there are more?"

"Oh, Susan, you're funny."

We turned onto Grizzly Court. The Jeep drifted to a stop in front of my B&B. Welcoming light streamed from its windows, painting the garden and gravel drive golden.

"I'm not— Did Chuck send Manchin to find the base?" I asked.

"Chuck always denied it. I suspect he didn't explicitly direct that rancher into those mountains. But I believe Chuck encouraged Manchin's search, and I'm not alone in that belief."

"Jane Thorpe is keeping Chuck's organization going."

She growled. "Is she now? How very interesting. And dangerous."

"Dangerous?"

Arsen set the parking brake. The jeep ticked, its metal contracting as it cooled.

"I won't ask how you got this number," she said. "I can guess. But don't call it again. I'll be changing the number."

"Dangerous?" I bleated to dead air.

Mrs. Steinberg had hung up.

"For Pete's sake!"

"What's dangerous?" Arsen asked.

I scowled at the phone. "That organization of Chuck's, I guess."

"Was Mrs. Steinberg helpful?"

"Until she hung up on me. She told me she thought Chuck might have been responsible for the death of that rancher, Topher Manchin. That must have been why Bridget was on the case. But it was old news. Chuck wrote about it in his book. And even if Chuck had encouraged Manchin to search the mountains for a secret UFO base, how liable could he really be?"

"In a civil court?" Arsen asked. "Who knows?"

"Could Chuck's death be some sort of revenge on behalf of the rancher?"

"Has he got any friends or relatives at the festival?" Arsen asked.

"Good question." I opened the door and dropped to the ground. The nearby rose bushes rustled in the warm breeze, scenting the air. Feeling suddenly awkward, I bit my lip. Should I ask him in? I'd asked him into Wits' End hundreds of times. He'd come uninvited hundreds more. Now, asking seemed fraught with awkward potential.

He yawned. "Pick you up tomorrow at the same time?"

It would be easier to get over him if he wasn't being so dratted conscientious. "If you want. You must have better things to do than—"

He revved the engine. "Sorry, can't hear you."

Giving up, I stepped away from the Jeep. "Okay, see you tomorrow." I shut the door and crunched up the gravel drive.

Arsen's Jeep didn't pull away until I was inside the Victorian. Dixie sat behind the front desk, her bare legs crossed at the ankles and boots propped on the desk.

Beside her, Bailey gave me what can only be described as the stink eye.

I knelt to pet the beagle. "Hey there. Who's a good boy? You're a good boy!"

His tail gave a single wag. The dog looked away, unimpressed.

"Oh, come on," I said. "Isn't this a little over dramatic? It's not as if I left you alone. Dixie's here."

My cousin glanced up from her phone. "Good thing I like overtime pay."

"How did it go today with Kayla? Any problems?"

She rolled her eyes. "Not with this bunch."

"And Kayla?" I loved my cousin, but she didn't always play well with others.

"She cl—helped clean okay. Any more murders?"

A warning note whispered in my head. To my everlasting regret, I ignored it. "Not a one."

"Darn." Her booted feet thunked to the rug. "Then I'm off. See ya tomorrow."

I saw my cousin out, then I walked to the kitchen and turned at the open door.

Bailey hung his head.

"Well? Are you coming?"

He lumbered to his paws and followed me to my private room, or as my Gran used to call the chic room, the parlor. Black-and-white toile paper lined the walls. I kicked off my shoes and dug my toes into the fluffy white throw rug, before dropping heavily onto the velvet couch.

Bailey curled on the ebony couch beside me, and I scratched behind his ears.

Cracking open Bridget's book, I skimmed for mentions of Chuck or the rancher.

They weren't hard to find. The reporter tore into Chuck as a fraud and a liar. According to Bridget, he'd manipulated people into joining his organization and handing over vast sums to learn the "truth" about UFOs.

But the dead rancher was barely mentioned, and that surprised me. If Bridget wanted to attack Chuck, a dead member of his organization seemed like a good way to do it.

Bailey whined and laid his head on my thigh.

"Do you want a treat?"

The beagle's ears perked.

He followed me to the kitchen, and I got him a crunchy bone from the top of the refrigerator. Grabbing my laptop off the kitchen table, I returned with it to the parlor.

I surfed the internet for the dead rancher's obituary. It was brief, speaking more to his life as a self-sufficient rancher than why he had been hiking in the mountains. One survivor was listed - his daughter, Margaret Manchin, who was training to be a nurse.

Bailey pushed through the half-open door into the parlor and settled in his dog bed.

I adjusted the velvet cushion behind my back and clicked a link. Another article popped onto my screen. The ranch had been foreclosed on six months after Topher Manchin went missing.

I ran an internet search on Manchin's daughter and came up with three different Margarets. None were nurses or lived in Nevada.

The internet had failed me and not for the first time.

Tasting something sour, I closed the laptop. There were only two days left of the festival, the sheriff was counting on me, and I had a sickening feeling that the murderer wasn't done.

But it was okay. I had a plan.

CHAPTER TWENTY-TWO

Arsen lounged against the kitchen counter and raised his oversized mug in a salute. "Outstanding breakfast, Susan, as per usual."

"Thanks," I said shortly, annoyed by my own pleased reaction. Why couldn't I *stop* reacting?

Bailey looked up from the linoleum floor and panted hopefully. Arsen was always the weak link when it came to sneaking the beagle scraps.

I groaned, arching my lower back, and set a soapy glass in the dishwasher. "Maisie called. You were right, the decision hasn't been made yet, so the festival is going on." And in my dark little heart, a part of me was relieved. No disappointed guests. No townsfolk with pitchforks. No suspects fleeing to parts unknown, or known, but unreachable to a busy B&B owner.

Another part of me was terrified. I wondered if the committee knew about last night's attempted sabotage of the stage. "I didn't plan for all contingencies."

A breeze tossed the curtains at the window over the sink. Bracing my hands on the butcher-block counter, I gazed out at Mr. Jonas, wandering in the rose garden.

"How could you possibly have anticipated what happened?" Arsen lifted a single brow. "You've done great. Dixie and Kayla are managing at the B&B. You stopped a saboteur. And the town and Wits' End have gotten a tourism boost. You got everything you planned for, and the rest is out of your hands."

"I didn't get everything." I'd never tracked down PB Gates. I pulled off my apron, smoothed the front of my green capris. Since it was going to be another hot one, I'd left my floral-print blouse untucked. "And I never wanted a murder. Murders," I corrected.

"Those weren't your fault. And they're not your responsibility."

"That doesn't mean I can ignore what's happening at the festival."

"I'm pretty sure it means you can."

Roughly, I stuffed what was left of my planner –in a new three-ring binder – into a beach tote. Why did we always cover the same old ground? Arsen told me to loosen up, and I told him to take things more seriously. It was time to break the pattern.

"About what I said the other day..." I shut the dishwasher. "I know I sometimes give you a hard time about work and things. But there's nothing wrong with you either. I like the person you are." My face heated, and I got busy arranging things in my beach tote.

"You haven't been wrong." He sobered. "I know I've gotten into the habit of sometimes taking things too easy since I, um, got back. It's nice to be reminded..." He trailed off.

"Of the rewards of hard work?"

"Let's not go crazy," he said hastily, and I laughed.

Bailey loosed a short bark.

"How is the security company going?" I asked.

"Right now, I'm sticking with security strategies and procedures and equipment. Those are the things small and mid-size businesses can understand and afford."

I cocked my head. Where *had* Arsen learned about security strategies? His website had been annoyingly coy.

I thought of that ice cream seller. He seemed to think Arsen had been in the military with that *Semper fi* comment. But that was ridiculous. Arsen would have told me something important like that. We were best friends, even if he did make me crazy.

I ran my finger along the edge of the butcher-block counter. "Arsen—"

He checked his dive watch and straightened off the counter. "Whoa. We should get going."

The porch door banged open. Sheriff McCourt strode into the kitchen. "You had to do it."

Bailey barked once and came to stand in front of me.

I edged away, so the dog wouldn't sit on my foot. "Do what?"

"Interrogate Mrs. Thorpe. Let's go." She jerked her head, blond curls bouncing, toward the porch door.

"Go?" I asked wildly.

"I'm arresting you." She said each word slowly, enunciating, and unhooked a pair of cuffs from her massive belt. "It's called interfering with an investigation."

I froze. "What?" She couldn't be serious.

"Whoa," Arsen said. "For talking to Mrs. Thorpe? They had festival business. I—"

"Was just about to drive me to the festival," I interrupted, before he could confess to aiding and abetting.

"That will have to wait." The sheriff folded her arms over her khaki shirt.

Arresting me? This made no sense. There had to be something else going on. The sheriff and I were friends. Sort of. Unless this was just her way to get me alone so we could discuss what I'd learned. That made sense. After all, how could I be a confidential informant, if everyone knew I was helping her? I could play this game. "But I really wasn't interfering—"

"Do I have to use these?" She dangled the cuffs from one finger.

"No!" Arsen and I said.

"We'll sort this out," Arsen said to me more quietly, and I nodded.

I followed her to her sheriff's department SUV. She opened the rear door, and I climbed into the caged area. The door slammed with an aura of finality.

She got in and started the SUV. The air inside the cab was stifling from the morning heat, and it smelled of disinfectant.

"Sheriff, what's going on?" She couldn't seriously be arresting me. Talking to suspects is what I do.

"What part of *you're under arrest* don't you understand?"

"Well, aren't you supposed to read me my rights or something?"

"Oh, yeah. You have the right to remain silent..."

I pressed against the seat. She was taking this arrest illusion a little far, but she hadn't cuffed me. Maybe she should have cuffed me? No. I didn't think I'd like that.

We traveled in silence to the modern police station, marched in silence up its steps, stood in silence in a grim, windowless, gray room.

The sheriff pointed to a chair on the far side of the table, opposite a mirror. "Sit."

I sat.

She scraped back the chair across from me and dropped heavily into it. "What the hell do you think you're doing?"

"Acting as your informant?"

"By harassing witnesses?"

"I don't think I was harassing Mrs. Thorpe. We had a nice conversation."

"Mrs. Thorpe told me all about your conversation."

Well, what was the point of me being an informant if the sheriff bothered my suspects with the same questions? "Did she tell you she's continuing Chuck's creepy UFO cult? Or that Bridget was asking a lot of questions about Chuck's past before she was killed?"

"No and yes. Not that the former has anything to do with anything."

"It does if she killed her husband for the money."

The sheriff rubbed her temple. "UFO cults aren't as profitable as you may think."

"You checked their tax records?"

She waved away my question. "I'm asking the questions."

I hate it when cops say that. Even in the movies, it's irritating. "Maybe Mrs. Thorpe just wanted her freedom. Or didn't want to deal with a divorce. Plus, I heard a rumor Chuck was having an affair with Aleta Bradford."

"Are you hearing anything I've said?" She banged one fist on the metal table and leaned forward, cords of muscle straining in her neck. "Interfering in a police investigation is a crime. It's none of your business who might have been having an affair with whom."

Even red faced and shouting, she knew her *who* from her *whom*, I thought irrelevantly, but my chest tightened with anxiety. The sheriff looked seriously angry. Had I misinterpreted her intentions?

Since I was embedded in the festival, I'd been sure asking around just made sense. But all I'd succeeded in doing was getting knocked down and pushed around and not stopping a single murder. I sank lower in the metal chair. The sheriff was right. I wasn't a detective. I was...

Nosy.

Oh, my God. I was turning into Mrs. Steinberg.

My cheeks burned. "But—"

"No buts! Just because you were moderately lucky in one investigation doesn't make you a junior detective. It makes you *under arrest*. Are you hearing me? Are you picking up what I'm putting down? You're lucky Arsen isn't in here too. I thought of running him in for operating a fraudulent security company, but with his record—"

"Arsen has a police record?"

"His military record!"

I gaped. Military record?

Of course. I swayed in my seat. *Semper fi*. The way he knew things about people with PTSD and security and... Why hadn't I seen it before? And why hadn't he told me? My hands clenched on the tabletop.

I couldn't breathe, couldn't swallow. I'd thought we were friends, but he'd lied to me all these years. Had he been laughing the whole time? How could he not? Here I was, a "detective," who couldn't see what was right in front of my nose. How could I have been so stupid?

Her nostrils flared. "Dammit, are you going to cry? Don't even think about crying!"

"I'm not crying," I snapped. But the backs of my eyeballs heated. "I'm sorry if I've made things harder for you."

"Tell it to the judge." She rose and stormed from the room, slamming the metal door.

My breath came in short gasps, realizations thudding into me like moths hitting a bug zapper.

Arsen had never joined the circus. That had obviously been code for military. And all his travels, working in those resorts – had those come after his military service, or had those been part of the cover as well?

Why hadn't he *told* me?

I forced myself to take deep, yoga breaths, and my head stopped spinning.

The wall clock was stuck on six-fifteen. It would be right at least twice today, so its track record was probably better than mine.

Pain swelled in my chest. I really had misinterpreted everything. I was the one who hadn't looked beyond the surface. And Arsen *wasn't* my best friend. A best friend wouldn't have lied about something so important.

But why? Why do it? Did he think I'd think less of him? Whatever he was doing couldn't have been super-secret, or the sheriff wouldn't have been able to get his record. What *had* he been thinking?

"Susan? Susan?" Someone shook my shoulder, and I started.

A cherubic blond deputy I knew slightly, Owen Denton, frowned down at me. "You okay? You looked kind of catatonic for a second there."

"What?"

"You can go."

"I made bail?" How was that even possible?

His brow puckered. "No," he said, drawing out the word. "Bail has to go through the courts. You're free to go. Arsen's waiting for you."

My gut tightened. *Arsen.* "But I thought I was under arrest."

"Do you want to be arrested?"

"No."

"Then come on," he said.

Footsteps dragging, I followed Deputy Denton into the sheriff department's high-ceilinged foyer. A beam of late-morning sunlight pierced the glass ceiling and pointed to a grouping of blue chairs. Beside them stood two men – Arsen and a lawyer we knew, Nick Heathcoat. Nick wore dress slacks, the sleeves of his button-up shirt rolled to the elbows.

"Susan!" Arsen strode to me and pulled me into a rough hug. "You okay?"

I stepped away and studied his face, sketched with concern. Was that real? Was any of it real?

Arsen wrung Denton's hand. "Thanks, man."

The deputy shrugged. "Hey, I just collected her. See you at Antoine's next Friday?"

"I'll be there," Arsen said.

I couldn't look at Arsen, so I turned to the handsome lawyer. "What happened?"

"You're out," Nick said, smiling. What looked like baby burp-up stained the blue fabric on his left shoulder.

"Do I have a court date," I asked, "or—"

"You were never charged," the lawyer said.

"But... the sheriff said I was under arrest."

"Nick changed her mind," Arsen said.

The lawyer shook his dark head. "I don't think she was ever serious about charging you. Too much paperwork. She just wanted to scare you."

"She's good at her work," I said.

Arsen frowned, "Hey, are you—"

A flash of red hair moved in the corner of my field of vision, and I turned toward the movement.

Maisie hurried past, her leg bumping one of the blue chairs. She yelped and rubbed the thigh of her white slacks.

"Maisie?" I asked. "What are you doing here? Is everything all right?"

Arsen and Nick shared a look, which I ignored. I knew what they were thinking – I'd just been busted for interfering in an investigation, and now I was pestering another suspect. But asking Maisie about being at a police station was only good manners.

"Oh. Hi, Susan. I didn't expect to see you here." She smiled at Arsen, and I didn't care. "I'm trying to get a police report on the tent fire for the insurance company."

"Shouldn't the insurance company be able to get that?" Nick asked, and I introduced them.

Maisie's smile was strained. "You would think so, but the adjuster seemed to think it was on me."

"Did the sheriff have any information about the sabotage of the stage the other night?" I asked.

Her shoulders sagged. "Just that if the saboteur had succeeded, the stage would have, and I quote, tipped like a cow. Is it small of me to worry that she doesn't know cow tipping is a myth? Cows are big animals. If you tried to shove one over, it would just look at you. What are you doing here, Susan?"

"Me?" I shuffled my feet. "Oh. Just... Uh, you know, witness statements and stuff. Statements about the person I saw beneath the stage last night," I said quickly, relieved I'd finally hit on a sensible explanation.

"Thank God you caught him in the act." She ran her fingers along her X-tranormal lanyard. "A collapse could have caused a stampede, not to mention people getting hurt on or near the stage." She closed her eyes. "All I need to do is get through two more days without incident, and the worst festival of my life will be over."

"You've done a great job," Arsen said. "What's happened wasn't your fault, and you've done everything you could to keep people safe."

"I'm sure Rachel appreciates everything you've done," I said.

She gave a little jump. "Right. Well. I'd better be getting back." She hurried from the station.

"Who knew a UFO festival could be so life threatening?" Nick shook hands with Arsen. "I'll see you around."

"Thanks." Arsen clapped him on the shoulder. "You're a life saver."

"Yes," I said, wondering how much the lawyer was going to cost me. Because I knew Arsen would try to pay the bill, and I wasn't going to let him. "I don't know exactly how you did it, but thank you."

We walked together through the sliding glass doors and to the parking lot, heat radiating from the pavement.

Nick got into his SUV, and Arsen walked me to his massive Jeep. I jumped into the passenger seat before he could help me inside.

Heart banging against my ribs, I buckled in and squeezed against the seat while he got inside. I knew the truth. Now what was I going to do with it? Pretend ignorance? My fingers bit into the palms of my hands.

"You okay?" he asked, starting the car.

"I'm fine," I lied, forcing a smile. "Thanks for breaking me out."

"Nick did it."

"I'll call him about the bill," I said, words clipped. I checked the dash clock. It was only ten AM. It had seemed like I'd been in the sheriff's station for hours.

"Where to?" he asked. "Wits' End or X-tranormal?"

I couldn't do it. I couldn't pretend. "Please take me home."

"Home?" He draped his left arm over the steering wheel and swiveled toward me. "Don't tell me the sheriff's got you running scared?"

"No." I rolled down the window.

"Then what's wrong? You're acting weird—"

"*I'm* acting?" I exploded. "Are you kidding me? You've been lying to me – to everybody – for years about where you've been."

"What do you—?"

"Oh, stop! Just stop. You weren't in the circus, you were in the military." I stared out the front windshield. A crow pecked at a furry bit of roadkill in the parking lot.

There was a long silence.

"How did you find out?" he asked quietly.

I shook my head.

"You know what my aunts are like," he said. "I couldn't tell them."

"But why didn't you tell me?" My eyes warmed, and I compressed my lips. I was *not* going to cry.

"I don't know. It didn't seem that important—"

"Not important? You made up an entire fake life. What's actually true? Any of it? Did you work as a dive instructor in Fiji?" I braced my arm on the open window. The metal was branding-iron hot, and I jerked away.

"I did some diving," he hedged.

"What were you? A Navy Seal?" In the hot car, a bead of sweat trickled down my back.

He didn't respond.

"I'd assume I was correct," I said hotly, "but you're a better liar than I ever gave you credit for."

"What does my old job matter? You know who I am."

"No, Arsen. I really don't. Will you drive me home, or should I start walking?"

His knuckles whitened on the wheel. But he pulled from the lot, and we drove up the mountain road. Soon, we stopped in front of my driveway.

"Susan—"

I leapt from the Jeep and slammed the door. There was nothing he could say. Not anymore. My crush – and that's all it had ever been – was dead. And a steel weight of misery pressed down upon my heart.

CHAPTER TWENTY-THREE

I paced my mod-Victorian sitting room, Bailey trotting at my heels. But all that thinking just made me angrier.

So, I drove to X-tranormal on an unsuccessful quest to find the elusive PB Gates. It wasn't that the Sheriff had scared me off our murder investigation. If she'd really meant to scare me, she would have charged me. But I felt I was at a dead end with the murders, and I wasn't ready to give up on PB.

By two o'clock I began to realize what a stupid idea this had been. I didn't even know what PB Gates looked like. I was hot and dusty, and I swear I was being followed by men in long white robes. Not mystical wizard robes. Bathrobes.

Yuri trudged past a head-in-a-hole photo cutout against an alien background. His briefcase bounced against the thigh of his rumpled brown suit.

I waved. "Hi, Yuri."

He flinched and turned toward me. His muscles relaxed. "Susan. How are you?"

"A little shaken up, I guess, after what happened at the concert."

His saturnine face darkened. "Our enemies are everywhere."

Our? "Er, yes. I saw you there. Did you see anything suspicious?"

His grip tightened on his briefcase. "No."

"Can I ask you a personal question?"

"You can ask."

"What's in the briefcase?"

He stared down at it. Swiftly, he knelt, laying it on the uneven ground, and snapped it open. A change of clothes. A flashlight. A notepad and pencil. A small cardboard box with...

I pointed at the box. "Is that a pinhole camera?"

"The aliens are able to block our technology. I thought, with something no-tech like a pinhole camera, the next time they take me, I might be able gather evidence."

"The next time..." I drew in a slow, unsteady breath. "This is a go bag." I had one myself, underneath my bed, in case a forest fire forced a quick evacuation.

Yuri snapped the briefcase shut and stood. "Yes." He checked his watch. "I'll be late for the next lecture. If you'll excuse me?"

"Yes, of course. I'll see you later."

I watched him disappear into the crowd. The poor man. What must it be like to honestly fear that at any moment, someone could snatch you from... anywhere and do awful things to you?

Scalp prickling, I glanced over my shoulder. Three robed men examined a stand selling alien bobble-heads.

I walked on and stopped in front of a hot pretzel stand. In the mirrored surface behind the rotating pretzels, the white-robed men were reflected. They spoke in low voices and shuffled their feet.

This was ridiculous. I spun on my heel and strode up to them. "What? What? Why are you following me?"

The robed men colored and muttered denials.

"Bull." I read their lanyards. "You've been following me for the last hour, Jim and Rick and Tran."

The tallest man, Jim, cleared his throat. Sunlight gleamed off his balding head. "In fairness, we are all walking a spiral path."

My muscles tensed. "That's not a denial."

Rick, the shortest one, stared at his leather sandals. His rope belt strained about his gut. "We should tell her before she calls security."

I jammed my hands on my hips. "Tell me what?"

"That security guy asked us to keep an eye on you."

"Security – Arsen?" I sputtered. "Arsen Holiday?"

They nodded.

Oooh! That... sneak! Even when I'd told him to leave me alone, he had an angle. And after my parents had hired a detective to follow me – but Arsen didn't know about that. I guessed we both kept secrets. But his was worse! I ground my teeth. "Why?"

"He said you might be in danger," the middle-sized man, Tran, said.

"Why you?" I jabbed my finger at Tran. "Who are you to Arsen? How does he know you? Are you part of his security company or something?"

Jim turned crimson. "Uh, he sort of arrested me."

"Arrested you?" I stepped backward.

"For going au natural."

I stared. "You're the sweaty naked guy?"

"He made me put on this robe." He plucked at the rope belt. "It's surprisingly comfortable when you're not wearing anything underneath."

"You're not... Oh, no." Arsen had blackmailed a streaker.

"These are light years better than our alien costumes," Rick agreed. "I thought I was going to have a heat stroke under all that silicone."

"We're converts to the robe," Tran said.

"Why the hell – no offense – would Arsen ask you to follow me?" I demanded. "Why you?"

The fireplug pointed at his tall friend. "Jim's a second-degree black belt in hapkido."

"Hapkido?" I asked. "That doesn't sound real. Did you make that up?"

"No," Jim said, affronted. "It's from Korea, and it's an extremely practical form of self-defense. Or offense."

"Right," I said faintly. "I don't suppose you've seen PB Gates around anywhere?"

"Oh," Jim said, "he left hours ago."

I massaged my forehead. "Great. Thanks. I'm leaving. And don't follow me, or I will complain to security and get you banned from the festival for good." I stormed out the gates. Beneath the UFO, I turned and looked behind me. The three weird monks were nowhere in sight.

Frustrated, I drove to Wits' End.

Dixie sat behind the desk, feet up, eating a hamburger. Bailey sat beside her chair and tracked the movement of burger to mouth. The vacuum cleaner roared upstairs.

Dixie froze, mouth wide.

Bailey leapt to his feet and raced to me, tail wagging.

My eyes narrowed. "Why is Kayla working upstairs while you're down here?"

"I'm taking a break," she mumbled.

The beagle woofed.

"But..." A bucket and mop leaned against the stairs. "Why isn't the cleaning done by now?"

She swallowed. "Kayla was late."

"But you were here." My neck stiffened. "What if a guest came back to an uncleaned room?"

"They wouldn't. They're all at the festival except for Mr. Jonas, and—"

My left eyelid twitched, and I pressed my hand against it. "Are you making Kayla do all your work?"

"No. I'm not making her do anything. She volunteered."

A headache beat in my temple. "I'm only paying her to work until noon. It's almost three."

"It's not as if she's slave labor," she said. "So, I subcontracted."

"You what?"

"I'm paying her—"

"I know what subcontracting is!"

The beagle whined and snuffled at my tennis shoe.

Something crashed upstairs.

"Don't worry," Dixie said hastily. "I'll take it out of her pay."

I growled, fists clenching.

"What's going on?" Arsen asked from behind me, and I jumped. Perfect, like I needed *him* to stick his oar in.

Dixie rolled her eyes. "Susan's mad because I'm paying Kayla overtime—"

"Oh," I said, "so you're paying her more than I am?"

Dixie flushed. "Well, no—"

"I can't believe you lied to me." I struggled to tamp down my rising hurt and anger. She wasn't Arsen. She was Dixie – twice as irresponsible as Arsen, but at least she had some excuse. Her parents had horribly neglected her, so she'd had something to overcome. Arsen had no justification.

"I didn't lie," she said, "not technically."

"You misled me." *Again.* True, this sort of thing was par for the course with Dixie. But we were family, and I knew Wits' End was important to her, too. I couldn't believe she'd be so cavalier about the work.

Arsen shifted his weight, looking uncomfortable. "Look, it wasn't right, but I'm sure there's no real harm done."

I whirled on him. "You don't get a vote."

"What did Arsen do?" Dixie asked.

"The point is the cleanup is two hours late. What if a guest had returned early like I had?" I clamped my mouth shut. Shouting at Dixie never helped anything, least of all my blood pressure.

"I'll be back," I said through gritted teeth and stalked into the cheerful kitchen, Bailey at my heels.

The porch door stood open. A breeze flowed through the screen door and made the curtains in the window above the sink dance. I pushed open the screen door. Bailey and I walked onto the porch and into the side yard. The faint smell of roses teased my nose. I paced the lawn, stopping beside some pink Eden roses climbing up the white-painted banister and closing my eyes.

"I know, I know, Gran," I muttered to the flowers. "I need to be patient. Dixie was just up to her usual hijinks, and no harm was done. But it's the principle of the thing."

Pink petals fluttered in the breeze, and I imagined my grandmother's response. *The most important principle is forgiveness.*

I hung my head. "But sometimes it's so hard."

A man cleared his throat behind me, and I started, turned.

Mr. Jonas rose from an Adirondack chair, hidden behind the curve of lawn and more roses. He held my grandmother's small book on Doyle UFOs loosely in one hand. "Sorry. I didn't mean to eavesdrop, but I thought I should alert you that you weren't alone."

My face warmed. "You must think I'm crazy."

"For talking to plants? Lots of people do it, though I've never heard of a rose variety named Gran."

"My grandmother planted these roses. I guess I feel closer to her when I'm out here," I admitted.

Bailey sat on my foot.

"And you were communing with her." He grimaced. "In that case, I'm doubly sorry I disturbed you."

"Don't be." I scrubbed a hand across my face. "I'm the one who was bothering you."

"Not at all." He motioned with the slim paperback. "Your grandmother wrote this, I take it?"

"Yes. I updated it to include the reappearance of all those people, but the rest is hers."

"It's quite thorough, and intriguing."

If only I could have gotten PB Gates to read it. I forced a smile. "How was your day?"

"Delightful, once I realized I didn't have to actually *go* to the X-tranormal festival. I didn't have to argue with people obsessed with fairy versus UFO abductions, or fight my way through crowds, or eat festival food. Then, the entire week seemed to fall into place. I attended for a few hours this morning and returned here."

In my opinion, festival food was a feature, not a bug, but to each his own. "So, what have you been doing?"

"Relaxing in your garden, mostly. You and your grandmother created something marvelous here. How is it that so many of your roses are still in bloom?"

I shifted my weight. "I have no idea. And I can't take any of the credit. Like I said, my grandmother planted this garden." A sudden ache of missing her made my eyes water, and I looked away.

"Are you all right?"

A chipmunk scampered across the lawn. Barking, Bailey leapt to his feet and charged after the tiny animal.

"Fine," I said. "Just a little stressed over everything that's happened at the festival. I know it's not my responsibility—"

"Why not?"

"Why isn't it my responsibility?" I thought about that.

He nodded.

"I... guess because everyone keeps telling me so," I said.

The chipmunk scurried up one of the porch posts and onto the shingled roof.

"But in fairness," I continued, "they're right. I may have been a big part of bringing X-tranormal to Doyle, but it isn't my festival. And it's the job of the police to investigate murders."

"But it's your community, and you care."

"Two people are dead. How could I not care?"

We said nothing for a long moment.

The chipmunk invader driven off, Bailey returned with a triumphant air and lay down on the lawn beside my feet.

"Did you know Chuck Thorpe at all?" I asked.

"Ye-es, somewhat. To be honest, I tended to avoid the man at conferences and events like these."

"Do you mind if I ask why?"

"Not at all. He's been murdered, and there's little sense keeping secrets. Not that this is much of one. Chuck was a master manipulator, and I didn't like it. It bothered me to see people fall under his spell, especially since I couldn't do anything about it."

"No one wants to believe they're being manipulated," I agreed.

"True. But once they do learn the truth - if they learn they've been deceived - the victims can be unforgiving."

Was that what had happened to Chuck? Had one of his victims fought back? "His wife is keeping his organization going," I said, brow wrinkling.

"Is Jane?" His nostrils flared. "In any case, I doubt she'll have Chuck's success. She's not the Svengali her husband was. Someone else will no doubt end up taking up the reins of power, or the organization will crumble. I hope it's the latter."

I did too, but the worry that had been niggling in my chest seemed to grow, hot and jumbled.

"Well, enjoy the garden." Thoughtful, I walked inside, holding the door open for Bailey.

Arsen lounged against the kitchen counter holding a bag of dog treats, and I stiffened.

"What are you doing here? I really need some space right now, Arsen."

He tossed a crunchy bone to Bailey.

The beagle leapt, catching it midair. Crumbs of faux-bone dropped to the linoleum floor.

"You've got a right to be angry," he said. "But I don't want to leave things this way."

"Like I said, you don't get a vote. Where's Dixie?"

"Upstairs, helping Kayla." He straightened off the counter. "Dixie was wrong. She should have told you what she was up to. I shouldn't have tried to get in the middle, and I should have told you the truth about my past. I'm sorry."

I folded my arms. "After all the lies you've told me, why should I believe that?" The circus. Who runs away to join the circus anymore? How could I have believed it?

He winced. "I didn't mean to lie. I was a kid when I left. I told everyone I was joining the circus just to piss them off. You know how my aunts were. Are."

"Yeah, I know they loved you and were devastated when you left." We all had been. It had taken me a while to get over his defection, at least until the postcards had started arriving from odd places. Postcards I couldn't respond to, because they never had a return address.

He looked out the kitchen window. A curtain stirred in the breeze. "At the time, I was dumb and angry. Angry my parents were gone, angry I was stuck in a place like Doyle while you got to escape to San Francisco once the summer was over."

Some escape. I paced the linoleum floor. "So, it's my fault?" I knew I was being irrational, but the wound of that sudden departure poured into me, taking my breath away.

"No." He clawed his hands through his wavy hair. "It's my fault. I didn't tell anyone for all the wrong reasons. And then when I joined up, and things started to get serious... I didn't want to be the guy people said, "thank you for your service" to. I didn't want my aunts bragging all over town about their nephew in the Navy Seals."

I stilled. Seals? He really had been a freaking Navy Seal?

"I'm proud of my service," he continued. "We did good work. But I don't want to..." His weather-roughened hands fell to his sides.

"To what?"

"I don't want to be *that guy*." He shot me a pained expression. "It's not why I joined up."

Nausea climbed my throat. "Why did you? Just to get away from Doyle?" *From me?*

"I wanted to be more than the town's orphaned rich kid. My aunts had everything planned out for me. I should have just told them *no*, but I was young and gutless. And I'd rather you not say anything to anyone about the Navy."

"Of course I won't. You know I can keep my mouth shut."

"I do. You can."

"You never used an APO," I said, accusing. If his postcards had been postmarked by an Army post office, I'd have noticed. I know, because I'd kept them all, my young self studying them for clues to Arsen's mysterious disappearance. Maybe a part of me had never bought his story.

"It would have been an FPO for the Navy."

I glared.

"But no," he said. "I didn't. It would have given it away."

"But why didn't you tell *me*?" I asked, anguished.

He stepped toward me and stopped. His hands clenched at his sides. "I'm sorry. At first, I just didn't have the nerve. The way I left everyone seemed the right thing to do at the time. Later, I realized how shitty I'd been. But when I finally returned, you seemed to have forgiven me for leaving and accepted my story. I didn't want to rock the boat. You like things a certain way, and—"

"And?"

Bailey whimpered.

"It's my fault and only my fault. Susan, I'm sorry. I hope this doesn't ruin our friendship."

"I don't even know who you are anymore."

"I'm exactly the same person I was yesterday."

"Do you even own a security firm?" At this point, I wouldn't put it past him to just buy the logo'd shirts and slap up a website. With Arsen, finances had never been a barrier.

"The security company's real. I've even got an LLC."

"Congratulations," I said dryly.

"Susan—"

"What about your barf bag collection? If you were in the military, you weren't flying on civilian planes."

"A civilian friend collected them for me. He thought it was funny."

"So, you did have civilian friends who knew you were in the military. Just not me."

"Susan—" He reached for me, and I stepped backward.

"I can't talk about this right now. I need to calm down." I stormed into my sitting area and held the door for Bailey. He looked between me and Arsen, gave a sad woof, and followed me inside.

I didn't slam the door, though I really wanted to.

The sitting room was elegant black and white, but I was starting to see that nothing else in my world was that clear. How could I have been so blind about Arsen for so long? I dropped onto the velvet couch.

And I'd thought I was a decent detective. *Ha.*

Bailey hopped onto the couch and laid his head in my lap. Absently, I petted the beagle's soft fur.

I sank deeper into the cushions. I'd seen what I'd wanted to with Arsen. I'd accepted the ridiculous explanations he'd given me because... Because why? Because I hadn't wanted to believe he'd lie? Or because deep down, I'd wanted to keep thinking of Arsen as... safe? It had been easier to keep him at arms-length that way, that he was just a friend, that nothing had changed.

An ache pierced my chest. I didn't want him as just a friend. I wanted more.

Bailey climbed onto my lap and pressed his head against my stomach.

I hugged the beagle.

Wait a minute... If Arsen had been in the Navy Seals... "Holy cow," I whispered. "He's a secret alpha male!"

My head swam. The signs had all been there. The mountain climbing, the extreme sports... But I'd only seen the lovable goofball because...

"I wanted to be in control," I told Bailey and groaned. I dropped my head against the back of the couch, not liking what this said about me.

I'd seen what I'd wanted to see about Arsen, just like I'd ignored the signs that Dixie had been up to no good. What other misperceptions had I indulged?

I jolted upright and cursed. A misperception... I was looking at the murders the wrong way. But how?

CHAPTER TWENTY-FOUR

I edged open the kitchen door.

Arsen was gone. Of course, he was gone, I'd sent him away, and my heart shrank. One way or another, the two of us needed to resolve our differences. But could we?

Depressed, I returned to the side yard. I snipped a handful of pink roses for the table.

Kayla scampered onto the side porch and into the garden. She turned to wave at the closing screen door. "Thanks, Dixie!"

"How did it go today?" I asked the teenager.

"Great. I didn't think the job would be this much work, but Dixie's letting me off early today."

I smiled bitterly. How generous of my cousin. "Mm, hm. Will you be able to make it tomorrow? It's the last day of the festival."

"Oh, yes." She glanced toward the street. "Dixie said I could leave early tomorrow too. Bye!" She trotted down the lawn.

Mr. Jonas ambled up to me. "Now there is a hard-working young woman," he said approvingly.

I scowled at the Victorian B&B. A figure shifted behind the curtained kitchen window. *Dixie.*

"I'd better get back to work myself," I said, motioning with the roses. "Let me know if you need anything."

"Will do." He touched his finger to the brim of his baseball hat.

I strode inside to face Dixie.

She tossed a giant yellow sponge into the kitchen sink. "I've finished."

"Great. Thanks." I yanked open a sky-blue cupboard and pulled out a vase.

She braced her hands on the counter and stared out the window over the sink.

Shooting her covert, sideways glances, I arranged the roses.

Dixie grimaced and edged away. "I thought she wanted the extra work."

"I know." I added water to the vase from the tap.

She turned to me and put her fists on her slim hips. "I mean, I thought it was a win-win."

In spite of myself, I felt a surge of sympathy. "I can see how you would."

"But Kayla couldn't get out of here fast enough when I offered to help her finish up." She blew out her breath.

Like me, Dixie had seen what she'd wanted to see. The last remnants of my irritation vanished. "There's no harm done. Just, next time there's a personnel decision, let's figure it out together."

She brightened. "Really?"

"We both loved Gran and want to see Wits' End succeed. That's what counts."

She polished the sparkling section of metal countertop with the sponge. "I don't know what I'd do without this place. Seriously. Your grandmother..."

"She considered herself your grandmother too."

My cousin cleared her throat. "What's with the flowers?"

"I thought I'd put them in the breakfast room."

Dixie rolled her eyes. "Like those nut jobs will even notice. Are you back for the day?"

"It looks that way."

"Good. I've got things to do." She grabbed her purse off the kitchen table and left. The screen door banged shut behind her.

Our moment hadn't lasted long, but it had happened. I hadn't imagined it. "Thanks, Gran," I whispered to the roses, then took them to the octagonal breakfast room.

I peered out a front-facing window. Arsen's Jeep was gone. He'd really left.

Well, what had I expected?

I returned to my private parlor.

Bailey raised his head from the black velvet couch to look at me, snorted, and flopped back down.

"I know. I've got one more relationship to repair. But at least you and I are okay again, right?" Because I still wasn't sure how to fix things with Arsen, or even if I wanted to. Confused, I picked up Bridget's book and began reading.

I'm not usually a non-fiction fan, but the woman could write. I felt another stab of regret that she was gone. "What did the killer have against you?" I murmured. And were there any secrets between the covers that might reveal why she'd been killed?

Bailey wriggled closer, laying his head on the thigh of my green capris.

I scratched his head and kept reading.

The page darkened. I looked up. The light had dimmed, the sun behind me dipping toward the western mountains.

My phone rang.

I shut the book and answered. "Hello?"

"Susan, it's Maisie. I just wanted to tell you that the committee decided not to cancel. We're on for tomorrow."

"Oh. That's good." It was, wasn't it?

"Are you all right?"

"I guess," I said, "I'm just worried."

"I'm not happy about it either, believe me. But it's out of my hands. So, see you tomorrow?"

"Yeah, thanks."

We hung up.

I walked to the kitchen and made myself peanut butter toast. After refilling Bailey's bowl, I returned to my parlor and Bridget's book. Finally, I reached the chapter about the rancher's death. And this time, I didn't skim. I read it carefully. Then I read it again. But I didn't find anything new. What was I missing?

I returned to the chapter's final paragraph and read to the beagle.

"Topher Manchin's body was found by hikers two years later. Too late for Topher. Too late for his daughter, Margaret. Chuck Thorpe's hunt for evidence of a UFO base had turned deadly."

Bailey sneezed.

I opened my laptop and found Topher Manchin's online obituary. The dates were the same. The description of finding the body matched up. The only real difference was it listed his daughter's name as Meg. That wasn't much of a difference at all, since Meg is short for Margaret.

But something nagged at me.

"I know I'm missing something. But what...?"

My lips parted. Once again, I'd misread everything, or technically, misunderstood. My mind raced, the pieces falling into place, but if that were true...

I called the sheriff.

If it was true, tomorrow there would be another murder.

CHAPTER TWENTY-FIVE

Morning sun reflected off the car's bumper in front of mine. I fumbled for my sunglasses. My cell phone rang, and I hit the phone button on my car's dashboard. "Sheriff McCourt? Thanks for returning—"

"It's Arsen."

"Oh." A tiny voice whispered in my head, *don't blow this.* But I wasn't in control here, wasn't in charge. I didn't think either of us was, and I gripped the wheel more tightly.

"Look, I don't know if you want to see me, but I just wanted to check in about the festival. It's the last day. I'm assuming you're going?"

I blew out my breath. "I'm going, and I do want to see you. I..." I still wasn't sure what I wanted to say. "I'm actually on my way to X-tranormal now."

A VW Bug, two dirt bikes on its roof, veered onto the mountain highway and nearly took off my front bumper. I slammed on the brakes.

"Susan? You okay?"

"I'm okay." I unclamped my fingers from the wheel. "I wanted to get to the festival when it opened. Are you going?"

"Yeah, I'll catch up with you."

We muttered strained goodbyes and hung up.

I glanced at the empty passenger seat beside me. I hadn't brought my purse, because I hadn't brought my planner. Today, I had no plan. Just a sick sureness that something awful was going to happen if I couldn't stop it.

I pulled into the dirt lot and hurried to the festival gates, flashing my lanyard badge at a security lady.

A cooling breeze snapped the flags atop the tents and kicked dust in my face. Rubbing my arms, I regretted my lightweight khakis and thin, olive blouse. I should have brought a jacket.

I strode through the festival grounds, past tents and wandering parents with kids in face paint and alien costumes. The crowds were thin at this early hour and flowed in the same direction - away from the entrance and toward the center of the spiral.

I walked to the small VIP food tent behind *Planet of the Grapes*. Mr. Jonas sat in one of the Adirondack chairs opposite Jack Bauer, wine glasses dangling from their hands. Fruit flies buzzed about their goblets.

I brought myself up short. These two weren't VIPs. What were they doing here? Not that I was an elitist or anything. It was just surprising. "Mr. Jonas, what—?"

"Am I doing drinking wine at this hour?" He flushed beneath his baseball cap.

"It's my fault." The leader of the fairy contingent scraped his hair back into a ponytail. "We got to talking, and it turns out we're not so far apart on the issues after all. I'm a big fan of his writing."

I blew out my cheeks. His writing? What writing?

"And in the grand scheme of things," Jack continued, "what does it matter if it's fairies or UFOs kidnapping people? You know, I've been reading your grandmother's book—"

I frowned. "Her book?" What was Jack doing with that?

"I lent it to him." Mr. Jonas shifted in the low wooden chair.

"And it's quite a remarkable document," Jack said. "You know, the Doyle disappearances really do have all the hallmarks of fairy abductions."

Jonas rolled his eyes, grinning. "Let's not start that again."

Jack laughed. "Anyway, I thought we'd make up our differences over a drink, but *Planet of the Grapes* doesn't open until eleven."

"Um, right," I said. "It's fine with me of course, but if Maisie sees you, she might kick you out since you're not VIPs. Have you seen her, by the way?"

"Maisie?" Mr. Jonas asked.

"The conference organizer," I said.

Mr. Jonas rubbed his jaw. "I thought Rachel was in charge."

"She was, but she had to..." Wait, how did he know who the conference organizer was? My eyes narrowed. "Maisie took over at the last minute. She's a redhead. About my height?"

Mr. Jonas's flush deepened. "I've been avoiding anyone wearing an official lanyard. The thing is, I *am* a VIP. I just haven't been attending the festival as much as I should. The lure of relaxing in your B&B was too seductive."

My brow furrowed. "You're...?" My breath quickened. No. It couldn't be. Could it? But it would explain a lot.

Mr. Jonas shook his head. "There's something I feel I need to tell you." He drew in a deep breath. "I'm PB Gates."

Mentally, I smacked my forehead. I'd been searching for him all week, and my quarry had been at Wits' End the entire time.

Jack chuckled. "Can you believe it? I love this guy's work." He raised his glass in a toast. Red wine slopped over the side, dripping onto his shorts.

"I've truly enjoyed your B&B," Jonas, aka PB Gates said. "I'd love to interview you about it."

An interview? OMG! PB Gates was my white whale, and this was... unimportant. "That would be great, but I need to find Jane and Maisie. Have you seen either of them?"

"Sorry, no." Mr. Jonas sipped from his glass. "I see you're busy, but we can do the interview whenever it's convenient. I already have plenty of material. And I'll certainly mention your grandmother's charming little book."

"Thanks." I glanced at the clock on my phone. "But I really do need to find Jane Thorpe."

"Chuck's widow?" Jack rubbed his round chin. "You know, I think I did see her carrying a box of books."

I snapped my fingers. "To the authors' tent?" Of course. "Thanks." I left the men and jogged to the booksellers' tent.

I walked inside and looked around. I was one of two potential customers inside the warming tent, and behind their tables, authors jerked to attention. The other potential customer stood in front of Jane Thorpe's table.

I tried phoning the sheriff again. My call went to voicemail. "Sheriff, it's Susan again. I'm in the bookseller's tent with Jane Thorpe. I'll let you know if she goes anywhere." I hung up.

Smothering a curse, I sidled up to Jane's table.

Her customer, in an old-fashioned waistcoat and top hat, examined Chuck's book. He rubbed his trimmed beard. "I dunno. It isn't signed."

"I'll be happy to sign it," Jane said stiffly.

The man tugged at the hem of his red satin waistcoat. "But you're not Chuck."

"I am his widow."

"I don't think the price will go up if it isn't signed by Chuck," he said.

She snatched the book from his hands and clutched it to the chest of her sleeveless gray tunic. "If you don't find the information contained inside valuable, then it's of no worth to you."

"Well, you don't have to get so huffy." The man stalked away.

"I don't suppose *you* want to buy another book?" she asked me.

"No, thanks. One was enough. And I read it," I added quickly. "Very informative."

"If you're looking for signed copies, I'm out."

"Yeah, you told—" I shook myself. "I just thought I'd say hello."

She swatted at the air. "Well, I'm quite busy," she said, motioning around the customer-free tent. "I really don't have time to chat."

"Right. Have you seen Maisie by any chance?"

"Maisie?" Her gray brows rose. "No, I have not. Why?"

"Just some festival sponsor details. Thanks anyway." I wandered to the next table and idly picked up a bright yellow pamphlet, keeping an eye on Jane. If my suspicions were right, I couldn't let her out of my sight.

"Are you interested in witches?" the zaftig blonde behind the table asked.

"Sorry?" I glanced at the title of the pamphlet I held: *The Realities of Witchcraft in California.* "Um..."

"There's all sorts of witchcraft in these mountains." She leaned closer and lowered her voice. "They're the ones who are really responsible for The Disappeared, you know. But don't tell that to the fairy contingent. They're very aggressive."

Ha. As if Doyle needed another excuse for its weirdness. But recognizing a woman desperate for conversation, I braced my hand on the black tablecloth. "Tell me more."

We chatted a good fifteen minutes. Feeling guilty, I bought her booklet and moved on to the next table, with similar results.

An hour later, I was juggling a stack of UFO books I didn't need plus the witch pamphlet. My sleuthing was getting expensive. Where was the sheriff? As a partner in crime solving, she was really falling down on the job. And how was I supposed to watch Jane if I was loaded down like a pack llama?

"There you are." Smiling cautiously, Arsen strode across the bookseller's tent.

My heart leapt. He was in his casual wear — khaki hiking pants and a matching long-sleeved shirt – and he looked good, strong and tanned and muscular. But he'd always looked good. I still couldn't believe I hadn't seen it before.

"Do you need some help?" He angled his chin toward the books in my arms.

"Thanks." Unsure what to say, I handed them off.

"Susan—"

"Arsen—" I said at the same time.

We laughed nervously.

"I was gutless." He shifted the books beneath his bulging arm. "I should have trusted you. And..."

"And?"

Our gazes locked, his hazel eyes glittering with an unreadable emotion, and my breath caught.

"I didn't want to lose what we had," he said.

What we had was a friendship. Was that all he was afraid of losing?

"I don't want to lose that either," I choked out. I glanced around the tent. No one loitered nearby. "Why *did* you return to Doyle?"

"It's home."

My heart compressed, and I looked at my sneakers. *For home*. Not for me.

"And you were here," he said, stepping closer, his voice lowering. Electricity seemed to beat between us, and I fought a wild desire to press against his muscular body.

"Oh." I swallowed. "Arsen..."

His bent his head toward mine. My lips parted. My heart thudded in my ears.

Two books slid sideways on the top of his stack. Arsen shuffled around, balancing them, and I shoved the books in place before they could fall.

He tapped his fingers on top of the stack. "I should probably unload these."

"Could you put them in your car?" I asked, snapping back to disappointing reality. Had I imagined our near kiss? Again?

"Good idea. Don't go anywhere. I'll be right back."

Skin tingling, I watched him stride from the tent. No, I hadn't been imagining things. He'd been about to kiss me. And I'd been about to kiss him.

I bounced on my heels. This was real. Why hadn't I gone with him to the car? Oh, right. Because I was on a stakeout. And Jane...

The widow strolled past me and out of the tent.

Jane was leaving.

CHAPTER TWENTY-SIX

I jogged from the booksellers' tent and scanned the crowd for Arsen.

Jane rounded a bend and vanished behind a churro stand. I moved forward. If I lost her—

Tom Tarrant stepped in front of me, blocking my view. The reporter smiled. "Hey, Susan—?"

"There's nothing wrong with my roses!"

He reared backward, and I scooted around him. Talk about bad timing. Now I understood why law enforcement and the press were so often at odds.

"And stay off my lawn!" I shouted over my shoulder for good measure.

Pulse quickening, I hurried after Jane.

Maybe I was wrong. Maybe I was paranoid. Maybe Jane was taking a bathroom break. But it was nine-fifty, the start of those sacred ten minutes when festival-goers migrated from one lecture to the next. This was when customers found their way into the booksellers' tent. It was an odd time for Jane to leave her table.

Jim wandered past, stark naked, his bald head gleaming.

I started, did a doubletake. A seven-inch flying saucer, girding his hips on two pieces of string, hung in front of his private bits.

Oh, no. Jim had renounced his robes.

A mother clapped her hands over her little alien's eyes. The child dropped his ice cream cone and burst into tears.

This was not going to end well. I clawed a hand through my hair. But Arsen was no longer working security, and I had badder aliens to hunt.

Jane veered left, toward the exit.

I followed, keeping a safe distance. Where was she going?

"Fairies and aliens can be friends," a purple-haired member of Team Fairy insisted to Yuri.

Expression desperate, Yuri slapped his briefcase against one leg and tried to catch my eye. The look was plain: *save me!*

I didn't break my stride. *Sorry, Yuri, you're on your own.*

Jane passed beneath the exit's metal arch.

I hurried through, smiling my thanks to the female guard.

I hesitated. "Um, Jim the nudist is nude again. He's got a UFO in front of his... er, but nothing else."

She made a face. "For the first time, I'm glad I'm covering the front gate. I'll let HQ know."

"Thanks." I trotted into the parking lot and called Arsen. Voicemail.

Jane strode through a sea of cars, their chrome and windows blinding in the sunlight.

I jammed my hands in my pockets. Maybe I'd been wrong. Maybe she'd left something in her car that she needed?

Pretending to be a fellow traveler, I pulled my keys from my pocket and riffled through them. I glanced up occasionally to track Jane's progress.

She walked past the last car in the lot, beneath a gnarled oak. Jane stepped over the low, red tape barrier, and onto the dirt road leading to the barn. The widow headed toward the ramshackle wooden structure.

My belly knotted. She was definitely up to something. The barn wasn't part of the festival. It belonged to the vineyard. I loitered behind an oak tree and watched.

Jane disappeared inside the open barn.

I called Arsen again. This time when it went to voicemail, I left a message. "Arsen, I'm at the barn outside the festival's front gate. Jane's inside. Something's up. Come find me."

I looked around. If Jane was meeting someone, they were either already inside or late, because there was no one in sight.

Keeping to the side of the dirt road, I jogged to the barn. I edged along its rough, unpainted wood walls. Ears straining, I bent my head, listening. The wind tossed the nearby oak, its branches scraping against the barn.

I crept to the open door and peeked inside.

Straw on the floor. A small, green tractor. Old-fashioned farm implements hanging from the walls.

And no Jane.

I stepped inside. A door banged shut, and I straight-jumped about a mile. The door banged again, and I looked around. Behind the tractor, a human-sized door swayed in the breeze. I caught myself rubbing my hands and dropped them to my sides. Dammit. Where had Jane gone?

"What are you doing here?" She asked from behind me.

I yelped and did another Olympian-worthy leap. Turning to face her, I pressed my hand against my chest, because my heart was trying to beat its way free. "Jane. You startled me."

"You were following me." Her round face wrinkled with annoyance. Her gray hair stood up in front, and I guessed the wind had done a number on mine too.

I smoothed my hair. "Um. Yeah, I was."

"Why?" She folded her arms, bunching the fabric of her tunic.

"Because I'm worried if you keep Chuck's organization going, you'll get hurt."

She blanched. "Is that a threat?"

"No! No. Not by me. It doesn't make a difference to me if you keep it going or not. But I think it makes a big difference to the person who killed Chuck and Bridget."

"What do you know about that?"

"I don't *know* anything. But I'm pretty sure Maisie killed your husband and Bridget."

She blinked. "Maisie? The conference organizer?"

"She wasn't supposed to be the conference organizer. A woman named Rachel was. Maisie asked her if she could run X-tranormal. She first told me Rachel'd had a family emergency, and that's why she'd taken over. But that wasn't true. Maisie asked for this job. Later, she told me she just needed the money. I accepted that at the time, but I don't believe it now."

"Why not?"

"First off, the rancher who died in the Nevada wilderness looking for Chuck's UFO base—"

"It wasn't *Chuck's* base." She sucked in her cheeks. "He had nothing to do with that crazy quest."

"It doesn't matter what really happened. What matters is what his daughter, Margaret, thinks happened."

A breeze scattered bits of straw across the floor, and the door banged.

"Margaret?"

"Maisie is short for Margaret."

She gave a tiny head shake, and her silver earrings bounced against her neck. "Ridiculous! Lots of women are named Margaret. That doesn't prove anything."

"No, but it got me thinking about names. Names like Rachel. After your husband was killed, I overheard Bridget telling Maisie that she knew about Rachel. I assumed she meant Rachel, the conference organizer. But Bridget meant Rachel, Nevada, the town where Maisie and her father, Topher Manchin, lived."

She paled. "Rachel."

The barn door banged, and we twitched.

"Bridget was signaling Maisie that she knew who she was. And Bridget needed a big story to get her career back on track. Chuck's murder by Topher Manchin's daughter would have been weird enough to attract lots of attention. What were the odds she was going to keep the murder quiet?"

She fiddled with her dangly earring. "But there's no proof."

"No, but it shouldn't be hard to confirm, and there's lots of circumstantial evidence. Maisie's truck has a Nevada license plate. She told me she was driving since the age of 12 - that's the sort of thing that happens when you grow up on a farm or ranch. She measures travel in time, not distance—"

"So?"

I exhaled loudly. "So, it implies she's used to wide open spaces. And she told me it's impossible to tip a cow - something most city slickers don't know. None of it's proof. But together, it points to a woman who grew up on a ranch in Rachel, Nevada, something you'd *think* the organizer of a UFO conference would mention. Instead, she pretended ignorance of all things UFO."

"Why pretending?"

"Even though Maisie claimed not to know anything about UFOs, she kept slipping up and demonstrating she did."

She pursed her lips. "You said you can confirm this theory?"

"I won't have to. The sheriff can, easily. I'd be willing to bet Maisie's drivers' license is issued to a Margaret. She was married, so her last name probably changed, but her real identity shouldn't be hard to trace."

She waved me off. "But what does any of that have to do with me?"

I sighed. Was this blindness or willful denial? "She killed Chuck to avenge her father's death. This has been a long time coming, and we tend to justify our bad behavior. I'd be willing to bet she's told herself she was saving others from becoming his victim."

"But why kill Bridget?"

"I imagine to protect herself. Bridget knew or suspected what she'd done. And if Maisie believes the ends justify the means—"

"Then I'm next," the older woman whispered and touched her wrinkled throat. She straightened. "No. I haven't done anything wrong. I'm not going to let her scare me off. And it won't matter anyway. Once I tell the sheriff about all this, she'll arrest Maisie and the problem will be solved."

Maisie emerged from behind the green tractor. "Or, we can solve it right now."

In her hand gleamed a long knife.

CHAPTER TWENTY-SEVEN

I couldn't speak, couldn't move. The gray shadow had me by the throat, my pulse beating helplessly against its grasp.

I'd rather face a gun than a knife.

At the time, I hadn't believed Arsen had known what he was talking about. Now that I knew he did, I stood like a block of ice, my gaze fixed on the long blade in Maisie's hand.

In control, I'm in control, I'm in control. But I wasn't in control. I'd never been in control. And I couldn't breathe couldn't think couldn't react. She'd kill Jane. She'd kill me.

Light slanted through the gaps in the barn's wood-plank walls. It made diagonal bars across Maisie's pixie-like face and set her red hair ablaze.

"Maisie!" Jane gasped, her face as gray as her tunic. "What are you—?"

In two strides Maisie was at Jane's side, the knife at the older woman's neck.

Jane went up on her toes. She arched away from the blade until her shoulder touched Maisie's. "Please!"

"I'm sorry you're caught up in this, Susan," Maisie said. "But I can't let more people get hurt."

Sweat burned my eye, and I dashed it away, the pain stiffening my spine. I breathed slowly, deliberately, forced the away the rising panic attack. *Don't think about what might happen. Focus on what* is *happening.* "Maisie—" I rasped and cleared my throat. "What happened to your father was terrible, but—"

"But what?" Her eyes blazed. "How can you justify what they did?"

"Not me," Jane said. "I didn't do anything."

"My father was unstable. But Chuck didn't care. He bled him dry and sent him to die in the desert."

"It wasn't like that." Jane's voice trembled. "Chuck had no idea what poor Topher had planned."

"Liar!"

Jane went higher on her toes.

"Chuck gave my father a phony map," Maisie said. "I saw it."

"But we helped search for your father after he disappeared," Jane said. "Chuck was devastated by what happened. If he had a map, your father must have gone off the trail—"

"Of course, he went off the trail," Maisie said. "That's what getting lost means."

I was in the moment. Focus on the moment. I breathed slowly, deeply. "Maisie, you don't want to do this."

"Stop telling me what I want to do." She pressed the blade against Jane's neck, and a thin line of crimson beads sprouted from her wrinkled flesh.

I sucked in my breath. "Okay. Sorry. I'm sorry." I raised my trembling hands to chest level, palms out. I wasn't in control of this situation, and I needed to let her know that. Wasn't that what they did in all those FBI hostage negotiations? *Keep her talking.* "What was your father like? All I know about him is what's been written in the papers and, er, Bridget's book."

"He was a wonderful father." Maisie gulped. "But UFOs became an obsession with him. He was convinced he was on the edge of some big government cover up, and Chuck fed that obsession, taking his money, egging him on. After my father died, there was no money left, and the bank foreclosed. I loved my father. I loved that ranch. And I lost everything."

A bird fluttered in the barn's rafters.

"That's horrible," I said. "Your father taught you to drive, didn't he?"

She nodded.

Jane closed her eyes, her lips flattening into a pained line.

"You must hate everything about this festival," I whispered.

"You have no idea," Maisie said.

"Setting a tent on fire," I said, "running the VIP tent down with a forklift... Was that all about making people think... What? An anti-UFO fanatic was on the rampage?"

"This festival is full of lunatics. I passed a streaker on my way here. Why not blame one of them?"

"But sabotaging the stage...? A lot of people could have been hurt."

"A lot of UFO creeps just like Chuck."

Behind her, Arsen crept through the open barn door. *Don't see him, don't hear him.* "But most people aren't like Chuck." I rose my voice. "Most people are at the festival to have a good time. Most people think the idea of aliens visiting this planet is just intriguing fun."

Maisie rolled her eyes. "Come on. Aliens can't get to Earth. It's impossible. Everyone knows it would take light-speed travel to get to Earth. That's just science."

Seriously? She was blathering about the light-speed travel canard? And why did I care now? I was losing it, and I clenched my fists to stop their shaking. "Were you the one who set Jane's car on fire all those years ago?"

"I wanted to show them that they couldn't get away with it, that there were consequences."

"I think Jane knows that now. Maisie, what is it you really want?"

"I want this all to stop," she said, her voice anguished. "I thought it was over when Chuck died, but then Bridget just kept pushing and prying. And now you!"

Jane jerked her head back, her eyes widening. A line of blood trickled down her neck.

I blinked rapidly. "You're in charge here. We'll do whatever you want. That knife's against Jane's carotid artery, isn't it?" I forced myself not to look at Arsen.

"Yes, I know exactly what I'm doing," she said.

I nodded. "I'm sure you do. As a nursing student, you knew something of anatomy and the femoral artery. You knew just where to cut Bridget."

"Did you know I had to quit nursing school after my father went missing? I poured everything I had into keeping our ranch going. But I lost it anyway."

The barn door creaked.

Don't look toward the door. Don't see Arsen. "I'm so sorry."

"Bridget's death was painless," she said, "and quick. I'm not cruel. Bridget wanted justice, like I do. She just didn't understand what justice really meant."

"Jane's decided against continuing Chuck's organization," I said. "You don't have to hurt her."

One corner of Maisie's mouth tilted upward. "Nice try. I heard the two of you talking before I came inside."

Hunched low, Arsen paced closer. Another bead of sweat dripped into my eye, and I blinked rapidly. He needed a distraction. If only I could get Maisie to move the knife from Jane's neck.

"But I won't," Jane squeaked. "I had no idea how much damage Chuck caused. Of course, I wouldn't let anything like that happen—"

"In other words, you'll keep taking suckers' money," Maisie said. "Not good enough."

Don't think about what might *happen.* I stepped toward Maisie, toward Jane, toward the knife, and the gray shadow fled.

"Get back!" Maisie pointed the blade at me.

Arsen grabbed her arm and shoulder. He spun Maisie in a tight circle, whipping her to the straw-covered floor. The knife flew from her hand and landed at my feet.

Jane shrieked and ran from the barn, the hem of her tunic top fluttering behind her.

Hand trembling, I pulled out my cell phone and dialed Sheriff McCourt.

Arsen lowered one knee to Maisie's shoulder blade. He maneuvered her arm into a complicated looking lock between his arm and knees.

"Are you all right?" he asked.

"I'm—" My voice cracked. "I'm fine."

Maisie burst into ragged sobs.

Arsen flushed, grimacing, and looked down at her. "Oh, hey. Sorry. Is that too much pressure?"

"It is not too much pressure," I shouted, and he blinked. Arsen was hopelessly chivalrous, but he obviously knew what he was doing, and... okay, a part of me felt bad for Maisie too. But she'd murdered two people!

The phone crackled. "So help me, Witsend, if you've been investigating—"

"Maisie just tried to kill Jane Thorpe."

And finally, the sheriff listened.

CHAPTER TWENTY-EIGHT

Arsen and I stood outside the barn, surrounded by black and white Sheriff's Department SUVs. In the distance, the festival tents looked like a medieval battlefield.

Sheriff McCourt interviewed Jane beneath a nearby oak. A light breeze shifted its branches, and dried leaves drifted downward. Jane brushed a stray leaf from the shoulder of her gray tunic, then buried her face in her hands.

Arsen clawed a hand through his hair. "Why the hell did you walk *towards* the knife?" Straight backed in his khaki hiking slacks and microfiber shirt, he even *looked* ex-military. How could I have missed it before?

"I needed her to get the knife away from Jane's neck, so you could take it."

He was close enough to touch, and on any other day, I would have buried my head on his chest. But I didn't know what we were to each other. Not yet.

"Holiday!" the sheriff shouted.

Arsen caressed my upper arms, his touch warm through my thin blouse. A shiver fluttered through me.

"I'd better go talk to her," he said.

I nodded and watched him stride toward the sheriff while Jane hurried off.

"Hssst!"

I looked around.

"Susan." Mrs. Steinberg peeked from behind an SUV and motioned to me.

Bemused, I walked toward the SUV. Mrs. Steinberg scuttled behind the barn, and I followed.

I found the elderly woman leaning against a tractor and smoking an e-cigarette. Her black skirts and scarf flapped in the breeze. "So, you finally got there."

My neck tightened. "Finally? If you knew Maisie was the killer, why didn't you tell someone?"

"I didn't know she was the killer, only that she was Margaret Manchin and had a compelling motive."

I folded my arms. "You could have told me."

"Margaret deserved some privacy after what she'd been through. And I didn't know, only suspected." She pointed her e-cigarette at me. "But you found the evidence."

"Not really." I shifted my weight. "Just lots of means, motive, and opportunity."

"It will be enough." She took a long draw on the e-cig and shot a stream of menthol-scented vapor into the air. "Your grandmother would have been proud."

"Maybe." I rubbed the back of my neck. "How culpable was Chuck in Topher Manchin's death?"

She chuckled, an unpleasant sound. "Oh, Maisie had the measure of the man, all right. Chuck took advantage of Topher Manchin's paranoia and his desire to believe he could do something big. Chuck bled Manchin dry. And I have it on good authority that Chuck encouraged Manchin's secret investigations in the mountains. Aside from Chuck, Manchin believed he couldn't let anyone know what he was up to when hunting UFOs. The wrong people might find out. But as it happened, if he'd told someone..." She shrugged. "Maybe he wouldn't have gone alone. Maybe someone would have stopped him. Maybe they would have had an idea where he'd gone."

"What about Bridget?" I asked.

"What about her?"

"If you'd told the sheriff all this earlier," I said sharply, "she might not have died."

Mrs. Steinberg raised a brow above her Jackie-O sunglasses. "You think so?"

"Well, yes."

"Bridget's fate was inevitable." She straightened off the tractor and dropped her e-cigarette in her massive purse. "She knew too much."

"Inevitable? What's that supposed to mean?"

"Your boyfriend's coming."

"Arsen?" I whipped around and saw the side of the barn. When I turned back, she was gone, leaving behind only the faint aroma of menthol.

I really hated it when she did that.

My face heated. And was it that obvious that Arsen and I...?

Annoyed, I stomped around the corner of the barn.

Arsen motioned toward the open barn doors and turned to the sheriff.

I watched his smooth, economical movements, his assured stance. I slowed to a halt. Even from this distance, I could sense the power coiled in his body.

Palms damp, I went to loiter beside a Sheriff's SUV. A gust of wind tossed my hair into my face, and I pushed it behind my ears.

The sheriff nodded. She and Arsen came to join me beside the black and white.

She smacked her wide-brimmed hat against her leg and glared at me. "Anything else you want to add? Like why you decided to tell Jane you thought she was in danger instead of telling me?"

"I called you over and over last night and this morning."

"And didn't leave a message."

"Did too. If this is how you treat all your confidential informants, it's a wonder you have any left."

Her nostrils flared. "You—" She placed a hand on my arm and shifted me sideways, then got inside the SUV. "I'll see you two at the station." She smiled unpleasantly. "There will be more questions."

Ah yes, the debriefing.

"Sure thing, Sheriff." Arsen looped an arm over my shoulder, and we backed away. "We'll drive straight there."

A deputy hailed her before she could close the door, and she spoke to him, the SUV's engine idling.

Arsen and I ambled down the road toward the festival parking lot. I leaned a little closer than I had to, enjoying his clean, uncomplicated scent. Soap. He smelled like he'd just stepped from a shower. The image of him stepping from a shower flashed into my head, and I stiffened guiltily.

"Is something wrong?" he asked.

"No. I mean, I'm sure she's going to huff and puff and pretend we're suspects, and our debriefing will take all too long—"

"Debriefing?"

"But I'm glad Jane's okay." Even if I still didn't like her much.

"At least it's over," he said, "including the festival."

I looked toward the tents. "Yeah. Dixie will be happy she can go back to her usual schedule."

"How are things between you and Dixie?"

"Fine. I mean, she's Dixie, and she loves Wits' End as much as I do." And even though she made me crazy, I loved her too. She was family.

"What about you?" His mercurial gaze sharpened. "Will you be happy?"

We were safe. Things were back to normal. But would things ever be normal between Arsen and me? I swallowed. "I found PB Gates. He wants to do an article on Wits' End and Gran's book about Doyle. So, I guess I got what I wanted."

"But?"

I stopped. "Arsen. You... You were amazing today. I mean, I know Maisie was only a girl and not even as tall as me, but she had a knife, and you got it away from her. I've seen you do things like that before, but I just didn't think... I feel terrible I was so blind. I—"

He placed his large hand gently beneath my chin and tilted it upwards. His lips brushed mine. My legs trembled, and I clung to him to keep from falling.

Arsen pulled me closer.

Unthinking, I returned his kiss. I was out of control, my mind spiraling. Arsen was kissing me. Arsen felt the same, and—

A horn blared, and we jerked apart.

The sheriff leaned from the window of her SUV. "Get out of the road!"

"Right away." Arsen swept me into his arms and laughing, carried me away.

The End?

SPIRAL GALAXY PANCAKES

Ingredients

Pancakes:
1 C all-purpose flour
2 tsp baking powder
½ tsp salt
1 C milk
1 large egg, lightly beaten
1 T vegetable oil

Cinnamon Filling:
½ C melted butter
¼ cup + 2 tablespoons packed light brown sugar
½ T ground cinnamon

Glaze Frosting:
4 T butter
2 ounces cream cheese
1 1/4 C sifted powdered sugar
1 tsp vanilla extract

Instructions:

1. Prep the cinnamon filling first: Mix melted butter, brown sugar and cinnamon with a wisk. Spoon the filling into a zip baggie and set aside to thicken. (You're going to use the baggie as a pastry squeeze bag later).

2. Make the pancake batter: Mix the dry ingredients in a bowl. Add the wet ingredients and whisk.

3. Prep the glaze frosting: In a medium glass or microwave-safe bowl, heat the butter and cream cheese in the microwave

until melted, using 30-second increments. Remove from microwave and whisk together until smooth, then whisk in powdered sugar and vanilla. Set aside.

4. Warm a skillet on medium heat. Once its ready, spray with non-stick spray and pour roughly ½ cup of the pancake batter into the skillet. When bubbles start to form, snip the corner of the bag containing the cinnamon filling, and create a swirl pattern in the center of the pancake. Be careful to keep the cinnamon from getting close to the edge of the pancakes, or things will get messy. Flip the pancake with a wide spatula and continue cooking for another 1-2 minutes until golden brown.

5. Plate the pancake and drizzle the glaze over it. Warm it if needed.
6. Be sure to wipe out the pan after each pancake and repeat the above process.

SWISS CHEESE AND PROSCIUTTO GALAXIES

Ingredients:

1 pkg puff pastry (2 sheets)
2 C Gruyere cheese, shredded
One 3-ounce package prosciutto
1 egg
1 T water
cooking spray
zest of 1 lemon
1/2 C chopped basil or fresh herb of choice

Instructions:

1. Remove 1 package of puff pastry from freezer (each package should have 2 sheets). Thaw the sheets for 45 minutes.

2. Preheat oven to 400-degrees F.

3. Spray a baking sheet with the non-stick cooking spray of your choice.

4. Rip the prosciutto into pieces.

5. Unfold both sheets of pastry once they have slightly thawed. Lightly flour a flat surface and lightly roll out the creases in the pastry sheets. Do not over flatten them.

6. Stab each piece of pastry with a fork a dozen times.

7. Layer half the shredded Gruyere cheese and then half the prosciutto pieces atop each sheet of pastry, making sure the cheese and prosciutto touches the edges of the pastry.

8. Roll each of the sheets into a tight cylindrical shape and cut each into about a dozen, ½-inch "galaxies".

9. Place each of the galaxies onto the baking sheet. (Make sure the end pieces are cut-side down).

10. Beat 1 egg and 1 T water in a small bowl. Brush each finished pinwheel with egg wash.

11. Bake for 16-18 minutes, until tops are golden. Remove from oven.

12. Serve cool and garnished with the zest of 1 lemon and minced herbs.

BLUEBERRY BUTTERMILK COFFEECAKE

Ingredients:

½ C unsalted butter, room temperature
zest from 1 large lemon
1 C sugar (set aside 1 tablespoon)
1 egg, room temperature
1 tsp vanilla
2 C all-purpose flour (set aside 1/4 cup)
2 tsp baking powder
1 tsp salt
2 C fresh blueberries, cleaned
½ C buttermilk

Instructions:

1. Preheat oven to 350°F.

2. Cream the butter, lemon zest and the 1 C sugar with an electric mixer until the batter is fluffy.

3. Beat egg and vanilla into butter mixture until thoroughly mixed.

4. In a separate bowl, toss the blueberries with ¼ C flour.

5. In another bowl, mix remaining flour, baking powder and salt. (So we've got three bowls going on right now).

6. Incorporate half of the flour/baking powder/salt mixture into the batter, stirring until it's well mixed in. Add the buttermilk and mix that in too. Add the rest of the flour mixture to the batter and stir until everything is well blended. Next, gently fold the floured blueberries into the batter, minus any excess flour left at the bottom of the bowl.

7. Grease an 8- or 9-inch square baking pan with butter or coat with the non-stick spray of your choice. Pour the batter into the pan, spreading it to the pan's sides. Now dust the batter with that final tablespoon of sugar.

8. Bake 35 to 45 minutes — the smaller pan will need more time. A toothpick will come out clean when it's done.

9. Set aside for 15 minutes or more before serving.

ABOUT THE AUTHOR

Kirsten Weiss has never met a dessert she didn't like, and her guilty pleasures are watching Ghost Whisperer re-runs and drinking red wine. The latter gives her heartburn, but she drinks it anyway.

Now based in San Mateo, CA, she writes genre-blending cozy mystery, supernatural and steampunk suspense, mixing her experiences and imagination to create vivid worlds of fun and enchantment.

If you like funny cozy mysteries, check out her **Pie Town**, **Paranormal Museum** and **Wits' End** books. If you're looking for some magic with your mystery, give the **Witches of Doyle**, **Riga Hayworth** and **Rocky Bridges** books a try. And if you like steampunk, the **Sensibility Grey** series might be for you.

Kirsten sends out original short stories of mystery and magic to her mailing list. If you'd like to get them delivered straight to your inbox, make sure to sign up for her newsletter at **kirstenweiss.com**

Feel free to follow her on **Twitter** or **Bookbub**, get in touch on **Facebook**, post a picture of this book to Instagram and tag her **@kirstenweissauthor**, or send her an email. She'll answer you personally... which may be a good or a bad thing, depending on your perspective.

Copyright

Visit the author website to sign up for updates on upcoming books and fun, free stuff: KirstenWeiss.com

Cover art by WickedSmartDesigns.com

misterio press / paperback edition April, 2019

ISBN-13: 978-1-944767-36-5

Made in the USA
Coppell, TX
18 March 2023

14418285R00142